Kick the Can

A NOVEL BY
Steven I. Dahl, M.D.

Other books by

Steven I. Dahl, M.D.

Chicken Fried Steak, Action-Adventure

HOA Gold, Action-Adventure

Picasso's Zipline, Adventure/Medical Mystery

Rattlesnake, Wait and "See"

To Lexi Ann Dahl

She stole our family's hearts, then left us for a better place.

Kick the Can

Steven I. Dahl, M.D.

A novel

The characters, events, institutions, and organizations in this book are strictly fictional. Any apparent resemblance to any person, alive or dead, or to actual events is entirely coincidental.

Kick the Can
Published by Sweet Dreams Publishing of Massachusetts
January, 2011

Cover Design: Dianne Leonetti
Interior Design & Layout: Dianne Leonetti

Editorial & Proofreading: Lisa Schleipfer, Eden Rivers Editorial Services, Karen Grennan

Photo credits: Dreamstime Photos

For more information about this book contact Lisa Akoury-Ross at Sweet Dreams Publishing of MA by email at info@PublishAtSweetDreams.com.

All rights reserved. No part of the material protected by this copyright notice may be reproduced or utilized in any form or by any means, electronic or mechanical, including photocopying, recording, or by any information storage and retrieval system, without written permission from the copyright owner.

To obtain permission(s) to use material from this work, please submit a written request to:
Sweet Dreams Publishing of MA
Permissions Department
36 Captain's Way
East Bridgewater, MA 02333

or email your request to info@PublishAtSweetDreams.com.

Library of Congress Control Number: 2011936156

ISBN-13: 978-0-9829256-5-2

Printed in the United States of America

Copyright © 2011, Steven I. Dahl, M.D.

ACKNOWLEDGMENTS

The second best thing about writing fiction is the encouragement one receives from family and friends to keep at it. My heartfelt thanks goes to those who have read, listened tirelessly to my rehashing the story, and made suggestions. Especially helpful was my beautiful wife Paula, who lived a part of this story's setting firsthand. Many thanks also to: Elyssa Bent, Andrea Allen, Tasha Dahl, Lyn Glenn, Dennis and Julie Toleman, Bob Aborn, and to my patient and thoughtful editor Lisa Schleipfer and my extremely patient and talented publisher Lisa Akoury-Ross.

CHAPTER 1

"Get your dang head down or she's gunna see you. Why are you such an idiot?" Ian said. His voice, the faintest whisper of contempt, wasn't two inches away from his younger brother's ear. "You're gunna hide by yourself from now on."

The next time Dalan Dawson stuck his head up he got a light slap on the back of the head—more like a thump—for his inattention. It was really more his curiosity that made him keep poking his head above the shrubs. The game had appeared so simple to him sitting on the front porch the night before, watching the older kids play after the little ones were called in for baths and bed. Ian had caught on to the game early and had bragged to their Mom all day long how these kids in Coolidge couldn't run fast enough to catch a turtle, let alone ever beat him at kick the can, their favorite street game.

"When you see me take off running toward the coffee can, you stand up and start screaming as loud as you can, but do not move from behind this bush," Ian said. "It'll distract everybody so they look at you instead of me. If I win again tonight, I'll tell Mom that you are the best player, and she'll have to let you stay up an extra half hour tomorrow night," he promised.

Dalan watched through the branches of the dusty oleander bush as the other kids got caught, one at a time. In order to win, they had to run from their hiding places into the gravel street and give the old, rusted Folgers coffee can a good kick without getting tagged by "It." A girl named Darlene was "It" at the moment. She looked like she could run as fast as any of the boys, even Ian, and she could. Not only could she run fast, but when she tagged out some of the bigger kids, she didn't just touch them; she would take a big swing, slapping them pretty hard wherever she could land the hit. Most of the other players already had been tagged out and were standing beside the big cottonwood tree stump watching and waiting for the game to end. It was getting close to bedtime for all of them.

"Get ready," Ian whispered. "When I count to three you scream."

"What do I scream?" Dalan asked, tugging on his brother's sleeve.

"I don't care what you scream dummy!" Ian complained. He thought for a second and said, "How about 'fire'?"

"What if someone calls the fire department?"

"Yeh, right. Just scream like you did when I stuffed leaves down your underpants," Ian said, grinning at the little brother who was growing up too fast. "One, two, three," and then he was gone, tearing around the side of the Goebles' front porch, cutting across their yard, around the two giant olive trees and heading for the middle of the street.

"Fire! Fire!" yelled Dalan, feeling pretty foolish walking out into the open just so he could witness the footrace between Darlene and Ian.

Darlene was nobody's fool and didn't fall for the ploy. She immediately cut off her search behind the Rawlings house and headed for the street. She was wearing a worn-out pair of Keds, which at one time were probably white, but now matched the reddish dirt that covered everything in town not paved or planted with Bermuda grass. Her sole was loose and made a flapping sound as she ran, but that didn't seem to slow her down.

Dalan heard a screen door open behind him, but he already had started another round of "fire" yells trying to distract Darlene from her pursuit.

Just as Ian was about to kick the coffee can and be home free, Darlene came flying out of a shadow, both arms extended, head tucked to the side, striking Ian waist high and knocking him off his feet. Both went tumbling into the dry grass, rolling twice before coming to a stop.

Dalan was truly impressed. That girl was faster than his old dog Bandit chasing after a cat—before the dog got hit by the car. He started to cheer when suddenly it occurred to him that he could now run to the unguarded can and give it a kick and win the game. He took off like a rabbit, and was almost there, when he heard the siren.

The flashing lights on the Ford LTD lit up the whole neighborhood as the sedan's tires screeched around the corner, turning off of Main Street and then crunching onto the tar and gravel road. Dalan was headed on a beeline for the coffee can when the car cut him off. As it turned out, he couldn't have kicked the can anyway because the left front tire ran right over the top of the thing, smashing it flatter than a tortilla.

It didn't take long before the police officer had all of the neighborhood kids lined up on the Rawlings' front lawn, shaking his finger and glaring at them. The old biddy, Mrs. Rawlings, stood off to the side ready to point her finger at Dalan, just as soon as the tired-eyed officer finished his lecture on the danger of playing in the street and the prohibition of trespassing in the neighbors' yards. When it was her turn, she started in on the danger of yelling the word "fire" when there wasn't one. The woman made a good point; yelling "Fire!" could very well result in one having to listen to a long boring lecture on not yelling "Fire!"

By the time Officer Roberts had finished his mandatory warnings, the neighborhood moms and dads had joined the crowd, patiently awaiting his closing argument. Cranky old Mrs. Rawlings didn't get a chance to hear any one of the parents agree with her or apologize for the tromping of her flower beds before they marched their dusty wards off to baths and bed.

"You would have won," she said.

Dalan turned toward the voice and came face to face with someone he had never seen before. She was a young girl about his age—a very pretty young girl. She hadn't been in the game, nor had he even noticed her standing by the tree stump. She was at least his height and had the longest silky-black hair he ever had seen. Her big brown eyes twinkled in the dim reflection of the only street light. Normally, he wouldn't ever have noticed a girl's clothes, but hers were different than the rest of the kids—newer, cleaner, and kind of cool looking. Her shirt had little lacey stuff around the sleeves and her pants weren't jeans like every other kid in town, but thin fabric that matched her light green shirt. Her shoes were canvas Keds with little flowers.

"What did you say?" he asked, his voice squeaking a little from a low to high tone. It had been doing that lately.

"I said you would have won if that police car hadn't run over the can. I saw you running and there wasn't anyone who could have stopped you. What's your name?" she asked.

Too surprised to answer at first, he yelled to his mom that he would be there in a minute then turned toward the girl. "I'm Dalan Dawson. I'm just Ian's little brother."

"No, you're not 'just Ian's little brother.' You don't have to be just anyone's little brother. Besides I don't even know Ian, I just know you," she said.

"Who are you?" he asked.

"Do you mean what is my name or who am I?"

"I thought they were the same thing," he said.

"My name is Marie Palermo," she said, holding out her hand to shake, "but as to who I am to you, that remains to be seen."

The girl was looking straight at him, waiting for him to shake her hand. She wasn't frowning, but it wasn't exactly a smile either. He reached out and shook her hand, which was soft, but her grip was firm. He glanced toward home knowing he was in for a scolding when he got there, but he didn't want to leave the presence of this new person. She was weird in a sort of a good way. He felt drawn toward her like a magnet. She was so pretty and she even smelled good.

"Dalan?" his mom called from the porch. "You need to come in now sweetheart."

Embarrassed by his mom's endearment he let go of Marie's hand.

"Do you want to play kick the can tomorrow night?" he asked over his shoulder as he walked toward his house. "I can teach you all of the good places to hide and the tricks to not getting caught."

When the girl didn't answer him he turned again to look, but she had vanished into the shadows.

Both brothers were grounded for the next night's game. The neighbor shrew came knocking on the door the first thing the next morning, blaming Ian and Dalan for damaging her tomato plants. Mom made them each take money out of their vacation piggy banks and go with her to the nursery to buy new plants, and she then made them go out in the blazing noonday sun to plant and water them. The following day was Sunday and they had to go to their Granny Peterson's for dinner. Dalan had been thinking about the brown-eyed girl all day long, but by the time they got home the street game was over and it was bedtime.

Monday was the hottest day of Dalan's life. It never had been this hot in Colorado. He had been ordered to mow the lawn every Monday with the old push mower. It used to be Ian's job, but the lucky duck had landed a part-time job bagging groceries at the air-conditioned Safeway store. He complained about having to get up on time and putting on a white shirt to go to work, but that seemed a lot better than yard work in the sun.

It was looking like this was going to be Dalan's fate all summer long—probably the rest of his life—pulling weeds and mowing lawns. The only good thing about working in the yard was that he didn't have to wear much in the way of clothes. Cut-off old Levis and a T-shirt were about it. And the T-shirt was optional. When he got too hot he would turn on the garden hose and put his thumb over the end, making it spray into the air and rain back down on him—something he would never have thought of doing in Colorado. His mom didn't even care that his clothes got wet. His dad had given him a summer haircut with the dog clippers, leaving less than a quarter inch of blond fuzz on his head. The first day after the haircut he got his head sunburned, so from then on he always remembered to wear his baseball cap, and when his hat got wet, it would keep his head cool for several minutes.

He finished cutting the back lawn and was about halfway done with the front when he saw the girl walking down the road. She was wearing a pink blouse and light blue pants that were pretty tight and came just below her knees—he thought his mom called them "bike pushers," but he didn't know why. She had on a matching pink baseball cap. He couldn't think of a major league team that had pink hats. She was whistling as she walked.

He didn't have his shirt on at the moment, and still hadn't developed much of a tan—his skin was almost as pink as her shirt. He was dripping sweat mixed with grass and dust. As she walked closer he started to worry that the fly buttons of his Levis had come undone again or that maybe he had forgotten to fasten all of them. That was a frequent problem.

It turned out that it didn't matter anyway, because she didn't stop to talk or even to look at him. He thought about hollering at her when she was down the street a couple of houses, but that seemed pretty stupid. He'd missed his chance.

The game got started early on Monday evening. There were still some pretty pink and orange clouds in the western sky, reflecting the hidden sun, so hiding was pretty hard the first couple of games and everyone got tagged out quickly. Ian had to do the dishes and wanted to watch a baseball game on TV, so Dalan was on his own. He was "It" for the third game. There were ten kids playing, some having shown up late. He had no trouble getting the first six players out, easily finding them and running them down before they could get close to the can, but as it got darker he had trouble finding anyone. Just standing by the can was against the rules. Besides, a game could go on all night if "It" didn't at least go looking and flush out the players. At the same time Dalan was searching, he couldn't take his eyes off of the can for more than a split second.

He was in front of the house across the street when suddenly his peripheral vision picked up the light blue flash of movement from the left to right, toward the can. At first, he thought someone had thrown a shirt with a rock in it, like he had seen Ian do a few nights ago, but then he realized that it was the new girl. He was pretty sure she said her name was Marie, but he had been a bit flustered at the time she introduced herself.

He turned and ran as fast as he could to cut off her angle of approach, but it was too late. Reaching out to tag her, he tripped over a ground-surface tree root. The laws of physics did the rest. His forward momentum and the pull of gravity reduced his body to a tumbling ball of flesh and bone. Just as Marie's shoe nailed the can, sending it flying into the dry ditch alongside the road, Dalan crashed into her left leg, clipping it out from under her.

He heard the gravel dig into his skin, and then he felt the pain. He started to scream, but something stopped him. That girl, Marie, was laughing, her mouth just inches from his ears. When they finally untangled their arm and legs and struggled to their feet, the can had been re-kicked back into the street and everyone was "in free." He was still "It."

"You didn't get me," Marie laughed, "but that was a good try. Are you hurt?"

Dalan looked down at his hands and knees where multiple, beet-red eruptions were pushing blood through his dusty skin.

"I'm okay. Sorry I knocked you down. Are you okay?"

She looked at her blue pedal pushers and gave a little gasp. The knee on the left had a two-inch tear with jagged edges.

"Mom's going to kill me. I just got these for my fourteenth birthday," she said.

"I mow lawns. I get paid on Friday; I'll buy you a new pair," he said.

"No, no, silly boy; you would have to mow lawns all summer to pay for these. Mom bought them at Neiman Marcus in Phoenix. I wasn't supposed to wear them to play in, but I wanted you to see me in them."

It seemed as if his pain had vanished. He looked at her in the reflection of the street lamp and smiled. He had never heard of a Knee Man Market store but he had heard her say she wore her new pants just for him. He blushed and tried to make words out of his confusion, but none would come.

"Do you have to mow lawns tomorrow?" Marie asked, turning her head so only he could hear their conversation.

"Yeh, I have to mow the next door neighbor's grass, and then Boyd and I were gunna go swimming at the city pool."

"I get out of my piano lesson at ten thirty. I need you to meet me at the Tasty Freeze. You can go swimming afterward. I want to show you something I found out by the old Indian Ruins. You can't say no. After all, you owe me," she said, pointing to her knee. "If what I found is what I think it is, we can buy all the clothes in the whole Neiman Marcus store."

Too shy to say yes and too smart to say no, he nodded and smiled his biggest smile. "I'll jest go swimming later in the afternoon," he said.

"You better go wash the dirt out of those cuts or you'll get tetanus or polio," she said. And then she was gone, into the darkness of the night.

Dalan took a long hot bath—something he was usually reticent to do—washing the dirt and grit out of the little gouges the gravel had made in his shins. His thoughts were torn between watching the TV shows starting at eight and thinking about the strange request to meet that girl tomorrow. He knew nothing about her or her family as he was the "new kid in town" in the little cotton-farming community.

His family had moved to the town from Colorado Springs just after school was out for summer vacation. It was tough leaving his friends behind, especially at his age, after he had grown up with most of them through grade school. Telling them about moving to Arizona though, well, he had made it sound like a wonderful adventure. He told them how he wouldn't be stuck in the big city anymore and how he would be the star of the football and basketball teams since he wouldn't have so many kids in his school to compete with. He had stretched the truth like a bungee cord, bragging that he might even get a new dog or even a horse when the family got settled into their house in Arizona.

His dad had found an excellent job working for the power and light company. He was a solid-built man with a quiet disposition and a keen mind. He had a degree in electrical engineering from Colorado State and ten years of experience in the power and light business. He was a traditionalist believing that the man should earn the bread and the woman should manage the home and nurture the kids. Now his wife could do just that. With Mr. Dawson's new job in Arizona, Mrs. Dawson wouldn't have to work for a doctor anymore. The payment on the new house was a lot less than it had been in the big city.

The move to Arizona was because their grandpa had died the previous fall and Granny Peterson was all alone and getting to be real old. She needed Dalan's mom close by to help take care of her if she got sick, and to buy groceries and help keep her house clean. Everyone considered the move a blessing except Dalan. He missed his friends and the mountains and streams where he could explore. To make it worse, his parents hadn't even asked his opinion on moving to the hot, dry desert town.

Ian didn't seem to care about moving from Colorado one way or the other. He had been cut from the football team last fall because he wasn't muscular enough; he didn't make the basketball team because he was too short, and besides, he didn't even have a girlfriend in Colorado. He had found the job at the brand new Coolidge Safeway store his first week in town and already had met some of the local high school kids. He even claimed that he now had a girlfriend, but he always was telling fibs.

That left Dalan sitting around the house all day long or being Mom's lackey. He couldn't believe how many things she could come up with for him to do. Just this afternoon she made him crawl under the kitchen sink to stuff old rags into the cracks around the pipes where they came through the wall. Another time she held a ladder for him while he vacuumed mouse droppings from on top of the kitchen cabinets and one day she gave him a bucket and a rubber thing she called a "squeegee," and had him clean all of the outside windows. The worst thing was the weed pulling. The home's previous owners had ignored the yard's garden and flower beds. Dalan had no reprieve; Dad left for work early every day but Sunday and came home late in the evening, so he was always too tired to do much around the house. Thus, Dalan had become the official yardman.

His parents seemed happy most of the time. His mother was an optimist by nature, but was involved with the challenges of a move to a new town and with a new job caring for an elderly parent. It took a lot of her time, as did Dad's new supervisor job. The family always tried to eat their evening meals together and they always went to church on Sundays. The parents had trusted Dalan, thus he had lots of latitude in the use of his free time in the afternoons and evenings. Life for him was generally good; it was just that all the new odd jobs Mom piled on were getting to be a pain.

She had promised him the morning off the next day so he could go to the city pool with his new friend Boyd, whom he had met at church. He had agreed to mow the neighbor's lawn, but he could do that early. Now, he just hoped he could stretch the time away from home so he could meet the girl—Marie. He also had to figure out how he could ditch Boyd when they were done swimming.

Marie Palermo had been stuck in the dusty little town of Coolidge since she was a toddler. Her maternal grandfather had come to the desert's agricultural-rich valley as a laborer, but soon had organized his own work crews to haul hay and to pick cotton. By the time he retired thirty years later he owned thousands of acres of cotton farmland and whole convoys of farm equipment. He had become one of the leaders of the community. Marie's mom was sent off to college in New York, something her parents never could have dreamed of. Marie's mom, Gina, and dad, Franco, had met at Cornell University while taking a biology lab. Franco's family business had nothing to do with farming, but when Gina's father had an unexpected accident, the young couple was expected to move to the desert to take over her family's business. Franco still maintained business connections with his family in New York, but the exact nature of it was never discussed.

Marie's house was a huge white, two-story colonial, with a wrap-around porch, white pillars, and balconies off each of the upstairs bedrooms. It was surrounded with manicured lawns, shade trees, and flower beds. In back there was a swimming pool with its own gazebo and pool house. The house inside was big-city elegant, having been decorated by a professional from San Francisco. The house was fancy and yet often empty. It sat at the end of a tree-lined, gravel road on the edge of town, surrounded by fields of alfalfa and cotton. Marie's only sibling, named Kristen, was really an older half-sister from her dad's high school goof up. She was gone most of the time with girlfriends or guys.

Marie's parents always were busy. Franco was a workaholic, running the family businesses, which included a lot of traveling. A couple of times a year he even went to Italy to see his grandparents, but had never taken Marie or her mom. Gina was a tall, beautiful, and talented woman. She was a good mother and a social butterfly. Since she had grown up in the town, she knew almost everyone and everything about them. She was on several community committees and was treasurer of the Country Club. Now that Marie was a teenager—all of fourteen—Gina and Franco felt she was old enough to manage her own time, so she did.

As far back as Marie could remember the family had employed domestic help, including someone to prepare a big noon meal and a light supper. Someone did the laundry, cleaned the house, did the shopping, and even made the beds. For Marie, life was a lark. Aside from caring for herself, she had no real responsibilities, except keeping up with her studies, including piano, voice, and painting. The downside was that she was bored. She woke up bored, she went through the day bored, and she went to sleep at night bored. She had dreaded the last day of school because it was followed by the first day of summer vacation, which she knew would be boring. This morning however, she was wired.

She woke up early and rather than pulling the soft duvet up over her head and drifting back into dreamland, she threw off the covers and jumped out of bed. She checked the clock and cussed under her breath—something she had learned from her sister Kristen. Two more hours until her mom would leave for Phoenix on her weekly shopping spree. Marie always was invited to come along, but she claimed chronic car sickness and was allowed to stay at home to practice her piano and voice. Her mother was already grooming her to be Miss Pinal County, and hopefully Miss Arizona, someday.

Marie loitered around the kitchen, taking so long to eat her Cheerios that the last few bites were soggy. Next, she wandered out to the six-car garage where her Dad kept his collection of old cars, which he claimed he was going to restore someday. So far Marie knew of just one that he had worked on, turning a rusting car body into a spectacular 1932 deuce coupe hot rod. Most of the cars were still junkers. The car she like most was her dad's new 1958 Corvette.

Franco had collected a vast workbench of tools, scattered here and there in no organized way. Marie picked through the inventory, selecting and then placing the chosen tools in her backpack. She wasn't exactly sure what would be needed for the task she had in mind, so she took a variety of chisels, pliers, and a small hammer. Carrying a full-size shovel would be impractical, so she raided her mom's gardening closet. Just as she suspected, all of the tools looked brand new—apparently they'd never been used. Her mother always was talking about the vegetable garden she was going to plant, and would often stop at the little nursery on the edge of town and buy tomato and chili plants, but they always died before she took time to plant them. Marie picked out two small hand spades, adding them to her backpack.

Back at the kitchen she gave her mom the obligatory peck on the cheek and walked to the car with her to wave goodbye. The cook had the day off from preparing a noon meal since her mom would be gone, and her dad planned to attend the Cotton Growers Co-Op luncheon, which usually lasted all afternoon.

Back in the kitchen she found a couple bags of potato chips and a package of Twinkies. Hefting her backpack onto her shoulder she drank a big glass of tap water, pulled on her pink Yankee's baseball cap and slipped out the door.

Dalan also had awakened early. The sun was shining through the thin curtain into his eyes. He lay in the bed thinking about the night before, the game of kick the can and the strange conversation with that girl. He tried to imagine what the heck she wanted to meet him for, but drew a total blank. He had asked his only friend, Boyd, about the girl when the boys met at the pool, but only got a shrug. He guessed the younger Boyd hadn't yet realized that girls could be kind of fun once you get to know them.

"Hi Mom," he said, wandering into the kitchen still rubbing the sleep out of his eyes.

"Hi sweetheart," Mom said. "What are you doing up so early?"

"The sun sure comes up early here," he said, matter of fact. "Has Dad already gone to work?"

"Yes, they agreed on a six o'clock start for the rest of the summer. That's what lots of people do here. That way they can get done with the outside work before it gets too hot. If you're going to cut the Goebles' lawn you might as well get started right after you have breakfast. I hate to see you out in the middle of the day baking in that sun. Ian has to be at work at nine. You could be done before he even gets up; of course the lawn mower might wake him."

And it did. Dalan was just making his first pass with the mower along the sidewalk when an old, shriveled-up grapefruit whizzed by his ear, splatting onto the mailbox in a dozen mushy pieces. He turned to see Ian standing on the front porch in just his boxer shorts, winding up to launch another fruit missile. Ian was a good brother, and almost never got mad—he just got even. Dalan guessed he deserved a little retaliation for waking up the neighborhood with the noisy mower, but he wasn't going to lie down and die for Ian without a little fun. Leaving the mower running he dove behind a pomegranate bush, coming up with a moldy pomegranate the size of a softball. He crept around to the side of the house then sprang out into the open yard, side-arming the crimson fruit toward the edge of the porch. His timing was perfect. Ian stepped out in the open looking for his little brother just as the juicy, over-ripe fruit arrived via air mail.

"You little creep," Ian yelled, clutching his chest in faux pain, inadvertently smearing the juice with both hands. "I'll get you if it's the last thing I ever do."

He sprinted off the porch toward Dalan and was gaining on him by the time they reached the Petersons' yard. They both heard their mom's voice at the same time. It wasn't the first time she had called one, or both of them, to repentance at 120 decibels.

Dalan made the mistake of stopping in his tracks. Ian had made several mistakes, the first being caught in broad daylight in his underwear a hundred feet from the house. The others all had to do with forward momentum and being the older brother.

When they collided, both went rolling onto the grass with Ian coming up on top. He was in the process of grabbing a handful of new grass clippings to stuff in little brother's mouth when the working end of the broom landed upside his head, knocking him off balance. Looking up from the ground, both boys saw Mom, hands on her hips, the kitchen broom still dangling from one hand.

"Tell me, Ian, are you trying to make a new fashion statement?" Mom said, trying to look mad but suppressing a grin.

Ian said nothing. He was busy rubbing the side of his face, more in hope of sympathy than in reducing the pain.

Dalan was doing his best not to start laughing. He did notice that Mom's face looked extra pretty out in the open air, a light breeze lifting her long auburn hair and pleated skirt. A ray of sunlight caught the small diamond in her simple wedding ring, giving her youngest son a flash of pride that his mom owned a diamond. She was the best and most beautiful mom in the whole wide world, until she turned her gaze on Dalan.

"And you, Mister Whitey Ford, I saw you throw the fruit at your brother like you were pitching the winning strike at the World Series."

Mom loved sports analogies almost as much as gloves and hats.

"He started it. I'm just trying to get the grass cut before it gets so hot that I have a stroke of sun," he said, staring at Ian.

"It's called heat stroke, retard," Ian said. "Mom, I was trying to get some sleep. You know I'm a working man now. That Mr. Taylor at the grocery store made me move a whole aisle of canned vegetables yesterday—eighteen hundred cans."

The lawn mower, which had been running on idle during the entire confrontation, sputtered to a stop and then backfired with a rifle-sounding burst.

No one spoke. The mower had finished the conversation. Ian headed for the house wiping his juice-stained hands on the back of Dalan's white T-shirt as he passed. Dalan merely glared at him.

"Boys, your dad is taking me to Phoenix for lunch. We have a meeting afterward with our attorney to draw up a new will. I should be home in time to fix supper. Try to stay out of trouble," she said, bending down to give Dalan a kiss.

Most boys his age would have detested the overt demonstration of affection, but Dalan loved his mom and cherished her attention when they were alone together. He started to give her a big hug, but she stepped back. You'll mess up my new outfit," she said, smiling and pointing to a glob of rotted grapefruit stuck to the shoulder of his shirt "Better be sure you put that in the wash before you go swimming. I'll leave a fifty-cent piece on the counter for you before I leave so you can get a hot dog at the pool."

He had trouble getting the mower restarted after it had run out of gas. He called his Dad, and did all the things Dad had told him to try, but nothing was working. Finally, in desperation, he knocked on Ian's bedroom door. His brother apparently had forgotten all about their fight and came out to the yard. Within five seconds Ian had the mower running—the kill switch was engaged. Ian didn't return to the house, but headed straight for his rusty old Schwinn and rode off toward downtown and work.

Dalan finished mowing and trimming the lawn by ten fifteen. When the sidewalk was swept and everything was put away he took a fast shower and was running out the door when he remembered to call Boyd.

"I can't go swimming until after two o'clock," he told his friend.

"How come? You promised to meet me at noon!" Boyd said.

"I can't explain now. I'll see you there. I might have a good secret to tell you by then," he teased.

The streets were sending off heat waves that looked like glistening pools of water from a distance. The tar on the roads was getting so hot that it was starting to make little bubbles from the intense summer sun. Dalan thought about riding his bike but didn't have a good lock, and he didn't know if the girl would be walking or riding. In the end, he decided to leave the bike in the shed beside the garage and cut through the back alleys, staying in the shade as much as possible.

He could see her from a block away. She was wearing a pair of dark blue jeans—the way his looked before their first wash. Her shirt was a fancy cowgirl kind with pearl snap buttons just like he saw the rodeo queen wear in the Memorial Day parade. She had on new-looking blue Keds and that pink Yankees baseball cap. It looked kind of funny because her long black ponytail was sticking out of a hole in the back. Her face was the prettiest he had ever seen and the sunlight made her even prettier than she was in the evenings when they played the street games. As he got closer, he again noticed that her eyes were a chocolate brown color. When she looked at him it seemed like he was looking into bottomless pools of water. When she saw him she gave a little wave, which he returned, but did so with his hand still down near his side.

"Hi," she said.

"Hi," he said.

"I was worried that you might not come," she said.

"I had to finish the lawn and then have a shower. My brother tried to beat me up this morning and smeared pomegranate juice on me."

"You're lucky you have a brother. How are your scrapes from the gravel last night?" she asked.

"I forgot I even had them," he said, glancing at his knees.

She laughed and started digging in the front pocket of her jeans.

"They have really good curly French fries here. Let's eat some and have a Coke then I'm going to take you to the coolest place you have ever seen."

He started to object, but then saw her pull a whole five-dollar bill out of her jean's pocket. He tried to help pay for the food with his fifty-cent piece but she refused, saying that since she had invited him, it was her obligation to pay. He didn't have enough money anyway, so thanked her and put his coin away. The food arrived and they dug in. He had never heard of curly French fries, but he loved them. "You are so right about these fries," he said. "They're the best. Thanks. Say, where did you get that weird hat with the hole in the back?"

"My dad brought it from New York when he visited his uncles. It's the latest fad. See, you can adjust the size with this plastic snap thing in back," she said, taking it off to show him. "It's perfect for my hair—keeps it out of my eyes. I'd like to cut my hair short but none of the kids in my family are allowed to have short hair. My dad thinks girls with short hair all want to be boys."

Kick The Can

"How many kids in your family?" he asked.

"Just me and my sister, Kristen," she said. "You'll probably never meet her. She is real old and doesn't like young kids."

Dalan dropped his gaze a little, thinking that Marie must think he was just a young kid too. They finished eating and went out the door and across the highway toward a farm road that ran along a high chain link fence.

"Here, you better put this thing on your head or you'll have blisters." She pulled a faded green hat from her backpack.

"Who's John Deere?" Dalan asked, squinting at the name on the cap.

"You are a city kid aren't you?" she said with a laugh.

The Casa Grande Indian Ruins were surrounded by a high, chain-link fence with a double strand of barbed wire running along the top. The first time Dalan saw the fence he thought the place was a prison. Marie explained to him that the site was an ancient Indian dwelling that at one time was over four stories tall. Before it was abandoned around 1430 A.D., it was the cultural center for thousands of desert-dwelling Native Americans who farmed the surrounding area and even invented an advanced form of irrigation to bring water from the mountains to the desert valley. Since 1918 it had been managed by the National Park Service.

There was a gate along the entrance road off the main highway, where the visitors had to stop and pay a nominal fee. There were lots of rules once guests arrived inside, all put in place to help protect the multi-story adobe and wood structure. It was surprisingly close to town and only a mile and a half from the Tasty Freeze where they met.

"Before the Federal government took over the place, it had been open to anyone who wanted to drive up the half-mile-long dirt road and wander around. As a result, there were initials and dirty pictures carved in the mud walls right alongside ancient petroglyphs. Some of the rafters were broken from kids climbing around on top like a bunch of monkeys," Marie explained to Dalan.

The two were standing in the shade of an old manzanita tree about ten feet from the back side of the park's square mile of property. There were NO TRESPASSING signs every hundred feet or so along the fence.

Dalan had heard about the ruins, but in the hassle of moving, Dad starting a new job, and settling into their new house, the family hadn't begun taking in the local scenery or attractions.

"That thing is really cool," he said, looking through the fence at the covered adobe ruin. "Have you been inside?"

"Sure, every kid in town's been there. It's an annual field trip for every kid in the county. You'll get to go inside once we are back in school, but that's not what I brought you up to see. Follow behind me, and from now on, keep your voice down to a whisper. One more thing; there could be scorpions, Gila monsters, or even rattlesnakes along the way so watch out where you step and where you put your hands. If you see or hear a snake just freeze and let me take care of it. I've killed lots of snakes," Marie said in a tone that left no room for discussion, but lots of room for worry on Dalan's part.

The two youngsters followed the fence line toward the west for a quarter of a mile where a deep gully dipped into the desert floor. There they half-walked, half-slid down a steep embankment to the wide sandy floor of the gully. It was full of tumbleweeds that had been blown in from the desert to the west. As they walked along the deep, natural canal Marie explained, "The 'Big House,' as it is known in English, is called *La Casa Grande* in Spanish. That is its official name. It was originally built on a raised *mesa*, or table top, overlooking the surrounding farmlands. This was done for protection from being attacked by surprise and to keep it from getting flooded. Where we are right now is called an *arroyo*. During the spring rains these arroyos sometimes fill with rushing water, flooding the surrounding desert valleys and eroding the soil. Last year this arroyo was like a fast-running river for almost two weeks."

Dalan was following her, listening to the school teacher-like lecture, but mostly watching where every step of his feet was landing. He was wishing he had worn his high-top boots and long jeans instead of his cut-off Levis and canvas shoes.

Three hundred yards up the gully, Marie stopped beside a cluster of four-foot diameter tumbleweeds. She retrieved a long stick from a cluster of bushes and pushed the tumbleweeds aside. There in front of Dalan's eyes lay an opening about the diameter of Ian's old red hula-hoop. It extended deep into the side of the hill in the direction of the ruins. Marie used the big stick to clear away some spider webs, then she reached into her backpack and pulled out a small flashlight.

"You didn't tell me to bring a flashlight," Dalan said, his worried eyes darting back and forth between Marie's hand and the dark tunnel opening.

"Don't worry about it," she said in the sweetest voice he could imagine, and then she clicked on the light. "Let's have a look, Doctor Livingston."

Dalan didn't have a clue who the doctor was that she mentioned, but not being in a position to chicken out, he ducked down and followed as she led the way into the cave. Her light offered only minimal illumination into the long, pitch-black tunnel. The floor of the tunnel was soft and the air was cool and felt good. They were some twenty feet from the opening when the daylight behind him disappeared completely. He felt sweat running down his forehead, but when he wiped it away, his fingers didn't feel wet.

"Have you ever been inside here before?" he asked, his voice quivering.

"Heck no! I'm afraid of the dark. That's why I brought you," she said, giving a tiny giggle.

CHAPTER 2

Harvey Grimes hated the dirty little desert town. His friend Melvin at boot camp used to live in Coolidge, and had told him what a swell place it was. Now he knew that the guy was an idiot. Melvin told him there were lots of great jobs to be had, which was true if your idea of a good job was shoveling ditches or driving tractors in the one-hundred-and-twenty-degree sun. Coolidge was half way between Phoenix to the northwest and Tucson to the south. "It's the perfect location," Melvin had insisted. "Halfway to paradise in either direction. There are college girls at ASU near Phoenix and at the University of Arizona in Tucson."

Harvey had taken the bad advice hoping the town would be the perfect place to get a new start in life. He now knew that he was sadly mistaken. He had been unemployed for two months after his dishonorable discharge from the navy. The court-martial-ordered rehabilitation clinic had helped him kick his drinking problem, but he didn't think his problem was that bad anyway. He had never touched liquor before he put on a uniform. What he needed when he got out was a job good enough to save some money and then he could go to California and get into college. The thing about Coolidge, Arizona, that Marvin forgot to mention was that all of the available jobs required actual physical work, and not one of them paid above minimum wage.

He had managed to find a room to rent in the home of an old widower named Fred Larsen. The room was nicer than any Harvey had ever lived in, even at home in Arkansas. It was clean as a whistle, and it had its own little bathroom with a shower and its own entrance with a covered front porch. Mr. Larsen was friendly and welcomed Harvey with a smile.

He even cleared off a shelf in the Frigidaire for him. Fred had lost his wife a few years before and didn't have any pictures of any other younger family sitting around on the piano or coffee table. He did have a black-and-white television, but it sat on a low stand just a few feet in front of an old, heavy, cracked-leather arm chair, with the telephone and a coffee mug sitting on an adjacent lamp table. Best of all, Fred didn't have an arms-length list of rules and regulations to worry about every minute, like they did in the navy. Harvey handed over most of his military paycheck to pay the rent for a month.

The best job Harvey could find was on the early shift at a local drive up hamburger joint called Bill's Biggest Burgers. He told Fred that he didn't really need a place with a kitchen, just a bathroom and a soft bed. For work he had to shave his red beard every morning before he put on the starched outfit Bill's manager required. He had to keep his hair short and his finger nails clean. Only when he got home from work could he put on his Levis and Razorback T-shirt.

Harvey had come to town on the Greyhound bus in late April with a hundred and forty dollars in his pocket. All of his worldly possessions fit easily into an old hard-shell Samsonite suitcase, which he bought at a garage sale for three dollars. Both the locks were broken but the snaps worked. Harvey had lucked out with both the job and the rented room. Had the local cops seen him wandering the streets with his battered suitcase, they probably would have driven him to the county line and told him to keep walking.

It wasn't as though he was a hardened criminal or anything like that; it was just that he started drinking too much when he was in the navy and it got out of hand. When he was arrested by the MPs onboard with a stolen bottle of Jim Beam from the base BX, the military judge gave him the choice of the brig or an alcoholic rehabilitation program along with a dishonorable discharge.

Harvey's new landlord was a friendly enough guy, and even let him know that should he ever need a ride to work, like on a rainy day, he just had to ask and Fred would run him there in his Plymouth Belvedere. Otherwise, it was walking or a rusty, used bike for Harvey. Fred didn't work anymore and didn't seem to have any hobbies. "Mostly I watch the TV, go for long walks, and read the newspapers every day."

Fred smoked an old hickory pipe, which for Harvey, was a real bummer. His last bunk mate had been a three-pack-a-day Camel smoker and left the open packs lying around. The guy never mentioned missing borrowed smokes since the tobacco companies were always giving the military guys free smokes anyway—to get them hooked. Since he moved in with Fred, he had—by financial necessity—quit smoking. It made him a Nervous Nelly but after a couple of weeks his craving started to wane.

He liked his new job with its free burgers, greasy French fries, and Cokes, but his work shift was over every day at five o'clock. This left him with nothing to do during the long evenings except watch television with Fred. There were only three channels, and channel five looked more like a snowstorm than a broadcast program. The only way to clearly see the picture was if you stood and held on to the rabbit ears. Both men had tried everything to adjust the darn thing, but it usually only worked well during the Drano and Ipana toothpaste commercials. They figured that the station managers must turn up the broadcast power during commercials, just like they did the volume.

Once the days became longer and school was out for the summer, Harvey had taken to sitting on the raised front porch, reading and watching the neighbors. There was a row of waist-high bushes all around Fred's porch making a sort of visual camouflage so people on the street couldn't see Harvey very well, but from the old oak rocker he had a good view of them. He found a rusty pair of war surplus navy binoculars in

Fred's garage and took them apart, cleaned and rebuilt them so they were as good as new. With the binoculars, he could see up and down the street for six or eight houses, and had a clear view of the intersection of Pinkley with Main Street—about two hundred yards to the east. Within a couple of weeks he knew which cars would turn into which driveways and whose kids belonged with each house. He could see the fire trucks and police cruisers zipping back and forth on Main and watched an occasional accident. The town had recently installed the only red light in town at that corner. No one was used to more than a stop sign, so there were lots of screeching tires and close calls.

In the evening, as the sun settled into the hills to the west, things in the neighborhood became more interesting. When there was no traffic on Main Street to watch, he could hear the conversations of couples walking up and down the street a few paces away. He even could hear and see some of the neighbors inside their houses—until they put down the blinds—if they remembered or cared. He watched some eat dinner at their kitchen tables and could clearly hear occasional family quarrels or a scolding if the kids didn't come in when called.

Lately, he had looked forward to the nightly street games that several of the neighborhood kids played. As long as there was sunlight they liked to play softball, usually just "flies-are-up," but as it got darker the kids turned to a hide-and-seek-like game. His favorite game to watch, and theirs to play, was kick the can. One night they came to Fred's front door to see if he had an empty Folgers coffee can. Why it had to be a Folgers can Harvey would never understand. All Fred could find was Maxwell House, so the crazy kids turned it down and went to the next house.

The kids playing the street games varied in age from nine or ten to sixteen. Once they or one of their friends could drive, they apparently never wanted to be seen in the neighborhood again. With his binoculars he could watch the kids' faces, examine their clothes and shoes, and sometimes he even recognized their names from seeing them at Bill's Burgers or hearing their names shouted by the others. He would try to figure out what their old man did for a living or how fat or skinny their moms were. He started to find that he had favorites among the kids, especially the boys who were athletic and even more specifically, the older girls. Not every one of the kids showed up each night, and of course an occasional dust storm or rare thunderstorm would put the damper on the evening's event.

His favorite observations were those interactions between teenage girls and boys. Watching them made him think back on his own high school days and how he used to wish this girl or that one would talk to or even smile at him. Sometimes, watching the street games, he would secretly root for one of his favorites to win. One night he even found himself standing up and cheering when the pretty girl with the long black ponytail collided with a punky kid, knocking them both down. She still got up and ran across the street, kicking the can to win the game. Afterward, he watched her take down her hair and shake it to get the grass out. It glistened like silk in the streetlight's glow.

That night he had followed her home, staying a long way behind so she wouldn't see him. She lived several streets away, past a cluster of big houses with large lawns and double garages. Her house was a mansion by comparison. It was surrounded by fields and had a pool in back. There was a brand new black Cadillac Fleetwood sitting out in front, and a four-wheel drive Ford pickup truck in one of the four garages. Best of all was his all-time favorite dream car, a shiny new 1958 Chevrolet Corvette.

He was standing across from the house, lost in a world of dreaming, when a police cruiser slowly rolled by. He stepped into the shadow of a cottonwood tree, but it was too late. The car came to a stop, and then backed up and the driver's window went down. A bright flashlight suddenly glared in his eyes and a voice broke the surrounding silence.

"Are you lost, buster?" asked the hefty voice behind the blinding light.

Harvey could hear the country western radio station playing a Johnny Cash song through the open window. He stepped closer to the car, and when the light was taken off of his face, he saw a shotgun in a rack above the officer's seat.

"No sir, I'm trying to sell subscriptions to the Tucson newspaper," Harvey said.

"Which one would that be?" asked the cop.

Harvey almost turned and ran, but then he was jolted with a moment of divine inspiration.

"Both of them, sir," he said, his voice cracking a bit.

"Well I'll save you some time and trouble. The people in this neighborhood already take whichever newspaper they want—probably a Phoenix newspaper—and I can assure you that they won't want to be bothered, especially after dark. You know you look familiar. Don't you work over at Bill's?"

"Yes sir, I do. I'm just trying to earn a little extra money to help my little brother get a brace for his leg. He had polio," Harvey lied.

His bad luck changed when the police radio squawked something about a fender bender at Main and Grant Street. The officer suggested Harvey contain his door-to-door selling to daylight hours, and pulled away, spinning his tires and making a rooster tail of flying gravel.

Turning to leave, Harvey glanced at the well-lit house and saw a middle-aged woman standing in the kitchen window. She was even prettier than the girl. She leaned closer to the window as though she could see him standing in the dark. She looked for several minutes, which made him afraid to move. Then he saw the front door open and heard the dog. It wasn't a usual bark but more the deep roar of a big hungry dog. He suddenly remembered the trained attack dogs back at the military base and a jolt of fear ran up his spine. He turned and ran like the wind.

CHAPTER 3

Dalan had felt his heart beat extra fast before, but never when he was just standing still. He wasn't sure if it was the darkness of the cave that he was afraid of, or letting Marie witness his fear and imminent cowardliness. It was so dark in the cave that when she tripped on a pile of round stones, dropping the light, he couldn't see her or even his own hands when he held them in front of his face. For a second he wondered if he had gone completely blind. No light was visible from the entrance, since they had navigated the small angled turn twenty-five feet into the cave. Though the opening had been tight, once they were well inside, the height increased to where the two could stand erect. There was a peculiar odor of fresh, wet soil in the cave mixed with a sour animal scent. Only the sounds of their own footsteps and breathing could be heard.

"How did you find this place?" he whispered, not knowing why he was trying to being so quiet.

"Last month my little dog that ran away from me. It was a Scotty with soft black hair. I opened the gate in the backyard and she took off and wouldn't come back. Mom and Dad were gone and just the housekeeper was home. Nobody would help me look for her. I was on my bicycle when I heard barking so I ran down into the gully. She wasn't here, but I saw a coyote pup run out of the cave. When I got closer to the cave it ran back in. I thought the mom must have killed and eaten my Scotty."

That just about did it for Dalan. He was turning to leave when she yelled for him to look. Deeper in the cave there was a dirt shelf cut into the side of the wall. It was a couple of feet off the ground and fifteen or twenty feet long. Glistening in the flashlight's beam they both saw a line-up of large, earthen pots. Some were the size of the gallon pickle jars at the grocery store, while others were two or three times that big. The first thing he noticed was how they were lined up so perfectly—almost like they were meant to be on display or part of some kind of ceremony. As Marie shined the light up and down the row they could see that the pots were covered with fine drawings of animals and people. There were geometric lines on some of the ancient-looking pots. Their base color was grayish red. Their surfaces were smooth, and though covered with a light layer of dust, the artwork was still visible. At the end of the row there were two that were different than the others—fatter, shorter, and on closer inspection, filled with powdery, gray dirt.

Dalan couldn't resist. He bent down and blew real hard on the edge of one of the larger pots. The dust flew away, revealing a smooth, glazed surface.

"Wow! They are beautiful. How old are they?" he asked.

"I don't know for sure, but I have been reading whatever I could find at the library and I think the caves must have belonged to the people who built the Casa Grande Ruins in the fourteenth century. That would make them over six hundred years old."

"Look at the pictures of the people and the horses, and look, there is even a dog. Did you ever find your black Scotty?"

"Oh, I forgot to tell you. By the time I got back home, he was lying by the gate, asleep."

Deeper in the cave there was some old rug-like material that was rolled up and tied with a hemp rope. Dalan hoped they would find arrowheads or even a spear, but the flashlight was getting dim. They came to the end of the cave about twenty feet from the pots and couldn't see any more treasure, so they turned to retrace their steps. They had become used to the darkness and the silence and to each other. A couple of times they had even held hands to help guide one another— probably not even realizing it at the time.

"This place is really neat," Dalan whispered, as they passed the pot lineup and headed for the entrance. "How many people do you think know about it?"

At first she acted like she didn't hear him. Just short of the entrance where they would have to stoop down to emerge to the outside, she stopped and turned to face him.

"I think we are the first people to see those pots in hundreds of years. Think about it. If anyone would have found them they would have taken them or broken them up. I think the entrance must have been sealed and then maybe the big flooding rainstorm we had last winter eroded away enough dirt so it opened up the cave."

"There was that much water in this gully?"

"Everything was flooded. They called it the hundred-year flood. Even the bridge on the road to Phoenix was washed out."

"So what are we gunna do?" Dalan asked, continuing to defer leadership to Marie.

"We need to come back with better lights and a camera. I got a little Brownie camera with special flashbulbs for Christmas. I don't use it much but I'll find it and get new flashbulbs and we can come back and take pictures."

"Shouldn't we tell somebody?" Dalan asked.

"Hell no," she said, surprising his tender ears. He couldn't believe that she had used a cuss word. His mom had washed out Ian's mouth with soap one time for saying "damn."

"If we tell anybody, the first thing that will happen is a bunch of high school kids will come in here and bust everything to pieces. Remember that I said these things could be like sunken or buried treasure? We can maybe sell them to a museum or some rich person."

"What about our parents? Shouldn't we at least tell them?"

"No! No, no. We don't tell anybody until we have pictures and a plan. When we get the pictures, we can write to a museum and find out exactly what they are and maybe offer them to the museum. At least they will be safe."

"Okay," Dalan said, not sounding convinced.

She grabbed his arms with both hands and pulled him close to her.

"You have got to promise me you won't tell anybody, not even your parents and especially not your brother. Promise?"

"Are you sure you don't want to tell your dad?" he asked.

"Nobody, do you understand? Nobody! Say you promise me! Cross your heart and hope to die."

He crossed his heart and mumbled that he promised.

"Promise me with a kiss. That's what my mom always makes my dad do."

He looked at her, startled, not knowing what he was supposed to do. He didn't have to wait long to find out. Marie leaned toward him and pressed her lips against his. His instincts told him to turn away, but he didn't. Seconds later she moved away from him and bent down to crawl out through the narrow opening into the bright sunlight.

They scouted around to make sure no one was in sight then carefully covered the cave's entrance with the large tumbleweeds, and brushed their footprints away with broken sticks. Not much was said as they walked the distance back into town. The summer sun was intense, and both were dripping with sweat by the time they got to Main Street.

"My friend, Boyd, is meeting me at the city pool for a swim. Would you like to come?" He asked.

"That sounds great, but my mom won't allow me to swim in the city pool. It's 'cause of all the polio. Did you know that we have a swimming pool at my house?"

"No kidding? So you can go swimming any time you want, even on Sundays when the city pool is closed?"

"Yes," she said, raising her thick dark eyebrows like it was the dumbest question she had ever heard.

"That's so cool. I've never known anyone who had their own swimming pool."

"I'd have you over to swim at my house but my mom and dad are both gone and I'm not supposed to have friends over when they aren't there. Maybe I can arrange for something in a day or two. I'll ask Mom. Are you going to play the game tonight?"

"Nothing else to do at night so I guess I'll see you there," he said, turning toward his house.

"Dalan!" she shouted, when he was already down the road a few paces. "Remember, say nothing!" She pressed her index finger to her lips, staring over the top of it.

He nodded in the affirmative, but in his heart was already beginning to wonder if he could really keep a secret of such magnitude. He couldn't remember the last time he had a real secret to keep. Ian was always swearing him to secrecy, but it always was over the stupidest little things imaginable. The last one was when he brought home a magazine full of pictures of girls in swimsuits and made Dalan promise not to tell Mom. There was no way Dalan would just walk into the kitchen and announce that Ian had a girl's swimsuit advertisement. Why should she care, unless it was to worry that Ian was considering buying a girl's swimsuit for himself? The thing Marie said about the pots being some kind of hidden treasure, now that was something important. He would love to tell Boyd, or even Ian, but since he had promised and crossed his heart, and even sealed it with a kiss, he would have to wait. He hoped he could.

CHAPTER 4

There was a late afternoon dust storm the likes of which the new folks in town never had seen. One minute it was hot and sunny, and the next minute a few small gusts of warning came. Immediately visibility dropped to twenty feet at best and the howling wind blew fine grit and sand into every open space in the county. Tin roofs flew down the open streets as if in a foot race with the blowing cardboard, paper sacks, and tumbleweeds. The wind and dust was followed by a lightning-powered cloud burst, which left the neighborhood dripping. The sun was still bright enough to peek beneath the clouds giving a fiery orange hue to the whole town.

An occasional car came down Pinkley Street, hitting the puddles, sending out muddy sprays as it went by the Dawson house. Ian stood by the street contemplating what the fenderless rear bike tire, combined with the muddy water, was going to do to the back of his shirt. He had to work late since the store always stayed open late on the first and fifteenth of the month. That was payday for the Levis Strauss plant—the only real industry in town. It also was payday for the bank and a few other businesses. On those days the parking lot was packed and there was a crowd waiting for help getting their bags to their cars. He could hear the voices of the kids sitting on porches waiting for the evening fun to begin. He hated getting old and having to work.

Only a few kids showed up at first to play kick the can, but by the time the sun was completely down and darkness set firmly in, the street was getting congested. The air was moist and much cooler than it had been for weeks. Dalan noticed several younger kids that he hadn't seen before. It took longer to play a game when there were so many, especially those who had to be taught or who cried the first time they got tagged. He was glad he didn't have to watch out for a younger brother or sister.

Dalan loved to win every time, but with so many kids it would take forever to play just one game. He suggested that they split up in two groups, divided by age, but they only had one can, and everyone complained about being split up from their best friend or older siblings.

Boyd took charge and immediately elected Dalan to be "It." Dalan would speed up the game if he did the searching. He already had learned all the good places to hide and he could run real fast. He closed his eyes and counted to twenty, then set out searching. After ten minutes the red can still sat upright on the middle of the tar and gravel road. The first person put out would be "It" for the next game, so it was a trick for him to try to tag the guy or girl he wanted to be "It."

He hadn't seen Marie arrive at the beginning of the game, and then all of sudden there she was, racing past him toward the can. At first he sprinted to catch her—then he had another idea.

"Ping!" went the can, bouncing onto the sidewalk and then onto the grass.

"You missed me," she chided, laughing as she bent down, hands on her knees, trying to catch her breath.

Dalan didn't stop to talk, but quickly rushed toward a big oleander bush where he knew three kids were hiding.

"You're out," he shouted, then repeated it twice more, tagging the kids on their shoulders. One of the shorter kids started to cry, and immediately the kid's big sister stepped from around the corner and slapped Dalan hard on the ear.

"How'd that feel you bully? Don't ever hit my little brother hard like that again!" she said.

Dalan was startled. He didn't think he had tagged the kid all that hard. He started to chase after the girl to tell her so when Marie grabbed him by the back of his T-shirt.

"Let her go. That kid is in the same grade you are. He's just a wimp and she is always using him as an excuse to smack somebody. Just keep playing."

The new game started with a count to fifteen. Next round it would be to ten and then five. As Dalan ran off to hide Marie charged right behind him. He snuggled into a tight spot between the bushes on the side of Mr. Larsen's house. Mr. Larsen was a friendly old guy who was always asking the kids to call him Fred, but Dalan's parents said to always call his elders Mr., or Mrs., or sir, or ma'am, out of respect.

"I've got this place," Dalan said as a warm body smashed up against him.

"Shush! There's room for both of us," Marie said, leaning on his foot with her hand.

It took a second for him to compute that it was her. He squeezed up against the wall to give her more room, but she just nudged closer. He could smell her Doublemint-gum breath and when she turned to look at the street, her hair brushed his face. It had a flowery smell that he knew he could learn to love.

"Can you get away tomorrow about three?" she asked.

"What for?" he asked with a whisper.

"I got some new flashbulbs for my camera and a new roll of film. We can go to the cave and take the pictures. I have dance lessons until two. I also found another flashlight and new batteries so you can have your own flashlight."

"What are we going to do if we get caught?" he asked.

"There is no way anyone is going to catch us. Nobody goes out in gullies during the heat of the day. Meet me at the high school football field. I'll be by the ticket booth. It is going to be so fun!" She gave his arm a squeeze and dashed out of the bushes heading for the Folgers can.

Dalan hid quietly while a couple more players were tagged out. Once, he could have sworn he heard the screen door behind him on Fred's porch, but from where he was hiding he would have had to stand up above the bushes to see where the noise was coming from.

The games finished early so he went in to take his bath. Mom poured his bedtime snack into his favorite Davy Crockett bowl. He loved Wheaties and hoped to grow up to be a track star like that guy on the box. He pulled his sleeve back and flexed his bicep like the super star, checking his reflection out in the kitchen window. When his mom came back into the room he blushed and tugged his sleeve back in place.

"Mowing lawns is making those muscles grow big and strong," she said, bending down to kiss his forehead.

"Mom, have you ever heard about any buried treasure around here? You know like old Indian stuff or Calvary guns?"

"Not that I've heard of. Have you, Ian?" she said, looking over Dalan's head to his brother, who had appeared in the kitchen doorway, still wearing his white apron from the store. He shook his head and turned away, revealing a thin line of mud spots going up the middle of his back.

"Why do you ask, sweetheart?" she said, bending down to give him another good night kiss.

"Oh, I don't know. Some kids in town were just talking. Did you know that the O.K. Corral and Tombstone are only a hundred miles from here?"

"There was no such thing," Ian said in a know-it-all tone. "That's just some story a newspaper guy made up. I swear Dalan; you're so dumb you would believe anything. You've probably already let somebody take you on a snipe hunt."

"What is a snipe?" their mom asked.

All three of them started to laugh.

❖ ❖ ❖

Harvey Grimes' day had started out good, but now he had a bad headache. His boss had been on his case all morning.

Bill, a short chubby man, first started griping about Harvey not putting the ketchup in the middle of the buns and then about not speaking clearly into the microphone when he took customers' orders. The complaints had gone on all day.

When he got back home he took a nap, then he tried to relax on the front porch. He had been caught in the rainstorm on the walk home from work and had forgotten to bring home a cheeseburger for supper. He had settled for a can of cold Franco-American spaghetti, which left him with indigestion and in a bad mood. He needed fresh air.

When he finally settled into the front porch rocker he heard a rustling noise in the shrubs below. He could only see one person, the girl with the long black hair, but then he heard the voice that he was sure belonged to the kid from across the street. They were less than eight feet away. He silently eased himself into the rocker to listen.

He had to carefully tune his ears into the conversation to make out anything. He came away with what he thought were just fragments, but the fragments were very interesting. He learned that they planned to meet the next day and go to some gallery or gully where there wouldn't be anyone to see them. He became especially interested when the girl said something about them taking pictures. His mind wandered until he realized she had said something about darkness and flashbulbs. When she mentioned the time of the rendezvous he immediately started thinking about getting off work.

He awoke the next morning, starving. His shelf in the fridge was practically empty. He poured himself a bowl of cold cereal and wondered how bad it would taste with just water on it. At the last second he moved his bowl away from the sink and snuck a little of Fred's milk. The bottle was almost full so he blew it off as tough luck for Fred.

Once at work he scarfed down a couple of fried egg sandwiches that a lady misordered, then he started planning his early departure from work. By two thirty he was holding his stomach and groaning about the pain. He hid out in the restroom twice and finally sat down in the corner of the kitchen and moaned until his manager asked what the problem was.

"I got food poisoning, boss," he said.

"You sure you don't have a stomach bug? Maybe you better go home and take it easy. It's not a good idea to handle food if you are sick. Just make sure you don't go saying anything about my food making you sick."

He couldn't believe how easy it was to get off of work. "Maybe too easy," he thought. Maybe they were trying to find a reason to fire him. He was too far along with his little white lie to quit now, so he hung up his apron and gathered up his stuff. Glancing at the clock he figured he had timed it perfectly. He could ride his bicycle to the high school in fifteen minutes.

"I'll run you home, Harvey," his boss said, dangling car keys in his fingers.

"Oh, that's not necessary."

"I wouldn't feel right making you walk home in your condition. Come on. I need to get right back."

His plan was ruined. The high school was in the opposite direction from Fred's house. He almost refused the ride outright but, in the end wised up and gave in. They were barely out of the drive-thru when he looked across the street and saw the girl. She was walking out of the restaurant's front door with a sack of food. She would have an insurmountable lead on him even if he used his old bicycle to try to catch up, then he remembered his bike.

"Hey boss, I just remembered that I have my bike out back. I better ride it home or I won't have a way to work tomorrow," he said.

"Not a problem my good man. I have a very large trunk."

The boss swung the wheel, almost running over the black-haired girl, and pulled back into the parking lot.

"Grab your bike and I'll open the trunk," Bill said.

Harvey again started to protest, but found the words wouldn't come to his mouth.

It was at least ten minutes before the boss pulled away from Fred's, leaving Harvey standing by the street. He checked his old scratched-up Timex and figured that the girl was too far ahead of him to ever find her. He pushed the bike up the driveway and leaned it against the side of the house. By now his stomach really did hurt. In his room he went to the window and started to pull down the shade—he needed a nap—when he saw the Dawson kid across the street. Dalan was heading out of his driveway riding a bike older and more beat up than Harvey's. He immediately changed plans and ran out the door to follow the kid.

He didn't want to get too close to Dalan. By staying back at least a block behind, he felt he wouldn't be seen. Luckily, the kid stayed on the back streets and away from Main Street and Bill's Burgers. The last thing he needed was to have the boss see him out riding his bike when he still had thirty minutes left on his shift and had faked food poisoning. As he approached the football field he fell back further, and finally stopped in the shadow of a big cottonwood tree. The boy had barely stopped when the girl stepped out into the open and held out something for him to see. Moments later they were headed out across an empty field toward the north. The kid didn't even take the time to lock his bike.

Harvey wished he had brought a hat and sunglasses. Not only would they have added a semblance of camouflage, but the afternoon sun was scalding hot and the glare off the desert sand was making his eyes water. As the two adventurers ahead walked further from the road, Harvey was forced to follow closer or lose them. This left him exposed in the open terrain. He crouched down like they had taught him to do in basic training—and as he had seen spies do in the movies—but he soon got a cramp in his back and had to stand up straight. He saw the girl's head turn backward to scan the area. Immediately, he had to fall to his knees, ducking behind a low creosote bush as he went down, his left knee landing smack-dab on a bullhead thorn.

They had walked at least a mile into the natural desert when the two disappeared from Harvey's sight. One minute the two kids were there and the next minute the only thing he could see were heat waves coming off the ground. Off to the right he could see a big, three-story mud building with a more modern wooden cover built over the top. He recognized it as the old Indian ruins. Slowly now, eyes watering, head burning, and knee stinging, he proceeded toward where he had last seen the kids. The terrain dropped abruptly away down a gradual incline and then into a deep ravine. Again, he crouched down behind a bush and scanned the gully. A path down the length of it was circuitous and varied in width from twenty to about eight or ten feet. It was full of weeds and old trash. There was even a washing machine lying on its side, full of bullet holes. He could only guess how many scary critters were hiding down there in the shade.

Harvey had never been much of an outdoorsman, but had read and seen enough to know that the tracks left by shoes could be followed—like in the movies. He climbed down into the dry stream bed of the ravine and looked for footprints. Sure enough, there they were. He hadn't gone fifty feet when he came around a slight bend and heard their voices.

Harvey had been told by the locals at work that one should never turn over a rock or stick in the desert without expecting to find something alive and dangerous. He didn't mean to move the tree branch as he crawled on hands and knees along the sandy bottom of the powder-dry gully to get a closer look, but when it happened it was too late.

The two-inch-long bark scorpion was minding its own business, hiding from the dehydrating sun until dark when it would venture out looking for tiny mites and perhaps, if it was lucky, a tasty cricket. When the giant monster's hand moved its shade away and came down on top of it, there was no choice. Sting, sting, sting, sting. Just like Mama said.

Harvey thought for a millisecond that he had put his hand on another thorn, but then he felt the pain like a bolt of electricity shooting up his arm into his brain. He thought the world was going to end. His hand and arm tingled and burned at the same time. He jumped to his feet and screamed out, watching as his right arm and hand jerked and shook as if they were possessed by the devil himself. Never in his life had he ever felt such excruciating pain. He had once stuck a hair pin in a light socket and was shocked, but that pain wasn't nearly this bad.

Finally, gathering a fragment of his senses he ran up the gully in the opposite direction from the kids' location. The kids instantly had become the last thing on his priority list. A half-hour later he was sitting in the waiting room of the town's only doctor, with a bag of ice on his hand and sweat beads dripping off of his forehead. The wrinkled receptionist had diagnosed his problem after hearing thirty seconds of the symptoms.

"Here is some ice and some aspirin. I'll hold the cup while you swallow the pills. I'd bet twenty dollars that you got stung by a scorpion. Did you see it?"

When he answered no, she rolled her eyes and told him he would have to wait for the doctor to return from the hospital.

"Shouldn't you call an ambulance?" Harvey asked, his voice weak and trembling. "Am I going to die?"

With another roll of her eyes, she said, "It would be a waste of the taxpayers' money. There's really nothing else to do for a bad sting."

All his life he had been told that a scorpion's sting was fatal, so now at last, hearing the words from an expert, his beliefs disproven, Harvey took a deep breath then just sat back on a plastic chair in the doctor's dingy office waiting for the end—for his heart to stop beating.

"Sir, I think you misunderstood me," the woman said, "It would be a waste of money because in a couple of hours you will be fine. Nobody dies from a scorpion sting."

❖ ❖ ❖

"Did you hear that?" Dalan asked.
They both froze. She definitely heard something as well.
"Turn off your light and don't move."
The two would-be junior antiquities thieves doused their flashlights. The scream was followed by some cuss words that never were heard in either of the youngsters' homes. In less than a minute the sounds abruptly stopped. In the silence the only sounds were of their breathing. It seemed like an hour, but mere minutes later Marie whispered, "I don't hear anything now, do you?"
Dalan nodded his head in agreement, and then realized that in the absolute darkness only words would work.
"No, I can't hear a thing," he whispered. "Maybe whoever it is left."
Her light clicked back on and her first reaction was to shine it in his face, causing a whimper of pain and instant halos to appear in his vision.
"Don't do that," he said, but of course it was too late.
He turned on his own light, but it still took a couple minutes before his eyes were adapted well enough to proceed deeper into the cavern. When they arrived at the widened chamber and saw the lined-up pots, they once again stood in awe. Not only were the hand-made earthen pots still in perfect condition, but they were so beautiful, even in the eyes of young, naïve teenagers. Marie leaned her light against the cave's wall, aiming its beam along the line-up of larger pots. To give them spatial perspective she took off her Yankee's ball cap and placed it in a space between two of the pots.
Her camera was a nifty, thin thing in which the flashcube clicked in place on top. As she began taking pictures, the four-

sided flashcube automatically rotated to a new unused side. She took pictures up close and far away and then replaced the flashcube with a new one and handed the camera to Dalan. "Take my picture."

She sat on the ground and put her face as close to one of the pots as possible then smiled a most magnificent smile. He clicked the button four times.

When she stood up and dusted off the seat of her pants, he called to her from the corner of the cave. "Now you take my picture."

She retrieved another flashcube from her backpack and snapped it in place. When she turned to face him, he was standing, cradling a large pot in each arm and grinning from ear to ear.

"You've got to be crazy!" she said. "You shouldn't touch the pots. Put them down right now."

"Not until you take my picture," he said.

In frustration she took two flash pictures, then laid down the camera and insisted on helping him gently set the pots back in their places. She was astounded at how heavy a single vessel was. She also was impressed at how strong Dalan must be to have lifted two of them at once without dropping them.

"That was stupid," she chided her new friend. "What if you dropped one and broke it?"

He didn't argue but picked up his flashlight and for the first time shined the beam down into the largest of the pots. Though each pot had its own unique shape and general configuration, each had a flared mouth narrowing for the upper third, then widening to a diameter five or six times the width of the mouth. Some had a single handle incorporated into the narrow neck, and two or three had double handles. Two of the larger pots had wider necks and squattier bodies, kind of like the ones his mom had sitting in the shade by the front door with petunias growing in them.

Shining his light down into the pot, Dalan gasped and withdrew his face and the light.

"Marie, they aren't empty," he said, his voice soft, with a hint of a quiver.

She picked up her flashlight. Holding it off to the side of her face and pointing it downward she looked deep into the pot and whistled. Without moving the light she turned her face to Dalan's, mere inches away.

"I think that they are bones. Look at the curved piece on the right. It looks like a broken cereal bowl with hair growing out of it."

Dalan had the sudden urge to pee. He shined his light in several of the other pots. He couldn't see into the bottom of the ones with the narrowest necks but each of the others held something which looked like bones. Each sight was spookier than the previous. In one of the pots there was a curved bone with a straight row of four yellow teeth stuck in it.

They inspected each of the pots where similar findings were noted. The largest pot had a neck big enough to stuff a volleyball into, and was nearly filled to the top with what looked like ash, with drumstick-sized bones sticking out of the ashes. Marie tried to tip the pot sideways but it was far too heavy to risk it rolling off the shelf and breaking it on the cave's stone floor.

"Are they all full of dead people?" he wondered out loud.

"Whatever it is, at least it all looks real old. I hope it's not some missing person or a murder victim like I saw on television," Marie said. "People like to hide bodies in very strange places."

"Maybe this place is haunted or has a curse on it or something," he said.

The ever pragmatic Marie scowled at Dalan. "There is no such thing as ghosts or a curse."

"But I read about the tombs in Egypt and how the first people who went in to inspect them all died. Even the man who discovered the burial grounds got sick and died from the creepy dead people. We need to be careful and not disturb things and wash our hands when we get home."

"I told you there are no such things as ghosts and curses," she repeated.

"You sound just like my mom," Dalan said, and gave her a friendly slug in the shoulder.

"Why did you hit me?" she asked.

"Sorry, it's just what me and my friends do," he murmured, turning away.

Left to their own thoughts, the two carefully made their way toward the entrance. It seemed that the walk out of the cave took longer than the careful entry into the cave. Marie held out her arm to keep Dalan behind her as they were ready to step into daylight. They both heard the sound of a truck's motor. Maybe it was the skill of hiding for the street games that saved them, or perhaps just good luck, but when they peeked out, a green National Park Service pickup truck was sitting on the opposite ridge of the arroyo. Inside the truck sat a tough-looking, older woman holding a pair of gigantic binoculars up to her face.

They ducked back into the darkness and waited. The cave entrance was hidden from the woman's direct view by the pile of tumbleweeds the kids had pushed away. The female park ranger was definitely looking for something, and the two explorers supposed that it had to be them. They stayed back in the shadows holding their breath in fear of getting caught. The waiting seemed endless, but finally the woman put down the glasses and ground the clutch, getting the old truck into gear. It pulled forward slowly and eventually drove out of sight.

"Quick," Marie said as they scurried out onto the dry stream bed. "Cover the entrance while I work on our footprints."

They made fast work of their camouflage and headed down the gully in the opposite direction of the truck. A lateral gully let them sneak up to the ground level of the surrounding desert where they could see for miles. The green pickup was nowhere in sight. Walking back toward the high school on a gravel road, they shared a drink of water from a small tin canteen which Marie had in her backpack. They were able to see the football stadium light poles when the green truck came over a small hill and headed straight toward them. Keeping their heads down, they trudged along until the truck pulled onto their path and the woman climbed out of the cab.

"What are you two doing out here in the middle of the day? And you, young lady, with no hat on?" the woman asked.

Marie felt her head then realized that her Yankee's baseball cap was still in the cave, sitting on the earthen shelf beside the pots. Dalan had taken a couple of steps back, more than willing to let Marie be the team spokesperson.

"We're just going for a walk," Marie said to the woman. "A friend told us there was a swimming hole out here somewhere by one of the irrigation pumps."

The woman was at least as tall as Dalan's dad and looked like she needed a shave. Her hair was dusty brown, cropped short, and she was wearing a green uniform, just like a man's. He couldn't remember ever seeing a woman wearing men's clothes before. For a second he thought he was mistaken and she was really a man with a woman's voice until he saw the badge sticking way out on her chest and a shiny brass name tag that said "Alice Brown."

"I need your names," Alice Brown said in an authoritarian voice.

"I'm Suzie, and this is my brother Tom."

Dalan was shocked at the blatant lie Marie had just told to the woman, but he didn't see any reason to not tell the lady their real names—until the woman pulled out a small note pad and wrote the names down.

"What's your last name?" she asked, stepping forward and looking directly at Dalan.

He stammered, looking at her name tag instead of her eyes. Then in desperation the name "Brown" popped from his lips.

"Really," she said. "Maybe your dad is my cousin."

"There are a lot of Browns in the world," Marie said.

"Well, whatever your names are and whatever you are doing out here in the desert, this not a safe place to be in the middle of the day. Get in the truck and I'll drive you home. You do have a home here in town, right?"

Dalan saw Marie start to move toward the truck so he blurted out, "Our parents forbid us from riding with strangers. We have a canteen of water and know how to get home. Thanks for the offer but we'll just walk." Immediately, Dalan started out on the gravel road in the direction of town. Marie hesitated for a second, and then followed him. The woman yelled at them to get into the truck, but they ignored her and cut across a small gully so the truck couldn't follow. The last thing they saw of the park ranger, she was talking into a two-way radio, probably calling her boss at the Casa Grande Ruins office. They were a quarter of a mile away when she finally drove off in the other direction, leaving a long thick trail of dust behind. A gust of wind caught the dust, spinning it into a dust devil.

CHAPTER 5

There were no written rules to the game of kick the can. Likewise, there was apparently no restriction as to who, or how many, could play. The number of players varied, and for no good reason, it didn't seem to matter. Some nights there would be ten or twelve and on occasion, like the night they showed a World Championship boxing match on the *Friday Night Fight* TV show, only the very youngest kids showed up. No matter who took charge, there were always little arguments—perhaps the kids were practicing to be adults—and they never seemed to get the game organized well enough to prevent it from fizzling out after an hour or, at the most, ninety minutes. It seemed that every night somebody would go home crying and then often an angry parent would come out and send everyone home whether they were their kids or not.

On the Thursday night before the big Fourth of July celebration the game was packed. Not only did Ian promise to come out after the dishes were done, but two older high-school-age girls showed up. Dalan had never seen either of them before. He could smell their heavy perfume as they stood right there, shoulder to shoulder in the game's organizing circle.

One of the girls was a tall girl with long blond hair and a very shapely figure. She said that her name was Kristen Palermo. Dalan immediately looked for Marie, but she hadn't shown up yet. The other girl was shorter and a little plumper looking. She had red hair, braided into two pigtails. She wasn't much taller than Dalan. They weren't bossy, like most older kids might be, but seemed really interested in playing the game and just being young kids again.

The redheaded girl asked Dalan his name and told him he could call her Candy, which made him laugh because he didn't know people named their kids after food. He for sure didn't know anybody named Apple or Beans or Gravy. She was inquisitive about him and his family, then asked him if it was his brother who worked at the Safeway store. Ian was still in the house eating so Dalan just pointed at the house. That ended the conversation with Candy, who didn't even say thanks.

They played rock-paper-scissors to decide who was "It," and everyone seemed to be having a grand time for the first couple of games. They were in the first stages of hiding in the third game when Dalan heard the roar of a car engine. Mr. Palermo's Corvette was the only one in town that Dalan had heard with a motor that sounded so powerful; he had seen the Corvette twice in front of Tag's, a café down on Main.

The car making all of the noise stopped near the corner and let out a passenger who walked quickly toward the coffee can. It was pretty dark by then, and Dalan was hiding behind a car in the Rawlings' driveway as he watched, and then recognized, the approaching person. When she was close enough to be distinguished, Dalan stood up from his hiding place to wave at Marie. He was immediately tagged out by Kristen.

"I've got to talk to you," Marie said, when the large gang gathered again around the battered coffee can. "I'm 'It.' Wait until after the next game," he told her.

"Wait for me," Ian called from the kitchen door. Apparently, he had finished the dishes and recovered from his day of stocking grocery shelves.

"Eleven, twelve, thirteen, fourteen, fifteen, ready or not here I come," Dalan yelled.

It didn't take long to catch most of the younger kids but he couldn't find Marie or Ian or the two high school girls. He was about to call "all in free," to end the game, when he heard and saw a car speeding around the corner. It had the unmistakable engine roar he had heard when Marie arrived.

At first glance it looked like an old Ford coupe that had been customized into a hot rod. It definitely had a loud engine, but didn't sound as smooth as Mr. Palermo's Corvette.

As the car got closer, the little Hansen girl was running for the coffee can in the middle of the street. When the car finally hit its brakes it did little good. On the tarred gravel there wasn't any traction to be had, which meant there was no screeching sound from the tires, just the crunching and grinding of the rocks as the car's tires tried to grip the surface—but twisted out of control instead. Dalan made a frantic dash for the child, grabbing her around the waist and jumping out of the car's path just in time. The car's flimsy-looking bumper plowed into the wooden picket fence and crunched into the side of the poplar tree in Mr. Larsen's front yard, finally bringing the car to a halt. A cloud of dust covered the street, and then slowly drifted away.

At first, amid all of the screaming, Dalan wasn't certain if all of the kids were safe, but to his relief no one was under the car. Everyone was standing on either side of the car staring with big eyes. Kristen and Candy ran to the scene, yelling at the two people in the car. Though the car's front end was a crumpled wreck, the little chopped-off doors both opened, and two guys got out of the hot rod and walked around cursing and inspecting the damage.

Candy followed the guy in the black leather jacket who had been driving, yelling at him, "You are a stupid idiot, Billy. You almost killed some of the kids."

The passenger backed away from the scene, then turned away completely and ran toward Main Street.

To everyone's astonishment the driver wheeled on Kristen and slapped her face. This startled Dalan. Then the bully started yelling at her and calling her nasty names. When he twisted her arm it was more than Dalan could tolerate. He picked up a piece of broken wooden fence about the size of a thin baseball bat, and with a home run swing, hit the leather jacket guy squarely in the side of his knee. He fell to the ground screaming and swearing.

"You little twerp, I'll pay you back for this," he said, lying on the ground, glaring up at Dalan.

Ian had run into the house to report the car wreck to his parents, who immediately called the police. When Dalan's dad came out of the house, the hot rod boy had twisted one of Dalan's arms and was screaming swear words that most of the children had never heard before.

The arrival of a real adult silenced the crowd. Mr. Dawson was not someone to mess with. He stood six foot two and had wrestled and played college football at Colorado State. Though soft spoken and friendly, he had a firmness in his voice that commanded respect. Dalan was released and sent to the house. The leather-jacketed guy was told in no uncertain terms to stand beside the car and not to move. Mr. Dawson asked the two older girls to remain there as well so that they could explain to the police what had happened. The rest of the large group was asked to go to their homes.

"Why can't we stay and play? It's not a school night," the little Hansen kid whined, still shaking from nearly getting killed.

"Your parents all need to know that you are safe," Mr. Dawson tried to explain.

"You're not my dad. You can't tell me what to do," the sassy-mouthed Darlene, a girl close to Dalan's age, said.

Fortunately, the arrival of the police cruiser ended the discussion. For the next hour the flashing lights from the dome of the Ford cast weird pale light over the neighborhood. Strangers came and went looking over the wreck; getting second- and third-hand stories from other voyeurs.

Dalan obeyed his dad and stayed up on his porch watching the chaos. Standing beside his brother, he looked out at the street scene and began to question his own sanity: First of all, for jumping in front of the moving car, but even more for hitting the bully with the broken fence stake. He didn't even know the girl, Kristen. Why had he come to her rescue? One of the older neighbor kids walked up to the porch and told Ian that the guy in the leather coat was Candy's brother and Kristen's boyfriend.

A few minutes later Marie came around the side of the house and hissed to get his attention. He looked to his side and saw her standing in the shadows. He was surprised to see she was still standing on the side of the street, but even more surprised at what she said. "That was a very brave thing you did. Stupid but brave," she told him, giving his dusty arm a squeeze. "His name is Billy Real. His family works on a farm ten miles from here. He was the star of the high school football team last year. Everyone in town thinks he walks on water. Candy, the redheaded girl, is Billy's sister. Kristen is my stepsister. You now have the honor of being hated and loved by the most popular teenagers in town."

"Why would anybody wear a heavy leather coat in the summer in Arizona?" Dalan wondered out loud.

"He thinks it makes him cool. The same with his long, slicked-back hair," Marie said. By now she was standing up on the porch with him in order to see the crowd, which was still growing.

"You never told me that she had a mean boyfriend," Dalan said. He was still standing close enough to her to touch shoulders and smell her shampoo. They watched as a tow truck arrived with its flashing orange lights, adding to the colorful reflections on the houses. The driver took his time hooking onto the hot rod, probably trying his best not to do any further damage to the glassy-smooth, candy-apple-red paint job.

"I haven't told you a lot of things. It's not like we're married," she finally said. Then she dropped the real bomb on him. "After all you're just my boyfriend."

Dalan had no response. He was in shock. He hadn't ever had a girlfriend and now the prettiest and probably richest girl in town was claiming him as her boyfriend.

People on the street kept looking toward the porch. His dad and Ian were out among the crowd, Ian introducing his dad to some of the older kids and a few neighbors he hadn't met. Billy Real was limping back and forth inspecting his car and listening to the policeman who was writing out something he made the guy sign.

It was half an hour before the tow truck finally hauled off the wreck. The neighbors still lingered out in the street, some of the men collecting the shattered white pickets of Fred's fence and putting them in a neat pile.

Dalan and Marie had finally sat down on the steps. She put her hand on his for a minute, sending chills up his spine, but he pulled it away when he heard his mom open the screen door.

"Oh, there you are Dalan," she said. "Hello, young lady," she said, changing her tone to one of sugar and spice. "Dalan, dear, why don't you introduce me to your friend?"

The introduction went very politely, but then Mrs. Dawson suggested that it was getting very late for a young woman to be out.

"Would you like me to drive you home?" she asked.

"No thank you ma'am. I'll just walk home with my sister."

"Well it was nice to meet you, Marie. I better go and get my men off of the street; they both have to go to work early," Dalan's mom said.

"How can Kristen be your sister if she has blond hair?" Dalan asked—his nervous words flowing out of his mouth without having given it enough thought.

"It's called bleach, silly boy. They call it 'bottle blond'. It makes black hair blond. Lots of the high school girls do it so they can look like the California surfer girls."

"Does she live at your house?"

"Kristen and her mom live out by the Country Club. I hardly ever see her, but when I do she tries to be real nice to me. Candy and Billy's parents are still good friends with my mom, who grew up here, but not with my dad. It's all very strange and complicated. You really don't want to know any more than that," she said, then stood and ran into the darkness up the street to the west.

Dalan didn't even have time to say good night. Life was sure different here.

Things on the street were clearing out. The tow truck and police cars were gone. A new black Lincoln arrived and the three older teens climbed inside. Apparently no sobriety test would be required. As he limped toward the car, Dalan saw Billy look toward the Dawsons' porch searching for the kid who had crippled his knee.

❖ ❖ ❖

Harvey Grimes had watched the entire fiasco transpire like a three-act Shakespearean play, which then morphed into a three-ring circus. From his vantage point on Fred's porch, he could see everything and even hear most of the conversation. His only distraction was his throbbing hand. It had swelled up to the size of a boxing glove, and had a constant tingling pain that ran up his elbow as though he had just hit his crazy bone. The doctor had given him pain pills that made him fall asleep for a couple of hours, but now the pain was too much to sleep through and the noise in the street wouldn't have allowed it anyway.

He was worrying about how he could go to work tomorrow with his swollen, painful hand, and even more so, what he would tell the boss. He had never seen a scorpion around Fred's and that was the only place he could say he had been when he was stung.

He watched the sandy-haired kid come out and join in the kick-the-can game, but didn't see his little pony-tailed, co-conspirator until later when the Corvette dropped her off. He was guessing that her daddy had brought her in the sports car—how he would love to get behind the wheel of that speed machine for a few hours. He could be on the beach in California picking up girls and surfing the big curls by tomorrow morning.

When he first heard and saw the hot rod accelerating around the corner, coming west and then veering suddenly away from the cluster of kids, he thought it was going to run right up onto his porch. Luckily for Harvey, the car spun-out, wiped out the fence and smashed into the tree. He was sure it had killed the little kid who was standing at the side of the street. At first he considered jumping up to help, but then he had second thoughts. The last thing he wanted to do was to be interviewed by the nosey police. Instead, he settled deeper into the rocker and watched the scene unfold.

He laughed when the blonde girl with the nice figure screamed at the hot rod's driver until he wheeled around and slapped her face. Again, Harvey almost jumped up to come to her aid. That's when the unbelievable happened. The skinny kid from across the street picked up a two-by-four cross rail from the splintered fence. He was barely half as tall as the big muscular teen in the leather coat. The kid looked like he was up to bat at Fenway Park. Harvey could hear the rail land home with a sickening thud to the knee. The bully hit the ground like a sack of sprouted potatoes and lay in the dirt crying like a baby at first, and then shouting profanities Harvey hadn't heard since boot camp.

Harvey's subconscious respect for the little kid across the street increased exponentially. He had more guts than anyone would have imagined. As the rest of the circus played out, Harvey continued to keep an eye on the whereabouts of Dalan and his pony-tailed girlfriend. The last he saw of them they were deep in the shadows of the Dawson's porch, probably planning another secret outing.

It was better than a Hitchcock movie, watching the interaction of the parents, the cops, the kids, and some of the uninvolved neighbors. All of them had a different version of the sequence of events. Before the tow truck arrived and the black Lincoln showed up to haul off the older teens, Harvey had gotten up and walked into the street. He wanted to hear all of the conversations and get a closer look at the damaged hot rod and the greasy driver. It never hurt to know the leading players in any game.

"Lot of excitement for a small town, don't you think?"

Harvey turned to stare face-to-face at a stout policeman in full uniform. He was pretty sure he was the same guy that questioned him in front of the Palermos.

"I'm glad no one was seriously injured," Harvey said, recovering from the surprise encounter.

"How goes the newspaper subscription sales?" the officer asked.

"I'm working full time now at Bill's Big Burgers," he said, realizing he had been recognized and wishing the cop would get lost.

"Don't let Bill hear you call the place Big Burgers, he's set on the name Biggest. My name is Officer Roberts," the man said extending his hand to shake, then seeing Harvey's bandage said, "Say, that hand looks pretty nasty. Black widow bite?"

"Scorpion sting," Harvey said, trying to keep the conversion short.

"I'd guess you were out in the desert. We never see any scorpions here in town or on the farms. They crop dust the fields around town and even the city park with airplanes. They use malathion or parathion for the boll weevils—keeps 'em outta the cotton. Also it kills the scorpions. So where'd you get it?"

A creepy feeling came over Harvey. He hadn't really done anything wrong, but was feeling guilty just the same. Getting caught in a lie by his boss was one thing, but lying again to this cop could bring on real trouble.

"I was out looking at the Indian ruins and sat on a rock when the thing stung me. Hard to believe something that small can cause so much pain."

Kick The Can

The cop finally lost interest and wandered over to another group of neighbors. Harvey slipped inside and locked the door behind him. Fred was asleep in front of the TV where he had been throughout the entire neighborhood excitement. Harvey picked up his binoculars and with the room lights out parted the curtains just enough to get a peek. He saw the two youngsters were still laying low in the porch shadows. He then turned the glasses toward the police car. Officer Roberts was standing beside his squad car staring directly at Harvey.

CHAPTER 6

"What do you mean you can't go?" Dalan asked, a tone of frustration in his voice.

"We are leaving tomorrow to go the beach in San Diego for a week. Mom insists that I go to Phoenix with her today to buy new swimsuits for everybody."

"But you promised last night that we could go back to the cave."

"I'll be back in just a week. Then we can make a plan for what to do with the pots and maybe find out what's inside of them."

"What about the pictures you took?"

"I had Dad drop them off at the Rexall Drug to get them developed; they said it would be at least four days so I'll pick them up when I get back. Don't you want to know which beach I'm going to?" she asked, trying to change the subject.

"I don't know anything about beaches. I've never even seen the ocean," he said, covering the mouthpiece with his hand for fear his mom might overhear his conversation.

"I didn't want you to know, but I guess I'll tell you anyway; we also are going to go to Disneyland," she said.

"Wow, that's really neat!" he answered with excitement in his words.

"I was thinking of getting you a present there. What would you like? They have big Mickey Mouse stuffed animals. In Adventureland they have old-fashioned rifles—flintlocks I think they call them."

"You don't have to get me anything," he said.

"I have a great idea. I want you to come by the house just before dinner tonight. I'm going to ask Mom if it's okay for you to be in charge of feeding our dogs. That way you can come and swim in our swimming pool while we are gone and you won't have to go to the city pool. I'll show you how to brush it and skim the leaves off of it. I'm sure she will agree. And my dad will pay you."

"That sounds good, but I thought you just had one dog, a little fluffy black Scotty," he said.

"Be here at my house at five and I'll introduce you to both of them. Okay?"

"Okay. I hope you have a nice time in Phoenix," he said, his spirits a little bit higher.

He hung up the telephone. It was the first time he had really talked to a girl on the phone. It would have been pretty fun if the news had been better. He could picture her sitting on her bed looking at all the pretty things in her fancy room. Her phone call had been a complete surprise. He didn't ask how she had obtained his phone number. He guessed it must not be that hard.

"Who was that you were talking to," his mom asked.

"Just a friend," he said.

Ian piped up from his bowl of Frosted Flakes, "Go ahead and tell Mom that you have a girlfriend."

"She's not my girlfriend," Dalan insisted.

"Is too. Everybody knows it, Mom. She's older than Dalan and even wears a bra. I heard she's real rich too and that her grandpa is some kind of powerful Mafia guy in New York City and that if he doesn't like somebody he just makes a phone call to one of his boys and has the guy murdered."

"You've been watching too much television," Mrs. Dawson said.

"It's the truth; Marie's grandfather is a Mafia boss."

"Shut up!" Dalan shouted, then got up from the table leaving his cereal uneaten and went out the kitchen door.

"Shame on you, Ian," said Mrs. Dawson. "You need to watch your words, young man. You don't want me to have to tell your father when he gets home. I need you to be nicer to your little brother. He's having a hard time adjusting to our new home. It's good that he is making some friends. The last thing we would want to happen is for the little girl's parents to think we are spreading rumors about them."

"Sorry Mom," said Ian, his face back into his bowl of cereal. "But it's the truth."

❖ ❖ ❖

That afternoon dragged by like a bad Sunday sermon. Dalan rode his bike by to see Boyd, but couldn't get anybody to answer the door. He had considered sharing his secret about the hidden pots with him, but he knew Marie would hate him for it. He went by the hardware store where he studied the knives and guns behind the glass cases, then wandered up and down the aisles until the manager asked to see what was in his pockets, suspecting he might be shoplifting. When all he could produce from his pockets was his lucky rabbit's foot and four worn nickels, the man apologized and asked Dalan if he wanted to earn a dollar by unloading some wooden pallets loaded with five-gallon paint buckets. He jumped at the opportunity to burn the clock and get some spending money.

The forty-pound buckets were heavier than he had imagined. There were thirty-six on each of the three pallets. By the time he collected his dollar and rode his bike home, he was ready for a nap. No one was home, so he ate a peanut butter and grape jelly sandwich and lay down on the couch. The next thing he heard was the screen door flap shut. He looked up at the mantel clock and immediately broke out in a sweat. It was ten after five.

"Hi son," his mom said. "Could you help me unload the groceries from the station wagon while I start dinner? Dad will be home early so he can go to his bowling league."

Dalan opened the car's rear door and nearly fainted. There were at least fifteen brown paper sacks to carry inside.

Fifteen minutes later and dripping sweat, he set the last bag of groceries on the table and ran out before his mom could ask him to put them away on the shelves. His bike didn't do well on the gravel road, nearly spilling him when he hit a spot where the rocks were deeper.

Not having a watch was a mixed blessing. He didn't know exactly how late he was for his meeting with Marie and he could always use the excuse that he didn't know what time it was. He parked his rattle-trap bike by the gate and started to open it when a giant, nearly horse-size dog came running around the corner barking the most ferocious bark he had ever heard.

Dalan hadn't ever had his own dog. He wasn't normally afraid of dogs either. But this animal wasn't exactly the neighborhood mutt. When he jumped up with his paws on the picket fence, his head—twice the size of Dalan's—was looking down at the boy and drooling like he had just found supper.

"Bad dog, Harley! Get down and stop barking!" The harsh voice was not Marie's. Dalan looked across the yard at a tall, muscular, dark-haired man about the same age as his dad. He was wearing a powder-blue shirt with a black tie and grey pinstripe pants. He wore a wide, black alligator belt, which matched his shiny black-and-white dress shoes. Dalan had never seen anything like them. The dog obeyed immediately, quickly moving clear of the approaching man.

"You must be Dalan," the man said, stretching out his hand in greeting.

"Yes sir. My name is Dalan Dawson."

"I'm a Franco Palermo, Marie's father. It's a nice to meet you."

Dalan nodded and tried to smile. He had never heard someone in real life speak with that funny New York accent. Once he had seen a movie on TV about Lucky Luciano, the mobster who helped the FBI guard the New York harbors during the Big War. Mr. Palermo talked just like Lucky and all the men the commentator interviewed.

"That is sure a big dog you have, Mr. Palermo," Dalan said.

"He's a Great Dane—actually a Harlequin Great Dane. He just barely reached full size. But don't be afraid of him. Marie's little Scotty is much more ferocious." Marie's not back from town yet. She said to show you around and to give you a key to the pool gate. We keep it locked so none of the field workers come by for a Saturday night bath." He laughed like he had just told a great joke.

By the time Dalan got the tour and the key and knew how much food to give Harley, and Scotty, he was anxious to leave. Marie obviously wasn't going to make it in time. He thanked the man and headed for his bike.

"Don't be shy about using the pool, and bring a friend or your family if they would like to swim—but don't let any coyotes in," Franco laughed and waved goodbye.

❖ ❖ ❖

"Kick the dang can!" Ian screamed at the third grader who had run into the road well ahead of "It," but then just stood there. The kid had come with his big sister, a fifteen-going-on-twenty-year-old whom Ian had invited to the street game earlier that day when he carried out her mom's groceries. They were part of another new family in town. Ian said they had a new Oldsmobile with lots of chrome and that the woman had a diamond ring as big as a walnut.

The kid jumped at the sound of Ian's harsh voice then started to cry. "Don't you dare yell at my brother!" the girl screamed, running out of her hiding place in Mrs. Rawling's bushes.

"Sorry," said Ian, "I'm just trying to teach your little brother how to play the game."

The girl put her arm around the howling kid and walked off down the street toward Main.

"Shit!" screamed Ian at the top of his lungs, knowing his chance to make friends with the girl was gone forever. "I was just trying to help," he yelled.

It was no use, the cute girl just kept walking and the brother kept howling. Everybody came out of hiding thinking someone must have been badly injured.

"What the heck happened?" Dalan asked his brother. Cuss words were never used in the game and the parents in the neighborhood would be mortified if they thought their tender little ones were being taught the words of the world.

"It's none of your business. I'm not playing this stupid kids' game anymore," Ian said, stomping toward the house, giving the poor coffee can a violent kick as he walked by. Everyone watched as he went into the house and slammed the door.

The reduced group gathered together and Dalan volunteered to be "It." The can was replaced in the middle of the road and they started all over. The first person to run in behind his back to kick the can was Marie. He hadn't seen her arrive and got a pleasant little chill when she smiled at him. Two games later they were hiding in Fred's bushes, together again.

"Daddy said that Harley and you got along great."

"Yeh, after I recovered from my heart attack. I'd never seen a Great Dane before, except in the encyclopedia."

"He is lots of fun. When you come swimming don't forget to let him in the pool with you. He loves to swim, but watch out for his toenails. If he rakes you with one you'll think you've been clawed by a bear."

"Thanks for asking your dad to have me feed him. When do you leave for California?"

"Very early tomorrow morning. We have to get across the worst of the desert before it gets too hot and the car heats up," she said.

He hesitated then said, "I can hardly wait until you get back so we can go to the cave."

"Me too! The first thing we need to do is take my pictures to the museum in Phoenix and ask somebody what they are and how old they are."

"Why not just take one of the smaller pots instead of the pictures?" he asked. "I'll think about it. You haven't told anybody have you?"

"Not a soul," he said, wishing she wasn't quite so bossy.

"Don't you dare go back there by yourself," she said.

He had heard enough instructions. When he saw his chance, he burst from the bushes toward the street and nailed the can with his left toe, sending it sailing clear into Mrs. Rawlings' yard.

❖ ❖ ❖

Harvey's right hand was lying in a basin of ice water as he sat on Fred's front porch watching the street games. He had called in sick again and the boss had dropped in on him to check his hand. The man even brought him lunch. They had to make the effort of looking for the scorpion before the guy would leave. Thank goodness Fred wasn't home to declare that there were no scorpions in his yard and never had been.

The kids had started the evening games playing dodge ball, which was more fun to watch. They had an old volleyball that was low on air and worn shiny with use. It proved to be too painful for most of the smaller kids, so after a couple of games the girls and little kids had opted out until it got good and dark, and then the real game—kick the can—could begin. The rusty coffee can was retrieved from the bushes and it started.

He noticed the tall, pretty new girl right away. He remembered seeing her at the hamburger joint a few days before. He laughed when the Dawson kid yelled at her little brother and she verbally attacked him. What high spirits she had. Maybe she would go for an older guy? It wouldn't hurt to try. Later he noticed the rich girl with the ponytail arrive quietly and sort of meld into the game. She had a habit of practically appearing out of nowhere.

When the two little lovebirds finally hid out in the bushes below his feet, he stopped rocking the chair and splashing his hand in the water. They were hot into a discussion when he leaned closer to the porch railing. They were plotting again all right. He heard "California" and "dog" and "photos" and then there was the whispered secret. The word "cave" was mentioned followed by the words "museum" and "ancient pots". What in the world had these two gotten themselves into? It had to have something to do with that gully out on the north end of town—the one full of scorpions.

He knew he had to return to work the next day and wondered how he could keep an eye on the two kids if he was stuck at the greasy burger joint. Then it occurred to him that maybe he wouldn't need the job after all, especially if these two kids were on to something profitable.

"Say something more," he mentally prodded the two conspirators, but quick as a cat, the boy was gone, dashing toward the coffee can. The girl stayed just a minute or two longer and then she too ran into the street.

He could barely sleep that night. Between his throbbing hand and the visions of finding lost treasure in a cave less than three miles from his house, he tossed around in the stuffy room until he was fully awake. He had to find out what those ancient secret pots were all about. And for sure he had to find out where the entrance to the cave was located. Just before his scorpion sting he had watched the two kids disappear around a bend in the gully. Whatever they found couldn't be too far beyond.

At first light, he got dressed in his work clothes, took two aspirins, and snuck out the front door. He had a little navy-issued flashlight and a pair of leather gloves. Heading off toward the ruins on his Schwinn, he was able to ride just two blocks before his hand started killing him. The bouncing on the handlebars sent electric shocks up his arm with every pebble in the road. He finally abandoned using both hands and struggled guiding the bike on the gravel road with just his left hand.

He had promised his boss that he would be there bright and early. He was over his stomach malady. Working with his swollen hand would be hard, but he would just have to make do for now. He had less than two hours to explore whatever it was those kids had found and get back downtown.

It was real quiet out away from town this early in the morning. He heard a barn owl protest his showing up and startling the field mice. He heard a distant train whistle as the Santa Fe freight train made a quick stop in town then chugged on its way to the northwest. He laid his bike down at the top of the gully where he had last seen the kids, and climbed down the steep side. Standing on the dry stream bed and looking up, he could see fading stars and the waning light of a quarter moon.

Using his flashlight he walked along the bed in the loose sand. It reminded him of the navy maneuvers and how he used to try to ditch the officers so he could lie on the grass while the rest of his company did KP, then show up just in time to eat, claiming he had been lost.

There was nothing in the gully but tumbleweeds and occasional trash where some loathsome jerk had backed a car or truck up to the edge and emptied all their garbage into the gully. Old refrigerators, mattresses, and piles of rusted cans littered the way. Many of them were full of bullet holes where target shooters had practiced their aim.

He came upon a mattress which didn't look too filthy. The lack of sleep was catching up with him and he considered sitting down to rest but thought about the scorpions and kept walking. He could not for the life of him find any sign of a cave. When he started running out of time, he began looking for an incline to get out of the deep gully, then he noticed something suspicious. Ahead was a grouping of tumbleweeds much larger than anywhere else. Close inspection revealed lots of footprints fifteen or twenty feet from the stack of weeds then the ground appeared smoothed over nearer the pile. He even found a long, out of place, mesquite branch lying up against the gully wall. This was it. It had to be.

Harvey shined his light through the weeds from several angles and finally saw what he had hoped for. There was definitely a defect in the dirt wall, but without moving a mountain of weeds he wouldn't be able to enter. He glanced at his Timex and made a tough decision. He would mark the site up on the bank of the gully above and return later with more tools, better lights, and something to carry away any loot he might find. He needed an old car or truck.

Work went okay that morning. His shoes were dusty when he arrived but he was a couple minutes early. The night manager was sitting at a table with her head in her hands waiting for the boss to show up so she could get home to her kids and then to bed. Harvey wiped off his shoes and pant legs then went through the "stale" food tray. It was stuff that had been cooked too long or people had returned because the order was incorrect. That's where he usually ate breakfast. He found two cheeseburgers and a fried apple pie, snuck a cup of Coke, and went into the bathroom to eat. The bumping and jolting of the bike handle had made his right hand so swollen it was essentially useless. It was much worse than the day before.

Finished eating, he washed his hands, letting the cool water run for several seconds over the swelling. As he opened the door he almost ran right into the girl with the black ponytail.

He excused himself and went behind the counter to start his shift. He couldn't believe his eyes; there at the counter was that beautiful woman he had seen at the ponytail girl's house. Her husband was standing right beside her looking like a Charles Atlas version of a Mafia murderer. Harvey had seen a James Cagney movie about the mob and was sure that this guy fit the profile. No one else in Coolidge ever wore clothes like this guy was wearing.

They were ordering food to go and said something about eating in the car on the way to California. When the teenage girl came around the corner he couldn't help staring. She was even prettier that he had thought. He had never seen her up close in good light. She was even better looking than her mom. She smiled at him then joined her parents.

As they gathered their sacks of food and drink the young girl turned to Harvey.

"Don't you live on Pinkley Street? I see you watching us kids play street games every night. You ought to come and join in sometime."

Not waiting for him to confirm or deny the question, or comment on the invitation, she turned and followed her dad and mom out the door.

"Well, look who came back from the dead," his boss said.

The man had slipped quietly in the back door and already had on his apron.

"Enjoying the morning view?" he asked Harvey, glancing at Mrs. Palermo as she leaned into the Cadillac, her tight skirt riding up the back of her tan legs.

"I'm ready to go back to work," Harvey said, ignoring the boss's comment. "My scorpion sting is much better. My hand is still a bit swollen but I won't let it slow me down."

The boss looked him up and down, reached over and grabbed the swollen hand to have a closer look, sending lightning bolts of pain up Harvey's arm.

"You'll live, Grimes," he said. "Fry up a new batch of potatoes. I'm starved."

CHAPTER 7

A really great secret is usually too good to keep!

Dalan awoke when he heard his Dad's car motor start and pull out of the driveway. He wondered why rubber car tires on gravel made so much noise. Going to sleep had been hard; going back to sleep would be impossible. He kept thinking about the pots and the bones or whatever that was inside. To wait more than a week for Marie to get back from the beach was going to be a killer. He had thought about telling Ian and getting him to come with him to the cave, but then Ian would probably want to do something stupid with the treasure—even sell it. Dalan had a better idea.

He started on the lawn mowing right after breakfast and then hopped on his bike and rode the three blocks to Boyd's house. It was in a little better part of town than the Dawsons' and was real pretty on the outside, but when his friend's mom opened the door and invited him in, he immediately noticed that Boyd's mom was a terrible housekeeper. The inside of the house looked like a dump. Boyd was just waking up, but when he heard about going to Marie's house to swim, he couldn't get his suit on fast enough. The boys took some dirty laundry to the cleaners for Boyd's mom and then were off on their bikes.

Harley had to be fed just twice a day so Dalan didn't worry that it was nearly noon when the sweaty boys arrived. The thermometer by the Palermos' pool house read 109 degrees, but the water felt relatively cool in the dry hot air. Once Boyd got over the shock of Harley's size and exuberance, the three of them had a grand time playing in the pool. The black Scotty didn't like the water so he just sat in the shade and watched.

The Palermos kept a small refrigerator in the pool house that was full of a variety of sodas and even a few bottles of beer. The giant bag of dog food sat right next to it. Out of breath and choking with thirst, the boys helped themselves each to a Coke and then stretched out on lounge chairs under the gazebo. This was the life. The dogs had both gone to sleep and the midday air was still. The boys didn't have a care in the world.

The sound of an approaching car stirred Dalan from his drifting thoughts. The sound of the engine had a familiar note to Dalan's memory, sending a chill up his spine. He looked up and saw the hot rod that had wrecked the other night driving slowly down the road. Its big block engine and full race cam left no doubt about its power or identity. The crumpled fender and grill left no doubt about how much trouble Dalan would be in if that town bully, Billy Real, were to catch him alone.

"Get down!" Dalan said.

"What? What's the matter?"

"The guy in that car is the guy I hit with the board. If he sees me he is going to beat me up."

"What if he beats me up too, just for being with you?" Boyd said.

"Just stay down and maybe he will go away."

The car circled around the block twice, then pulled into the long driveway stopping near the back of the house. Harley and Scotty both immediately barked and ran toward the gate when Billy and Kristen Palermo got out of the car. The two young boys rolled onto the ground and scurried behind a huge built-in brick barbeque grill which was bordered on two sides with tall shrubs, adding privacy to the pool area.

"You sure your dad won't mind us swimming?" they heard Billy ask.

"Just because I don't live here doesn't mean I don't kind of own the place," she said. "See, the dogs are happy to see me."

As they came through the gate into the yard, the dogs gave them both a good sniffing then took off running around the barbeque and started barking at Dalan and Boyd.

"What are they after?" Billy asked.

"They are probably after a ground squirrel or a bird. Come on, let's go swimming; I've got to be back in forty-five minutes."

The boys had a good view of the couple through the branches of the shrubs as they went into the unlocked pool house. Luckily, they didn't notice the boy's bottles of Coke sitting on the glass table between the lounge chairs, and the sun was so hot that the boys' wet footprints already had evaporated. Seconds later, the teenagers came out with Billy holding a bottle of what Dalan was sure was beer. Kristen was wearing cut-off jeans and a loose T-shirt; Billy was wearing just cut-offs.

They ran to the pool where Kristen was pushed screaming into the deep end. Billy took a couple swigs of the beer and then, putting his thumb over the opening of the bottle, jumped in after her. There was a lot of splashing, giggling, and then a few minutes later a loud scream. All of a sudden a wet T-shirt came flying out of the water landing on the edge of the barbeque, inches from the boys' hidden faces.

The two stared at the shirt, then at each other, eyes big and hearts pounding.

The splashing in the pool stopped and they heard Billy say, "What's the big deal?" The next thing they witnessed shocked them like nothing they had ever seen in their young lives. Kristen was cussing and calling Billy every bad name they had ever heard. Then to the boys' astonishment, she stomped up the pool steps out of the shallow end of the pool and walked straight toward the boys' hiding place. She was still swearing and squinting in the bright sun as she wrung the water out of her long blond hair. She was naked from her cut-off jeans up—her light pink skin outlined with dark copper-colored tan lines. The next sixty seconds held an experience like they had never imagined. In spite of the fear of being seen, their bodies and their eyes didn't move an inch.

Keeping her back toward Billy, totally unaware of the four young eyes less than five feet away, Kristen slowly squeezed the water out of her T-shirt. She shook it out, then pulled it slowly over the top of her head carefully straightening it as the fabric fell downward, finally covering her abundant bosoms.

"Get out of the water and take me home right now, Billy," she demanded, finally turning her back on the boys. "If you ever do something stupid like that again I'll tell my dad. You have no idea how mean he can be."

Dalan and Boyd stayed in the bushes until the sound of the hot rod's engine was long gone. Boyd was practically shaking from the ordeal and wanted to leave. Trying to relax from all the excitement, Dalan fed the dogs again then said, "They won't be back. Let's swim some more."

The boys played Marco Polo and shot baskets at the poolside hoop. They went back for another Coke and finally got out and dried off in the sun. Before they left they threw away the pop bottles and fetched Billy's beer bottle from the bottom of the pool. Neither boy mentioned a word about Kristen—perhaps not wanting to blur that image—but they did mention Billy.

"I couldn't believe how big his muscles were when he took off his shirt," Dalan said.

"I couldn't believe how black and blue his leg was where you hit him with that board."

Both boys laughed.

Maybe it was the relaxed aura after their adrenaline rush or maybe the bonding of what they had seen together, but Dalan's resolve not to tell anyone his and Marie's cave secret began to erode. He really liked Boyd, who, kind of like Dalan, was relatively new to town, this being only his second summer sweltering in the desert.

"Do you ever go out exploring in the desert?" Dalan asked as the boys locked the pool house door and headed for their bikes, which they had luckily laid down flat in the tall grass by the ditch.

"What's out there to explore?" Boyd asked.

"Oh, you know, looking for things, maybe animals or old stuff. I heard that real live cowboys and Indians used to live around here. Maybe they left some guns or arrows or some other kinda stuff lying around."

"My mom told me to stay out of the desert because there are rattlesnakes and coyotes out there. I hate snakes. Me and my dad saw a dead rattler alongside the road to Tucson one time. Dad stopped the car and we got out to look at it. It still had its rattlers on but we didn't have a knife to cut 'em off and Mom wouldn't let Dad bring the whole snake in the car. I had a bad dream about snakes that night."

This was not the direction Dalan had hoped to go with the conversation. He was hoping for information—trading something for what he knew. But maybe he wasn't asking the right questions to the right person.

"Have you ever seen any real Indian stuff? You know, like cooking pots, or plates, or maybe even real people bones. Anything?"

"Sure. Over at the museum by the Casa Grande Indian Ruins they have a building with lots of that real old junk like spears and arrows and stuff. We took a field trip there last year. It was okay but they didn't have any bones. How come you want to see bones?"

Dalan hesitated, took a deep breath and almost chickened out but then said, "If I tell you a secret will you promise not to ever tell anybody?"

"We're friends right? That's what friends do—they keep secrets with each other."

A wave of guilt swept over him unlike anything he had ever felt. Marie was his friend: She had taken him into her confidence, shown him the cave, given him a promise kiss, he was swimming in her pool, drinking her sodas, playing with her dogs, and yet he was ready to betray his solemn promise to her not to tell anyone about the cave.

"What is the secret?" Boyd asked, holding his bike up, ready to get going.

"Just a second," Dalan said. "I'll be right back."

He went back into the pool house and into its little bathroom. He needed a minute to think. If he told Boyd the secret, then they could go explore the cave right away and Dalan would not have to wait seven days for Marie to return. If however, Marie came back and found out he had told Boyd she would hate him forever and tell everyone at school he was a liar. The acid from his stomach came up into his throat nearly making him throw up. His hands were shaking. He washed out his mouth with water from the sink then flushed the toilet.

"Come on, we need to go right now," he yelled, coming out the pool house door and locking it behind him.

"Wait a second, you didn't tell me the secret."

"I'll have to tell you later. I think I'm getting sick. I want to go home. I'll tell you some other time. It's not that great a secret. Meet me here tomorrow at five. That's when I have to feed the dogs. We can go swimming again."

The boys threw Harley his rage bone so he would let them out the gate without slobbering on them, then got on their bikes and headed off their separate ways. Boyd hadn't seemed to mind too much, not hearing the secret, and by the time Dalan rode into his garage he felt one hundred percent better. Being a true friend was a good thing. He actually felt a little tingle of pride for having the personal courage to be loyal to Marie.

❖ ❖ ❖

None of the older kids showed up early for the street games that night. Lots of folks had gone on vacation and the day had been especially hot. Dalan waited until the sunset had faded before he went out looking for Boyd. He couldn't find him,

Kick The Can

but did spot the older guy who lived across the street with Mr. Larsen. The man was standing on the covered porch holding a pair of binoculars. He thought the man must be in college or maybe a soldier home for the summer. He thought it was weird that he had never seen the man do anything but ride his old bike around town or sit out on the porch.

Feeling bored, lonesome for Marie, and just wanting to talk to someone, he wandered across the street and stood on Mr. Larsen's driveway where he could see the front porch. He looked at the guy who was still just standing there. He was looking back at Dalan, but didn't smile or say anything. The pair of binoculars, now sitting on the porch railing, was bigger than any Dalan had ever seen. He took a big breath and strolled toward the porch.

"Those are sure some cool looking binoculars Mister. Would you mind if I look through them?"

The man looked at Dalan, then slowly stood up, picked up the army green glasses, and walked to the stoop. He didn't say anything but held them out.

Dalan thanked him and then spent several minutes looking up and down the street. He couldn't see a lot of things because it was dark but he could see in his kitchen window. The stupid cat Mom let in the house was on the table licking the sugar bowl. He could see a lady with her hair up in curlers standing in the doorway under a porch light a couple doors down the street. He saw a cop car cruise by on Main Street and then he saw Billy Real sitting in that '32 Ford hot rod with the crumpled fender, looking straight back at him with his own pair of binoculars.

Immediately he put down the glasses and walked to the stoop.

"Thanks Mister. I'd like to borrow them again sometime when the moon is up. I'll bet it looks pretty neat."

"Come over anytime. What's your name?"

"I'm Dalan Dawson. I live right there," he pointed at his house across the street. "My brother's name is Ian; he works at

Safeway bagging groceries and putting cans on the shelves. What's your name?"

The man hesitated at first then said, "Harvey Grimes."

Dalan put out his hand to shake but the guy didn't reciprocate, leaving him slightly embarrassed. He wanted to learn more about the man but didn't know what to say. He glanced down toward Main and saw Billy's car still sitting there.

"How come you're not kicking the can tonight?" Grimes said.

"I don't feel so good today." He paused for nearly a minute then said, "The truth is, Mr. Grimes, I don't want the bully sitting in that hot rod down there to see me. He'll come up here and beat me up."

Harvey pondered his potential relationship with the boy, finally deciding that this could be a golden opportunity.

"That was a mighty brave thing you did the other night, saving that little girl and then helping that older girl."

"You saw what happened?" Dalan said.

"I was sitting right here on the porch, just like most every night. That's about all there is to do in this dead-beat town."

Dalan was astonished to think that in his boring first few weeks in town he had never paid any attention to the man living across the street. He seemed pretty neat for an older guy. He squinted to see Harvey's face better in the dim street light. He didn't know anything about the man, but knew he needed to find out something. His mom or dad would for sure want to ask questions.

"How long have you lived here, Mister?"

"Just call me Harvey. That Mister thing sounds like I'm still in the navy. I moved in just before you did. I saw the moving truck unload your furniture," he said.

"Wow! You were really in the navy? Did you go on a battleship and shoot the big guns? Or were you a pilot on an aircraft carrier?"

"Nah, kid. I was just a grunt. You know what that is? It's the guy who swabs the decks and paints the latrines—you know, the toilets. Sounds like fun, huh?"

"Is Mr. Larsen your dad or uncle or something?"

"Jest my landlord. I jest rent a room from him. How old are you kid?"

"I'm in sixth grade. Do you do some kind of work?" Dalan asked, getting braver with each question.

"I'm between professions right now. For the time being, I work at the burger joint, so's to have something to fill the day. You ever been in there? It's called Bill's Biggest Burgers."

"That's a cool job. Do you get free burgers and stuff? My friend Boyd says they have hot dogs on wood sticks with some kinda stuff cooked on them. He says they taste great!"

"They call them things corn dogs, 'cause it's dipped in a corn batter and deep fried. I eat them all the time. I've never seen you at Bill's. Your dad ever take you there?"

"Mostly we eat at home. My mom is a really good cook," he said, dodging the fact that he only knew about Bill's Burgers from seeing the place driving by on Main and from Boyd.

"I work in the mornings and afternoons. Next time you and that little girlfriend of yours get hungry come by, and if the boss ain't looking I'll give you both either a doubleburger or a corn dog to try. You'll have to buy your own drinks though, 'cause they count the paper cups."

"Wow! I'd like that," said Dalan, wondering how this man knew anything about Marie.

From across the street Mrs. Dawson stepped outside the door and whistled twice, immediately getting Dalan's attention. It was the family come straight home signal—never to be ignored. He waved at her, a little surprised that she saw him so quickly. He started to say goodbye when the man—Harvey—spoke out.

"Listen kid. If that bully there in the hot rod ever bothers you, just let me know. If he so much as touches you or any of your friends I'll kick his butt to the other side of the county. I've had military hand-to-hand combat training. I know how to kill a man with one finger," he said, pointing his thick index finger straight toward the end of the street where the hot rod was last seen. The muscles on his arm and shoulder were flexed and bulging under his tight T-shirt.

Dalan stared at Harvey, who suddenly had a vicious scowl on his face and was now holding his swollen right hand with the index finger pointing toward the starlit heavens.

"Just one finger, kid. That's all it'll take and he's a dead man. You just let me know, and tell your cute little friend I'll keep her safe too."

CHAPTER 8

The little Coolidge branch of the county library was in a brick building next to the fire station. The main library was in Florence, the county seat, fifteen miles away. Florence also was the site of the state prison. In territorial days, Tucson and Florence were in competition for either the prison or the University of Arizona. Florence won the coin toss. The old-timers remember when the library was not just new, but when it was the repository for all of the most important news and literary print within fifty miles. Nowadays, it was the victim of budget cuts and entropy. Walking into its lobby, one was accosted with sights, sounds, and smells of which someone from a large city might wonder if they were from a previous era. Dust and the smell of mildew, hundred-year-old paper glue, and the overuse of Evening in Paris perfume by Miss Grange, the octogenarian librarian, made Dalan's eyes water as he perused the main room.

Along one side of the room were glass display cases, jam-packed with preserved small desert animals and birds, all from the local hills and nearby mountains. There were stuffed rattlesnakes fat as a man's leg, and scorpions with long hat pins stuck through their bodies, suspending them above display boards with Latin names written below. Off in one corner of the room there was a small display of Indian art. This was what he was hoping for. There he found blanket-like weavings, articles of clothing, and some ancient cooking utensils among which were several small clay pots, none even close to the size or beauty of those in the cave on the outskirts of town. Next to the display was a selection of books about the ancient Indians.

"May I help you, young man?" the blue-haired woman asked from her dais in the center of the room. Her voice was weak and warbled as she spoke.

"Yes please. I want to know if you have any pictures of the Indians who lived in the Casa Grande building and what their house looked like inside." His voice broke from a high-tone "yes please" to his normal voice as he formulated his sentence. He had practiced the question in his mind while riding his bike to the library, but the words had come out differently.

"We have some fine drawings of what the historians thought the people looked like, but unfortunately, neither Mr. Kodak nor Mr. Edison had been born yet, thus, there were no cameras. It is speculative as to the ancient dwellers real appearance. One can only suppose from the few rudimentary petroglyphs and paintings on pottery what they really looked like or how they lived. Very little actual art work has ever been discovered."

Dalan wasn't sure what the lady meant with her answer. Some of the words she used he had never heard before. He watched as she creaked to her feet and shuffled toward one of the tall shelves. He was certain that the eyeglasses dangling on the tip of her wrinkled nose would lose their battle with gravity, but they remained in place as she stretched to full height and retrieved a thick reference book from the shelf. He was surprised at its weight as she handed it to him and motioned toward a study table. She followed him and again motioned, this time for him to sit. Standing over his shoulder she reached down and as if by magic, opened the book to an exact page displaying a pencil-drawn picture of an Anasazi domestic scene.

"Is this what you had in mind, young man?" She asked.

He looked at the drawing, astonished to see the human figures sitting on mats or blankets preparing a meal. At their side was a varied array of large pots the same size or larger than the ones he and Marie had seen and touched in the cave. Even the paintings and geometric figures on the pots were the same.

"How do they know what the pots looked like?" he asked, getting right to the point.

"Archeologists have found fragments of the pots in the desert. Only a handful of intact vases, or pots as you call them, are known to exist," she warbled.

"Where can I see one?"

"The few that exist are in private collections, but there might be a few in the Natural History Museum in Chicago or in the Smithsonian Museum in Washington, D.C.," she said. "You also might try the small museum just up the road and the Casa Grande Ruins. They don't have any intact vessels but have some partial pieces that they have glued back together from pot shards local folks bring in. You should ask your parents to take you there since you are so interested. May I ask why are you so interested?"

He spent the next hour reading chapters in books about the ancient Anasazi people and their culture. The whole time he kept glancing at the old lady. He couldn't get out of his mind her question as to why he was so interested in the ancient people and their pots. He would have loved to show Marie the pictures and artifacts right then. He was tempted to check out a book and take it home, but he had second thoughts, suspecting that Ian would get nosey about his new-found interest in archeology. The entire time he was there, not a single other person came into the library. As he left he heard the heavy breathing of the dozing Miss Grange.

❖ ❖ ❖

For the next few days Dalan was busy mowing lawns, reading everything he could get his hands on about the history of the area, and exploring his new town. Some of the older neighbors had noticed him working in the yard at home and requested he come to work for them. By the end of the day on Friday he was exhausted, but he noticed his tan was darker, and his biceps and chest muscles seemed bigger. What really surprised him was how much money he had accumulated in the peanut butter jar he used for a piggy bank. He never dreamed of being so rich.

He got out the Sears, Roebuck catalogue and sat in his dad's recliner looking at all the things there were to buy. He could easily spend his thirty-seven dollars on a single order. Then he saw what he needed. On page 323, among the sleeping bags and camp stoves was a special high-powered headlamp. It ran on flashlight batteries one clipped onto a belt and had a nifty headband to hold the light. It would be perfect for exploring the cave. He tore out the page with the light as well as one of the ordering pages. He put on a pair of shoes and walked across the street.

"Hi, Mr. Grimes," he said.

"Hey there, kid. Didn't I ask you to call me Harvey?"

"Sorry. My dad is a real stickler about showing respect for adults."

They were standing in Fred's driveway. Dalan had watched for the neighbor to see if he was out on the porch, then he rushed across the street to ask him for some help. He was carrying the folded catalogue pages and a pencil.

"What do you have there?" Grimes asked.

"Some pages from the Sears catalogue. I was wondering if you know how to order things? I want to get a present for my dad's birthday," he lied. "I want it to be a surprise."

"What are you getting him?"

"It's a really nifty headlamp. It runs on flashlight batteries that you clip on your belt. I earned the money mowing lawns. I tried to figure out how to do this, but I'm afraid to just put the money in the envelope; somebody might steal it."

"Come on up and sit on the porch and let me try to figure this out," Harvey said. After reading the paper and thinking for a minute, he said, "you probably need to get a money order at the grocery store. Then you can mail it and the order form into the company. When's his birthday?"

"It's not for a couple of weeks. Do you think that's enough time?"

"I doubt it, but you can always try," Harvey said.

"What a lucky break," thought Harvey. "There is no way this headlamp is for his dad. This kid is going to use it in that cave, wherever it is, and I'm going to follow him regardless of the hazards." He glanced down at his hand, still swollen from the sting.

"You better tell your dad to be careful around here, especially at night. There are lots of scorpions. That's what happened to me."

"Wow! That still looks awful. I remember seeing it the other night. Where did you get it?" Dalan asked.

Harvey paused for a minute trying to make up a good story, wishing he hadn't mentioned his hand. "Just back behind Fred's. You kids need to be careful hiding in the bushes around here. You never know what you might be close to."

They sat on the porch as the sun began to set, filling out the order form. Harvey was used to ordering things from Sears and Montgomery Ward—he had even bought a gun and a hunting knife through the mail. He hoped that the kid wouldn't wait for the headlamp to arrive before he and the girl went back to the cave. That could be weeks.

The next morning, Dalan took his money to the Rexall Drug store and purchased a money order. He took the envelope with the order form and the money order to the post office, bought a stamp and sent it off to Chicago. In his mind he hoped that the package with the lamp would arrive at Mr. Larsen's the next day. Harvey had volunteered to watch for the package; after all it was a surprise for Dalan's dad.

❖ ❖ ❖

By Saturday, all the contracted lawns in the neighborhood were already neatly mown and edged. Boyd dropped by and suggested that the boys go for a swim at the Palermos' pool. He had been calling or coming by all week trying to get Dalan to go swim, but Dalan was always mowing grass.

They made a picnic of tuna fish sandwiches on Wonder Bread and Nabisco ginger snaps. Then they headed off on their bikes. They hoped that there would still be sodas in the pool house fridge. Dalan had been feeding Harley and the Scotty twice a day as agreed. Twice he had his mom drive him to the Palermos' and once he had brought Ian to let him swim. Each of those times it was after he had seen the hot rod cruising the streets and he had been afraid to go alone. It had been nearly two weeks since the car wreck. Maybe Billy's leg had healed and he had forgotten about it being smashed with the picket fence stake and who gave it to him.

The boys played with Harley, swam, and ate their picnic lunch. For some reason there were a lot fewer sodas in the fridge, and no beer left. They each drank a soda anyway. They looked in the garbage can but no bottles were found. Probably Billy and Kristen drank the beer and kept the bottles for the penny deposit. If Mr. Palermo asked about the Cokes, Dalan decided he would ask him to take the cost out of his pay.

The boys were sitting in the shade looking at an old magazine when they heard the hot rod. They looked at one another and panicked. Their bikes were sitting out by the gate in plain sight and their lunch bag was lying on a table beside the pool. They ducked into the pool house then realized too late that they were trapped.

The first voice they heard was not the familiar voice of Billy, but that of a strange man. Dalan peeked out the open door and saw a short, fat guy with a bald head and sun glasses, wearing dress pants and a blue dress shirt. He was throwing a ball for Harley to fetch and laughing. Billy closed the gate and the two headed for the pool house. The young boys went into the toilet room and locked the door. Moments later they could hear voices on the other side of the thin wall.

"How much can you sell him for?" It was Billy's gruff voice.

"I go to the dog shows all the time," the stranger said. That dog is really rare. I can get at least eight hundred dollars for him, maybe more. I'll split it with you fifty-fifty. All you have to do is to bring him by my motel room tomorrow night about eight."

"I want a hundred dollars right now and four hundred in cash when I bring him by, and it has to be tonight. I'm not going to steal the dog then have him stolen from me," Billy said. "I can't wait until tomorrow night. The owners will be home."

"That's not how I do business." The man's voice was getting angry.

"Well then there won't be any business," Billy said.

"Okay, okay. Here's a hundred bucks. I'll have the rest for you at eight. Make sure you bring the sack of dog food. Hungry dogs are dangerous and they bark too much. And while you're at it bring that little Scotty. He's worth a couple hundred. I'll give you half."

To the boy's surprise, the would-be dog thieves left without another word. The hot rod's noisy engine rattled the pool house windows then shot off down the dusty side road.

"Wow," Boyd said. "I feel sorry for Harley. What if they sell him to somebody mean who keeps him in a cage?"

"I'm not going to let anybody steal him or Scotty."

Boyd looked at Dalan like he had gone nuts.

"We need to find his leash or a long piece of rope. We'll hide him so they can't steal him. I'll find the leash. You put some dog food in our lunch sack."

Ten minutes later the pool house door was locked, the trash cleaned up, and Harley, Scotty, and the boys were headed down the road. Boyd carried the dog food and could barely keep up. The huge Great Dane was pulling Dalan's bike without him even having to pedal. They crashed twice on the way home because they needed to go right, and Harley turned left.

Dalan hid the dogs in the garage and waited for his Mom to come home. Boyd, being a basic chicken liver, dropped off the sack of dog food and left. At three o'clock sharp, Mom pulled into the driveway and got out to open the garage door. Dalan ran out of the house.

"Don't open the doors, Mom," he yelled just in time. "We found a runaway dog and put it in the garage."

"Well, I'll just call the dog catcher and have him come by for the poor thing," Mom said.

"No, no, no! There are two of them. I know who they belong to. It's the dogs I've been feeding for the Palermo family. The big one, his name is Harley, he keeps getting out. They will be home tomorrow night. Can't we keep them here just for a day or two?"

Mom, sensing something was amiss, was an easy sell. Dad was harder to convince when he got home from work. Both dogs already were barking up a storm, so Dalan had tied them up in the backyard with a clothesline cord.

"Why don't we take them back to the Palermo house and tie them up in their yard?" his logical-thinking father said. "They'll be a lot happier there in a familiar place."

Dalan couldn't say why, but he definitely didn't want to tell the story of hearing Billy's plan to steal the dogs. Dad would probably want to call the police, who wouldn't do a thing until the dogs were actually gone. He was about to lose the argument and would be forced to tell the whole story, when he was saved.

"That's a mighty fine-looking dog you got there, Dalan," Harvey said. He was standing by the back gate looking into the yard at Dalan and his Dad. "Where did you get him?"

After a fragmented explanation and an awkward introduction to his dad, Harvey offered to put the dogs in Fred's garage for the night.

"Fred is hard of hearing and I sleep like a rock, so their barking won't bother us a bit," said Harvey.

"That's mighty neighborly of you, Mr. Grimes. If you're sure Mr. Larsen won't mind, that would be a big help to my son and to the whole family. Maybe in return the Mrs. can fix you a plate of cookies?" Mr. Dawson said.

"Oh, that's not necessary. Actually, I'm trying to lose a few pounds. It's hard to keep in tip top shape when you work in a food establishment."

Dad accepted the offer without so much as a glance at his son. Harley was led out of the Dawson's yard, across the street, and disappeared into Fred's faded clapboard garage. Dalan played with the Scotty for a few minutes then took him over as well.

Dalan moped around the house the rest of the late afternoon. He was feeling guilty and afraid. *What if Billy found out what he had done? What if Harley got out during the night and ran away?* Also, it bothered him how Harvey was so anxious to take the dogs. Maybe he would sell them. As darkness fell, he couldn't stand it any longer and went across the street to check.

The street games were in full fury. Dalan knocked on Fred's door but no one answered. He already had seen that no one was on the front porch. No lights were on. He twisted the latch on the garage side door and slowly opened it to look inside. Not a sound was heard. He called Harley's name, but again there was only silence. He felt around inside the door until he found a light switch and clicked it on. A single bulb dangled from a wire in the middle of the dirt-floored room.

Dalan didn't think Fred or Harvey had a car, at least he had never seen one and there were no recent tire tracks on the dirt driveway outside, but there in the middle of the garage sat an old Plymouth Belvedere, shiny as the day it was first painted. In the corner of the garage was an old faded green canvas draped over what looked like a motorcycle. Lying beside it was a plaid blanket. Curled up on top was a very sound-sleeping Harley cuddled beside a black ball of fur.

"It turned out Fred could hear the barking after all."

Dalan nearly jumped out of his skin, turning to see Harvey standing in the doorway.

"It's an old trick my dad taught me years ago. Dogs love corn flakes and milk. I just added an ounce of Fred's medicinal whiskey and your dogs there curled up for a long nap. They were probably tired from all the excitement anyway."

Dalan bent down to pet them both to assure himself that they were still breathing.

"So how about telling me the truth about why you brought the dogs home?" Harvey probed. "I've seen the fence around the dogs' yard and know they couldn't have gotten out on their own."

Dalan had told enough white lies for the day and was relieved to share the story of Billy and the potential theft of the dog and how he worried that the Palermos would blame him when the dog was gone. He mentioned that his friend Marie said that her dad could be very mean. He also mentioned that the guy with Billy was even scarier than Billy.

"You did the right thing. I have the day off tomorrow. When the Palermos get home, you come and get me and I'll go with you to take back the dogs. If Mr. hot rod shows up we'll take him back to Mr. Palermo as well."

"Thanks for helping me, Mr. Grimes—I mean Harvey. You are a really nice guy for an adult."

"Don't mention it, kid. Let's go sit on the porch and watch the game."

CHAPTER 9

Marie arrived home just before dark on Sunday night. The distinctive tail lights of the big Cadillac were visible with the binoculars from Fred's porch as the car drove up the far end of the street. Dalan immediately dashed across the street to get his bike. He couldn't wait to get Harley back to the Palermos' fenced-in yard. His stomach had been in knots all day. He was fretting because the dogs were still asleep at ten in the morning and might never wake up from their drunken stupor. When he got home from Sunday school, Billy was parked half a block down the street, just sitting in the car, watching the neighborhood.

The biggest worry came when Harvey's boss drove up about two o'clock and asked him to work the evening shift. Someone had called in sick. Five minutes later they drove off. Harvey had left the glasses on the porch and had told Fred not to worry about the dogs and that the neighbor boy would be around the house.

Without his new friend there to console him, Dalan was afraid. He felt that at any second Billy would be out of the car with a baseball bat or even a knife, ready to make hamburger out of his face. He considered telling his dad or even Ian about his worry, but they were into watching football on the fuzzy-screened TV and seemed frustrated enough. Mom was in her room sewing a new dress. When he couldn't think of anything else to do he put his pocket knife in his hip pocket, got a longer rope out of the garage, and headed across the street to get the dogs.

Harley wanted to run and was not to be denied. It was all Dalan could do to steer his bike and miss the bigger ruts in the road on the way to the Palermos' house. He had taken the rope off of the Scotty, who was content to run and bark alongside the bike. With less than two blocks to go, the rumble of Billy's big-block Ford engine became louder than the dogs' barking and the bike tires crunching on the gravel road. Dalan put his head down and tried not to look to his side. He didn't think the idiot would run over him, but then again he had to be pretty mad that the dogs he intended to steal had disappeared.

Marie's house popped into view at the end of the long lane just as the front of the hot rod nudged Dalan's tire, sending him skidding sideways toward a vacant field, then flipping and twisting and rolling to a stop. The dog's long leash was still wrapped around the handlebars of the bike, so in spite of the bike's front tire being twisted sideways, it kept scrapping and bounding down the road toward the Palermos', Harley putting his shoulders into pulling the weight.

The head lights of the stopped car were shining up the road illuminating the fleeing dog and bike. The next thing Dalan saw as he lay on the ground was Billy's desperate attempt to run after the dog, still trying to steal him. He was completely ignoring Dalan and the Scotty. He was yelling for the dog to stop, but it wasn't working. He was a hundred yards away when he finally caught up enough to grab the back tire of the bike, which stopped the dog as well.

Dalan moved his fingers and toes, arms and legs, then finally felt his face and head for bumps or scrapes. Luckily, everything was intact. He looked at the hot rod just feet away from him. No one was inside. Billy was at least three hundred feet away and was in the process of getting his pant leg shaken by the angry Dane. The Scotty was nowhere to be seen. This left Dalan with the only option his brain could conjure. He pulled out his pocket knife and leaning down close to the car, plunged the blade into the right rear tire. Gaining confidence he attacked the right front as well then dashed across the street into the shadows and ran as fast as he could sprint for the Palermos' house. He didn't have to ring the bell. Before he got to the front gate Marie and both parents were coming out the door to see what all of the ruckus was about.

Out of breath, his Sunday clothes covered with dust and grass stains and with his eyes full of tears, Dalan told the story in bursts and sputters. He told of the planned dog theft and of hiding the dogs at Mr. Larsen's garage. Then, failing to hold back the sobs, he told of being run down in the street by the manic Billy Real. He started to tell about seeing Billy and Kristen at the pool house drinking beer, but stopped short when he remembered his and Boyd's erotic exposure to reality. No sooner had he finished his story and was beginning to answer questions, when Harley and the Scotty galloped up onto the porch, jumping up on Marie, nearly sending her to the ground. Twenty feet behind him was Billy with a big smile on his face. The idiot hadn't seen Dalan, who had put Mr. Palermo's big frame between himself and the approaching bully.

"Wow," blurted Billy. "That dog almost ran away from me. Some kid was trying to steal him so I stopped and asked him where he thought he was taking your . . ."

At that moment Dalan stepped into the light. Billy turned white as a sheet. Mrs. Palermo and Marie had disappeared into the house after whispering something into her husband's ear. Marie knew better than to interfere with any matter her father was in control of. Her father told Billy to have a seat on the stoop and then turned to Dalan and gave him a cursory exam. Both knees were bleeding through his pants. He had a flap of skin dangling on his elbow. Both knuckles and palms were scuffed.

Mr. Palermo helped Dalan into the house while Marie was sent to get a wet washcloth and some Band-Aids. With first aid supplies at hand, Marie's touch was soft and gentle as she dabbed at the little cuts and scratches. Dalan winced as she scrubbed the wounds, but he wasn't about to let her see him shed any more tears.

Outside Billy tried to make an argument for leaving the scene. "I better go now that I know that the dogs are safe. My car is still sitting in the middle of the street," he said.

Mr. Palermo stood on the porch, hands on his hips, as he questioned Billy, who merely glared back at him. Finally, disgusted and cautious about controlling his anger, Franco muttered a bone-chilling warning to Billy, then opened the front door and went inside.

❖ ❖ ❖

It was pitch-dark by the time two cars pulled up to the front of the Dawsons' house. The occupants got out of the cars and were having a quiet discussion as they walked up to the lighted porch and knocked on the front door. Officer Roberts fell back a step to allow Mr. and Mrs. Dawson to embrace their son. At first Mr. Palermo had resisted calling the police, but when Marie conveyed Dalan's fear of Billy to her mom, Franco was forced to give in and the police and the Dawsons were called. With the parents' arms around their son, introductions were made among the adults, skipping the sulking Billy who was sitting in the shadows.

"Mrs. Palermo and I want the two of you to know what a brave boy your son is," Franco said.

"He's a good, reliable kid," Dalan's dad said. "I'm sorry he had to be involved in this kind of thing at such a young age."

Officer Roberts asked Dalan several questions, glancing over at Billy at times to watch him squirm as his indictment was laid out before the gathering. The entire time Marie stood quietly, smiling from time to time at Dalan.

No mention of arrest or formal charges was mentioned. Technically, the only provable crime was reckless endangerment—following too close—with Dalan having the resultant bike crash. With a nod of his head, Officer Roberts sent Billy off toward the patrol car to wait. They would soon discover the hot rod's flat tires, and a tow truck would have to be called.

"Dad! Don't forget," Marie said.

Franco nodded and reached for his wallet. He bent down and handed Dalan two crisp twenty-dollar bills.

"Thanks for taking such good care of the boys," he said. "I'll have a look at your bicycle in the morning and have it repaired or get you a new one. Sorry you had to get hurt, kid. Don't you worry about that hoodlum bothering you again. He'll get the message to leave you alone."

The Dawsons looked at the man, surprised at his implication. Then to everyone's surprise, Marie stepped forward and gave Dalan a kiss on the cheek.

CHAPTER 10

Monday morning Dalan slept in. When he finally woke up, he could barely get out of bed. Every muscle in his body hurt. He counted the Band-Aids Marie had stuck on him and stopped at eleven. His mom had wanted him to take a bath the night before, but he was too tired. Now he had lawns to cut and it was already hot outside. The grass didn't stop growing for anyone. As he washed his face and brushed his teeth, he thought about Marie. He needed to have a private conversation with her and thought about calling her, but before he had a chance she was knocking on the front door.

"I baked you some chocolate chip cookies," she said, when he opened the door.

"Thanks," he said, taking the cookies. He couldn't remember ever getting a gift from a girl.

"Who is it?" Ian said, rushing into the foyer. He took a look at the cookies and then at Marie, then reached into the basket and grabbed two of the warm delicacies.

"I wish I'd a gotten hurt. Thanks anyway," he said in a mocking tone, then was gone out the door.

Mrs. Dawson came into the living room and insisted that Dalan invite the cute girl in, but Marie declined, saying she had to get to her piano lesson. Dalan walked her to the driveway where her shiny new Schwinn was parked.

"We have got to meet so we can plan our expedition," he whispered, looking up and down the street for any signs of danger.

"You mean looking in the cave," she laughed. Her smile was so radiant.

"I've been at the library studying while you were gone. I know all about the Anasazi and about those pots. They are very rare and worth a lot of money. I sent away for a nifty headlamp; it should be here any day. It's real bright. Did you get the pictures developed?"

"They are on the roll of film that I took to the beach. I'll try to pick it up at the drug store today. Maybe we should tell our parents about the cave," she said.

"No way! If my dad found out we were crawling in old caves he would ground me for the rest of the summer."

"Well, when do you want to go again?" she asked.

"Tomorrow will work for me. If my head light's not here yet I'll get my dad's flashlight; that way we'll have two lights. Make sure you bring your camera. When can you go?"

"Meet me at the hamburger place, Bill's, at two o'clock. You can buy me a corn dog now that you're rich," she smiled. "By the way, Daddy took your bike to his machine shop out at the farm yard. He said one of his hired hands was good at fixing things and could make it as good as new. He even said he would have the man paint it."

"That's great!" Dalan said. "So I'll be there—at Bill's. What about tonight? Are you coming to play kick the can?"

"I don't know if my parents will let me out of the house at night. They were pretty upset about you getting hurt last night." With that said, she got on her bike and rode off.

❖ ❖ ❖

Harvey had heard all about the bike wreck and the tires on the hot rod getting stabbed. He didn't hear it from Dalan, but from his boss and from several of the regulars at work. It was the talk of the little town. He couldn't wait to get off work so he could get home and hear about it firsthand. Harvey watched and waited for Dalan to come out at sunset, but the kid never showed. Maybe he was too beat up to play. He almost went over and knocked on the Dawsons' door, but just as he was starting across the street, those two older girls—

the ones from the night of the car wreck—walked down the street and joined in the kick-the-can game. One of them—the redhead—had on tight short shorts and a shirt which was tied across her abdomen, showing her belly button. The bleach blonde wore skin-tight pedal pushers and a white T-shirt. It wasn't dark yet so Harvey decided to head back to the porch and put his binoculars to work.

After a while he got tired of watching the girls and he started hoping that the bully with the hot rod would show up again. It had been a long time since he had had a good tussle with a tough guy. When he was in boot camp he would regularly single out one of the wimpy recruits and goad him into a fight. They were some of his fondest memories of the navy; that and shooting the M-16 and Colt 45 at the practice range. Too bad he didn't have one of those guns now. Wouldn't these kids be impressed if he had a nice shiny automatic rifle to show off? As he was day-dreaming, a skinny ten-year-old fell down early in the game and hurt his wrist. It looked broken to Harvey. So many wannabe-doctor parents showed up that the game broke up before it was even dark.

On Tuesday afternoon, Harvey was about to start the last hour of his shift when the two neighborhood kids came in. He had been thinking about them all day. Then, low and behold, there they were, like two little love birds, standing at the counter ordering food just like big folks. He stayed back out of sight watching as Dalan paid for the corn dogs and Cokes with a new crisp twenty.

"Hi there, Dalan, you're looking pretty rich today," Harvey said, coming out to the counter. "Who's your friend?"

"Hi, Mr. Grimes—I mean Harvey. This is Marie. They were her dogs that you let me keep in the shed."

"Hello," he said, extending his hand. "Dalan told me you were on a trip to the beach. Did you have a good time?"

She was polite but quiet, and once her order was ready she headed for a table at the front of the restaurant. Grimes got an ugly look from the cashier and glanced around to see if his boss was watching.

"So where are you two off to today?" he asked.

"We're just getting a snack and then riding around," Dalan said. "Her dad had my bike repaired yesterday. It's just like new."

"Pretty hot out there to just be riding around. I'll bet you have a favorite spot."

"Sorry, but I need to go. She gets real nervous if I leave her alone," he said.

"Well, I gotta work for another hour so I better get in the back. I'll see you back in the neighborhood. Sorry I didn't see you earlier; I mighta been able to sneak you something to eat."

The kids sat at the table visiting and eating the hot, greasy food, not looking at anyone. Harvey just knew that they had to be plotting something. He had known Dalan long enough to recognize a kid with brains, and the girl didn't act like a dummy either.

He was working in the back, which made keeping an eye on them difficult. He went to open a new box of hamburger buns and sure enough, the next time he looked up the two were gone. He quickly walked out the back door carrying a box to the dumpster, craning his neck to see which way they had gone. Too late, they were nowhere in sight. Then he remembered the girl was carrying a heavy backpack, like the kids nowadays used to pack around their books, but it was summer vacation. They had to be headed some place special. It had to be the cave.

❖ ❖ ❖

Marie was suspicious regarding the guy at Bill's. "Who was that creepy guy anyway?" she asked.

"He's just a guy who lives across the street from me," Dalan said.

"I don't like the way he looked at me—like Sylvester looking at Tweety Bird," she said.

"He's real nice. He helped me keep Harley and Scotty safe and he is protecting me from your sister's boyfriend."

"Kristen? She's not my sister. She is my half-sister. She hates me and my mom and only talks to my dad when she wants money. The reason she hangs around with Billy is to annoy Daddy."

"Well, don't worry about Harvey. He's okay. In a way he's like a grown up kid. I'll bet he'd love to play kick the can with the rest of us if he was allowed to."

"He could be the Easter Bunny and he would still give me the creeps. I guess 'cause you are a boy you wouldn't understand."

They were riding their bikes toward the high school as they talked. At the last minute Dalan had an idea.

"Follow me for a minute," he said.

She had fallen too far back to ask why, so she turned down Center Street. Dalan stopped his bike in front of the post office and yelled for her to wait. Two minutes later he came out of the building wearing a huge grin. In his hand was a small box. He pulled out his pocket knife and sat on the steps. Opening the package he produced a headband, then a square box with a belt clip, then two D batteries, and finally a small light, which looked like the end of a flashlight, but with a three-foot-long cord attached. Quickly he assembled the head light and put it on to adjust the headband. Joyfully, he clicked the switch on the box and the light came on.

"Isn't this the coolest thing you have ever seen?"

Marie rolled her eyes and got back on her bike. She was sure her flashlight would be all they needed. She told him to hide the light. "You are going to look pretty funny riding through town in the bright sunshine with that stupid light on your head," she whispered.

He looked around to see if anyone was watching then pulled it off and stuffed it into the inside of his T-shirt.

She took the lead, heading once more toward the high school football field on the edge of town, and ultimately toward the hidden cave.

They stashed their bikes in a group of bushes behind the bleachers, then half-walked and half-ran the quarter mile before they descended into the arroyo. They kept looking for the park ranger, praying they wouldn't run into her again. It had been over a week since their first visit to the cave, and with a couple of windy days and one evening thunderstorm, the gully had accumulated lots more tumbleweeds. It took them extra time to find the opening. This time they didn't just go in; they pulled the tallest weeds into the opening behind them. With their lights on, and a stick Dalan had left by the entrance to knock down cobwebs, they proceeded into the cave. "It looks smaller," he said, wiping new spider webs from their path as they progressed.

"Things always look smaller than the first time you see them. How is your head light working?"

He turned to look at her and nearly blinded her with the direct glare.

"Stop looking at me! Every time you turn your head toward me your light shines in my eyes," she protested.

"Look, they are all still here," he said, walking up to the tallest of the pots and examining it under the bright light.

"They look even better than the ones I saw in the pictures in the library books. Now what are we going to do?" he asked.

"I brought a tape measure and a notebook and a pencil. We need to measure each of them and make some notes. That's what good archeologists always do when they make a discovery."

"Who's going to read the notes? I think we need to figure out a way to get the things out of here and find out what's inside of them."

Marie gently put her hands on one of the smaller pots and started to lift it. Immediately she stopped and stepped back.

"This thing weighs a ton! There is no way we could carry one of these smaller ones, let alone the biggest ones."

"They have a thing with wheels at my brother's store that you slide under boxes so you don't have to lift them. It's called a dolly. Maybe if we ask Ian to help he could borrow the dolly and we could lift them with it."

"Then what are we going to do with them? Set up a table alongside the road and try to sell them like the five-year-olds selling lemonade?"

Her sharp sarcasm was unexpected. He turned away feeling like he had been slapped. He walked off to the far end of the room and pretended to examine the furthest pot. He couldn't believe that he actually had watery eyes from her curtness. He was afraid to ask her any more questions.

"Sorry," she apologized a couple minutes later, reaching across the pitch-black void and touching his arm.

"How about your dad?" Dalan finally asked. "He maybe knows somebody who would like to buy the pots for decorations, and we could dump the bones and whatever else is in the pots into a cardboard box and give them to the museum. That would make the pots a lot lighter."

"Daddy would just call the park rangers and turn everything over to them and we wouldn't get anything," she said.

"I know! We can get Harvey to help. He knows how to drive a car and maybe he can borrow a truck and we could load the pots in the truck then we could hide them until we find someone who wants to buy them."

"I told you that guy gives me the creeps. How can we trust him when you barely know him? He sounds like the weirdo guy that my mom said was standing in front of our house a few weeks ago, staring in our windows. He would probably just steal everything and sell it himself. He looks just like a crook to me," she said.

Undecided about what to do, they spent the next hour doing just what Marie suggested. Just like good archeologists, they took an inventory, measuring and estimating weight and re-photographing the pots. Dalan became bored watching her write and needed to pee really badly. He wandered off into the deepest part of the cave, about fifty feet from Marie and the chamber containing the pot shelves. He was unbuttoning his Levis when he saw the body.

At first he thought it was just a pile of old rags and turned his head—thus his light—away from the mass on the ground. Concentrating on the job at hand the previous mental image remained in his mind like an old photographic negative. Something wasn't right. Turning his headlamp's beam back toward the pile of rags, he saw a hand.

"Marie!" he screamed, running and buttoning toward where he had left her at work.

Moments later they were side by side, bending over the clump of old clothes staring at the desiccated body. The head was shrunken and twisted to the side. Hanging around the neck and mostly covered by the ragged clothes was a golden chain with large links. They could only see a couple of inches of it. The hand, however, protruded clear to its wrist from the sleeve of a coarsely-woven brown robe. There was no remaining flesh on the bones, but it was still articulated, the tendons all white and taut holding the bones in place. On closer inspection they could see a large gold ring on the third finger, which may have fit well at one time but now dangled freely. It was wide like a wedding band and on its surface there was an engraved, official-looking crest. Dalan reached down and gave the ring a tap, making it spin round and round on the dry bone.

"Look out!" Marie said.

They both jumped back and watched a family of scorpions march out of the dusty sleeve and across the cave's stony floor. That was enough shock for the moment. They retreated, backing out of the narrow portion of the tunnel. Dalan stopped once, shining his headlamp along the walls looking for any more surprises. His hands were shaking when he picked up the spider web stick which he had dropped onto the dusty cavern's floor.

"Let's get out of here," he whispered, again shining his bright light on Marie's face.

This time, she didn't protest, but closed her eyes, revealing the tiny tracks of tears running down her cheeks. The look on her face made him realize that she felt just as frightened as he did. For some reason he never would be able to explain, he took a big deep breath and made a decision.

"If we run out of here now, we might never come back," he said. "We need to finish writing down everything and taking pictures of everything in here. Then we need to get some help."

She didn't argue, but instead handed the camera to Dalan, insisting he be the one to go back and take pictures of the ancient person's body. "Make sure you get a close up of the hand and of that gold chain around his neck."

He nodded in agreement, his light creating strange flashes and shadows in the cave. This time with the five-foot-long staff in one hand, and the camera in the other, he headed back into the deep cave. As he walked, he began to see more evidence of what struck him as recent activity. There were lots of animal footprints. About ten feet from the body lay a green glass bottle, not shiny like a pop or beer bottle but lime green in color and opaque. He rolled it over with his stick then returned it to its original place. His memory flashed back to a sentence he had read in one of the books in the library, about how the great archeologists took special care never to disturb the site of an ancient find.

He began to study the body, starting with the ring. It had to be gold because in spite of the layer of dust everywhere else, the ring was shiny. Afraid to touch the skeleton's hand, he lifted it with the edge of the stick, which produced a crunching sound up under the robe. He scanned for more scorpions but none were visible. Braver now, he lifted the edge of the robe, bending his head down to look beneath its folds. There, looking back at him, were the hollow eyes of an empty skull. Lifting the fragile cloth further another golden reflection was seen. Links of the chain led down deeper into the folds to an elaborate gold cross embedded with red, green, and deep blue stones, each the size of M&Ms.

"Don't move. I'm right behind you," Marie whispered, leaning down nearly cheek to cheek with him.

He should have jumped or been startled by her sudden appearance, but he was so absorbed with what he was seeing, he instead continued his examination of the gold cross.

"That thing is beautiful! Look how big it is. It's got to be ten inches long," he said.

"Are those real jewels?"

"They must be. He must have been a priest or a monk. You think the Indians killed him?" Dalan asked, finally turning his head toward her.

"We better not disturb anything else with that stick. Step back so we can take some pictures," she said.

They took photos from several angles and then retreated into the main cavern. As much as Dalan was trying to resist touching anything, he had to know what was in the pots. Careful not to tip over the largest pot, he found a small stick and dug down into the substance inside the pot, adjusting his headlamp to improve his vision.

"It looks like a combination of ashes and sticks or maybe bones. I wish I had a soup can or a fruit jar so I could take some of this stuff out into the sunlight and then take it to somebody who knows what it is."

"Just leave it. When we come back we'll bring something to put it in," Marie said. "I'm getting more nervous every minute that we are inside this cave. I need to get out of here and into the sunlight."

Careful this time, they peeked out of the opening, checking for the Park Ranger or anyone else who might be wandering by. "What are we going to do?" she asked as they peddled homeward.

"We need help," he said. "And we need it before someone else finds the cave."

CHAPTER 11

Harvey was hopping mad. Not only did he miss the chance to follow those two sneaky little kids on their secret adventure, but the boss asked him to work a double shift. On top of it all, his hand still hurt like heck and was still so swollen that he kept dropping things. His back-up plan was to ride out to where he thought their cave was located and catch the kids as they were leaving. He muttered to himself all afternoon, as he slammed things around in the kitchen. Then, to make matters worse, business got really slow and the boss ordered him out to the front to scrub down all of the tables.

"Do you mean, wipe them down, sir?"

"No, Grimes, we wipe them down several times a day. I mean scrub them down with a brush and scalding hot water and disinfectant soap. That's why we are a successful business, because we are cleaner than the rest of the greasy spoons."

Thus, on bended knees and while dripping sweat, he started in one corner of the eating area and began scrubbing. The tables were actually quite filthy, especially along the edges and just under the lips. When he looked underneath one table it was so disgusting that he gagged. Balls of chewed gum and smeared food were everywhere. His hand was killing him and he was talking himself into faking a seizure or a heart attack when his luck changed.

He heard the sweet sound of a big block V-8 just as it pulled in the parking lot. He stood up and watched the hot rod head for the drive-through lane, but at the last second it stopped and the driver revved the engine, backing up as if to leave. Then, even better for Harvey, it pulled forward and parked right in front of the door. Out of the cramped driver's seat crawled the greaser, Billy Real.

Harvey watched as Billy straightened his jacket, tugged down his tight jeans then walked inside, still limping from Dalan's attack. Trailing several feet behind him were the greaser's redheaded sister and the blonde Palermo girl, the one the bully had slapped the night of the wreck.

"These tables are getting cleaned right now, you need to sit over by the window," he mumbled loud enough to be heard.

"We'll sit wherever we want to," Billy said dismissively. "I want fries, two double cheeseburgers, and a large cherry Coke—and get something for yourselves," he said to Kristen. "Oh darn," he said with a laugh. "I guess I forgot my wallet."

She and Candy headed for the counter. Billy plopped down in a booth, which had just been scrubbed, but not wiped down. It glistened with soapy water, which caused Billy's hand to slip. He reached to catch himself but smacked his shin on the edge of the table, then fell flat on the wet floor. The girls and the woman at the counter looked at him then pointed at him and laughed.

He blurted out a string of profanities as he got to his feet and charged up to Harvey, accusing him of neglect.

"I told you and your friends to sit on the other side of the room," Harvey said. "There is even a sign there on the floor warning you that things here are slippery."

The girls were placing their orders when Bill came through the door from the back to investigate the clamor.

Billy had clambered to his feet and was leaning right into Harvey's face, berating him as "a low life janitor," "a grade school dropout," and "a dumber than a door-knob idiot," among other insults.

Harvey, having gone through the navy's basic training, was used to a drill sergeant's hazing, and ignored it until one of the girls spoke up and told Billy to behave. Billy turned on the girls, shouting loud and vulgar. Next, the boss got into the mix, insisting that Billy leave the premises. That's when

Billy made his worst mistake, taking a step backward in preparation of throwing a punch at Bill. As his fist flew toward the manager, Harvey's hand shot forward like the strike of a cobra, grabbing the fast-moving fist, and with a practiced twist and downward jerk, forced Billy's arm downward, causing his hobnail boots to lose traction. Just before his body met the floor, there was a sickening snap and a scream of pain. The bully's wrist was definitely broken.

The next hour was a cacophony of crying, yelling, sirens, and finally pats on Harvey's back, not just from the owner Bill, but from Officer Roberts, who had documented a long list of grievances against Mr. Real. Harvey had saved the day. Billy was arrested for disorderly conduct, and because the handcuffs wouldn't go on his swollen wrist, ankle bracelets were applied before loading him ceremoniously in the black-and-white cruiser.

Kristen and Candy had retreated to the corner of the room originally suggested by Harvey, their order of food lying cold and abandoned nearby. At the last minute Candy had the presence of mind to retrieve the keys to the hot rod from her brother, but they couldn't leave until the police car blocking them left.

"Call your dad and tell him to come down and bail me out," Billy shouted to Kristen as the police goose walked him out the door and into the back seat of a cruiser.

Once the police car pulled out onto the highway, the crowd of gawkers began to leave as well.

"Back to work," Bill hollered to his staff. "You, Grimes, get those ladies' orders replaced."

He was about to defer to the girl at the register when Candy appeared by his side, and gently touching his arm, told him to skip the burgers. That just Cokes and fries would do. While the girls ate and the place began to get busy, Harvey finished scrubbing the tables and chairs. Eventually, the two girls finished their food and left, grinding the gears of the hot rod as they backed up and pulled onto the highway. Harvey noted that neither one of them had gone to the pay phone to call for help for Candy's brother.

That blonde girl was sure starting to grow on him. The long blond hair, red lips and fingernails, and those long tan legs—too bad she is so young.

Time flew by and he was well into his second shift when the boss tapped him on the shoulder. "I just got a call from Officer Roberts. The greaser is already out of jail and is at the hospital getting a cast put on his arm. It might be a good idea if you go out of your way to avoid the hothead. Roberts claims the guy is spouting off to everyone that he is going to get even with you. I don't want you riding your bicycle home in the dark. I'm ready to leave for home. Go punch out and throw the bike in the back of my car. Good job today."

❖ ❖ ❖

Dalan and Marie were sitting on the pool's edge talking about what to do about the cave and the new finding of a skeleton, when the hot rod drove up the gravel road toward the Palermo house. Dalan was surprised to see that the fender already was repaired. He would have been afraid of the approaching car, but Mr. Palermo had recently arrived home and had waved at Dalan, again thanking him for taking good care of Harley. He was sure that Billy wouldn't touch him with Mr. Palermo at home. He was happy when the hot rod's occupants turned out to be Kristen and Candy—no Billy in sight.

The girls went into the pool house and seconds later came out in bikini swimsuits. They pretty much ignored the presence of Marie and her friend. The older girls talked back and forth about the incident at the hamburger joint and finally swam over to the steps and shared the story with the youngsters.

"Who was it that hurt Billy?" Marie asked.

"Some older guy. I've seen him working there before. He's kind of cute and looks tough like a soldier or boxer. He sure put Billy down in a hurry," Kristen said.

"Billy is going to kill him," Candy said, with all the passion one might put into asking for the salt and pepper to be passed.

It wasn't hard for Dalan to guess who the fighter at the fast food place was. When the girls described the fight in detail it made him wonder more about Harvey.

It was getting to be dinner time, so Dalan dried off and put on his shirt and canvas shoes. As he was leaving, Marie tugged on his sleeve, nodding toward the far end of the yard.

"We've got to make up our minds and agree on some kind of a plan," she said. "What should we do?"

Previously, she always had taken the lead and made all the decisions about the cave. Now she was deferring to him. He was a little confused about the transfer of leadership.

"We need help and I don't know who to turn to except our parents. We are never going to be able to sell any of those things; besides, they belong in a museum, and they should be studied by a real archeologist."

Marie hung her head and paced in a small circle on the grass. "Daddy probably knows somebody in New York," she finally said. "We could ask him to talk to them. The problem is that if I tell him about the cave he's going to get mad that I went in there in the first place."

"What about the park ranger lady we met the first time?" he said. "Maybe we could talk to her."

"You decide what we should do," she said.

Dalan thought about it for a minute then went on, "No one is going to believe us unless we can show them the pictures. Why don't you get the photos and then we can talk to either our parents or the park rangers—there have to be other people who work at the ruins besides that grumpy woman we met. She gave me the creeps," Dalan said. "Just like you said Harvey did for you."

"Okay, but it will take a few days to get the pictures back," she said.

"I know! Let's ride our bikes out to the national park ruins tomorrow and go into their museum. I have money for the admission. Maybe that will give us more ideas and maybe we'll meet somebody we can trust to help us," he said, as he waved good bye to the older girls. He smiled at Marie as he pushed his bike out to the road. "I'll meet you at the Tasty Freeze at two."

❖ ❖ ❖

The bad news that was waiting for Dalan's return home couldn't have come at a worse time. When he walked into the kitchen his dad was sitting at the table informing the family that his favorite uncle finally had died after a long bout with cancer. He said that the whole family needed to go to the funeral in Colorado. They were leaving the first thing the next morning. It would take all day to get there.

Dalan was in a panic. He had to get word to Marie. Standing her up tomorrow would be horrible. Ian was on the telephone calling to get off of work and Mom was waiting her turn with a long list of relatives to call.

He thought about the street game but it was probably too early. Mom had fixed a light supper, which she told him and Ian to go ahead and eat. Afterward he ran out the front door looking for Marie, hoping that she already had shown up. It was still pretty light out and just the little kids were milling around. Back in his yard, he stuck his head in the door and yelled to his mom that he had forgotten something at a friend's house and would be back in twenty minutes. He wasn't sure she had heard him, but he wasn't going to go in and be denied leaving. He headed down the road on his bike as fast as he could ride.

The lights were on in the swimming pool and pool house. He hoped she would be out there so he didn't have to go to the front door. Mr. and Mrs. Palermo were still pretty intimidating. He parked his bike along the fence hoping Harley would bark, calling attention to his arrival. No such luck. With the yard still quiet, he went through the gate toward the pool. Just before he stepped into the light from the pool house he heard the voice of Mr. Palermo talking on the phone.

Dalan froze in place. As the one sided conversation continued he backed up a few steps. He couldn't help hear what was being said.

"You know I been patient with the kid but frankly he's gone too far this time . . . No, I haven't decided what to do about him but this last stupid trick crossed the line. I'll let you know after I decide. I gotta go; they're waiting dinner on me in the house."

Dalan heard the phone slam down, and then saw the lights all go out. He was standing right in the middle of the path to the main house and had no choice but to dive into a clump of shrubs. He could feel the breeze from Franco passing by and then smelled the strong cigar. Palermo was still muttering to himself when he went into the house.

"Now what? What kid is he talking about?" Dalan wondered. He wasn't left with a lot of choices. He crawled out of the bushes and walked to his bike. He pushed it around to the front of the house and rang the doorbell.

Immediately, he heard both dogs barking, and then to his relief Marie answered the door. She was dressed in a Sunday-looking skirt and sweater and even had on fancy shoes. She looked two or three years older than a few hours before.

"Hi," she said, stepping out onto the porch and pulling the door partially closed.

"Hi. Sorry to bother you at dinner time, I guess you're just starting dinner. I came by to tell you some bad news. My dad's uncle died and everybody has to go to the funeral."

"I'm sorry that he died; you must really be sad," she said.

"That's not the bad news. I mean it is bad news, but I didn't really know him; it means that we can't go to the museum tomorrow. I won't be back for five or six days."

"Do you want me to go by myself? You know, to collect information?"

He couldn't believe that she was still asking him to make the decisions regarding their secret.

"You can if you want to," he said. Then a thought came to mind. "Maybe you could go there and maybe make friends with that ranger lady. She might be a lot nicer to you than any of the men that you said work there."

"I can do that. But I'm not going to tell them anything or show them the cave without you being here," she said.

"I'll try to let you know the minute I get home. I should know after we've been there a day or two. Maybe I'll send you a postcard with a picture of Pike's Peak and tell you what day I'll be home."

"That would be great."

"You sure look pretty all dressed up. Are you going to a party somewhere?"

"No, Mama makes me dress up for dinner every night," she said blushing.

"Any chance you're coming to play the game tonight?" he asked.

"I hope so. If I can come, I'll see you in an hour, but don't count on it. My dad is really mad about Billy getting in a fight at Bill's Burgers," she said. "When he's in such a bad mood, it's best if I stay in my room or go shopping with my mom."

❖ ❖ ❖

Harvey sat on Fred's porch scanning the cars going up and down Main Street and listening for the hot rod's throbbing engine. He was dragging the blade of his double-bladed diving

Kick The Can

knife back and forth across a whetstone. With each slow swipe he was making the knife sharper and sharper. He held up a piece of paper between his two fingers and without it even bending, sliced the knife through the sheet. As he worked he thought about the future—his future.

As much as he had come to dislike Billy, he loved the bully's car. He was even starting to dream of ways to steal the car and just leave this loser town. California was where the action was. Fred had a little radio that he let Harvey use. The rock and roll songs all sang the siren song of California girls, hot rod races, and surfing. It would be pretty cool to drive along the beach or up and down Sunset Strip in Billy's hot rod. He really needed to get out of this town.

Owning a gun was out of the question for Harvey. Although he wasn't really on parole or anything, the navy judge had warned him about getting caught with a firearm. Now a knife—that was a different thing. Deep in the bottom of his navy rucksack he had stashed his dad's old skinning knife. He kept it rolled up in an oily rag with a piece of wire wrapped around it. Tonight after Harvey's boss, Bill, brought him home, he dug down into the bag and retrieved his only weapon; he borrowed the whetstone from Fred's kitchen drawer.

Sitting in the dim light he watched and waited. The street games were underway, but none of his favorite players had shown up. The younger kids all got hurt easily and never stuck to the rules. Probably they didn't even know them. When the teenagers arrived was when the real action began.

The knife was razor-sharp by the time he saw Dalan walk out of the kitchen door. There was no sign of the cute, black-haired girl, but walking up the street, silhouetted by the fading sunset, were the two older girls last seen at the fight at Bill's Burgers. The two stood a few feet away from the dented coffee can until the present game was over then asked the bossy Darlene if they could play.

The redhead was appointed "It," so she stood counting to twenty as the others scattered. Harvey thought it hilarious to watch her try to tag the younger, faster kids. She stood a full head taller than most of them. He had his binoculars up watching her bounce as she ran back and forth, failing to tag even the youngest of the kids.

"What's so funny?" came a voice from the bushes below.

Harvey hadn't seen Dalan sneak into his favorite hiding place at the base of the porch.

"I'm laughing at that redhead girl making a fool of herself. Do you know who she is?"

"She's the sister of Billy, you know, the guy who drives the Ford hot rod? Her name is Candy Real."

"And who is the blonde?" Harvey asked.

"She's Marie's sister, Kristen Palermo, but they don't live at the same house. It's complicated. She's Billy's girlfriend, but her sister claims she really hates him 'cause he is always being mean to her just like the other night. Remember?"

"You're a whole encyclopedia of information. How do you know all this stuff?"

There was no answer. Dalan was sprinting across Fred's lawn toward the can. Wham! He kicked it so hard it caved all the way in on one side. Candy made a last second reach to tag him out but missed.

Marie didn't show up and the older girls lost interest quickly and headed off to find something more interesting to do. Harvey put away the knife and sat in the rocker listening to KOMA. It was an Oklahoma City radio station with a disc jockey named Wolfman Jack. Yeh, California was the place for a guy like Harvey. "Three girls for every guy," one song promised.

❖ ❖ ❖

The drive to Colorado was torture. The Dawsons' car didn't have air conditioning and the back seat was crowded. Ian kept complaining that he needed to lie down and sleep and insisted that Dalan sit on the floor. The car overheated on one steep mountain pass so they had to sit by the road for what seemed like hours, waiting for someone to come by with a water bag. A front tire blew out north of Santa Fe, but the worst part of Dalan's trip was Ian. He had taken upon himself to annoy Dalan the entire time. Ian found an old buzzard feather by the roadside, and every time Dalan would try to fall to sleep, Ian would tickle his nose or neck or even slip it into his mouth. The car noise was so loud with the windows down that his parents completely ignored the ruckus in the back seat. Dalan would beg for cessation of the annoyance of the moment, only to have Ian dream up some other kind of torture.

The funeral was morbid. His dad had insisted that the boys walk up and look into the coffin at the wax-like face of the dead uncle. Dalan didn't know a single person there and everyone else with kids had been smart enough to leave them at home. There was, however, one highlight. Next door to the funeral parlor there was an antique store. During the viewing, he snuck away and went into the store. The place was like a museum for dust and cobwebs. The shelves were cluttered with useless but interesting junk, with the exception of one high shelf. It was toward the back of the store. There sitting all alone was a clay pot. It was about two feet tall and about as round as a volleyball. It looked real familiar.

"Can I help you, sonny?" came the voice of a stooped old woman.

"I'm just looking," said Dalan.

"Well, if you see something you like just ask," said the friendly old lady.

"That pot up on the shelf, it looks real old."

The woman pulled a rickety wooden ladder away from the far wall and leaned it against the top of the shelf. She nimbly climbed four rungs up the ladder then dragged the pot out to the edge. Cradling it in one arm, she climbed back down to the floor and set the dusty pot on the counter. Dalan was sure she was going to drop it. Next, she dusted it off with an old damp rag, enhancing its earthen smell and bringing out the detail of paintings on its surface. There were pictures of horses, men in robes, and children running away from men with spears.

Dalan took his time examining the ancient relic, carefully turning it so he could see the full circumference. "How much would it cost to buy this pot, ma'am?" he asked.

"Oh, I can't sell it. It's against the law to sell American antiquities," she answered, noting the quizzical look on his face. "*Antiquities.* That's the word for old stuff buried in the ground by people who died a long time ago. My late husband traded this for his pickup truck."

"So it's okay to trade the thing but not sell it?"

"Well I don't know about that but I can't even trade it. The bank loaned me money for my store, but said that the pot was part of the store—part of the collateral. So I have to keep it up there on the shelf. I only brought it down 'cause you seemed so interested. Most people don't even notice that it's there."

Dalan didn't quite get the idea of collateral, but guessed that the pot was valuable only as something to look at, especially if it was against the law to sell it. He looked at the clock up on the wall. He needed to go back to the funeral home.

The voice of the woman stopped him as he was stepping out the door.

"Ten thousand dollars," she said. "Find me more of these pots in good condition and I can get you ten thousand dollars. But you can't tell a soul."

"Ten thousand dollars?" The number cycled around Dalan's head for the next several days. It was enough to buy three new cars or even a new small house. It was enough to pay for his mom and dad to go on a ship to Paris or Hawaii.

It might be enough to even pay his way to college so he could become a doctor.

As hard as he tried, he couldn't get the idea out of his head that he and Marie should sneak one or two of the pots out of the cave and trade them for ten thousand dollars. *Wow! Wouldn't Mom be surprised with a new fur coat?*

CHAPTER 12

The morning after they arrived back home, he was out of bed early. The thermometer on the front porch read 102 degrees. It would be 113 before the day was over. The lawn looked like it had grown a foot since they left. Dalan was torn between cutting it right now before it got even hotter or trying to see Marie to tell her his plan.

His dad made the decision for him on his way out the door.

"Get that mower going, son. Mr. Peterson up the road wants you to cut his grass too. That was him on the phone a few minutes ago. I knew you wouldn't mind. He said he would pay you seventy-five cents extra if you finished it today."

The last thing he wanted today was another lawn job. Why should he waste his time cutting lawns when he and Marie could make ten thousand dollars trading just one pot? It made no sense.

The mower's engine stalled twice, he burned his hand on the muffler, Ian had thrown an old dried-up orange at him for waking him up with the noise, and Mom had made him stop in the middle of his work to eat pancakes and take his cod liver oil. Relieved when he was finally done with the front grass, he was cooling his face and hands with the garden hose when a car honked and pulled up to the curb. The electric window went gliding down and there was the smiling face of the prettiest girl in the world.

"When did you get home?" Marie asked. Her mom was behind the wheel of the shiny Fleetwood Cadillac and was smiling at him as well. They didn't seem to be in any hurry.

"Hello, Mrs. Palermo. Hi, Marie. We got home last night," he said, realizing that he had water dripping off of the end of his nose.

"You didn't miss anything while you were gone. I went to the Visitor's Center at the Indian Ruins with Mom. It was really interesting. We met a really nice lady there. She is a park ranger," Marie said, giving him a noticeable wink.

"Next time we go you should come with us," Gina Palermo said, her face all smiles.

Dalan figured that Marie was giving him some kind of coded message, but he wasn't sure just what it was.

"Mom has a dental appointment in Phoenix, so we're off until two. Hopefully I'll be home for the kick-the-can game at three," she said.

There it was. No one had ever played the street games during the daytime.

"I hope you don't have to have any fillings," he said as the car began rolling forward, the window on its way up. "I hate going to the dentist. Bye, Mrs. Palermo. Bye, Marie."

She kept her eyes on him through the tinted window until the car was to the corner, then she was gone for now, but the exploration was still a "go."

With no further communication he made his plans. He charged back and forth across the necessary lawns, hardly noticing what he was doing as his mind organized the needs for later in the day. He felt like he had to go for a quick one-hour swim with Boyd, when his friend wouldn't take no for an answer. He didn't want to lose the only guy friend he had, but Dalan needed time to organize his backpack. His list included: putting new batteries in the family flashlight and his head light, getting a canteen for water, and getting several pint-sized Mason jars to collect samples of the contents of the pots. The last thing he wanted to do was to bring one of the pots home, empty out the dirt, and find a human hand or foot or even a head.

The house was empty when he got home from the city pool. His mom often went to Granny's during these long hot hours, and Ian and his dad were at work. He went through the kitchen drawers trying to think of other things he might need. A knife would be good. He picked out a butcher knife with a seven-inch blade, some candles and matches—why hadn't they thought of candles before? They would be perfect, giving off plenty of light without using up all of the battery's power.

He stood at the kitchen sink and ate a snack, then hefting his stuffed backpack onto his shoulder; he headed off to meet Marie for their long-anticipated adventure.

Marie hadn't called, but he had faith that she would get home in time to meet him under the eucalyptus tree by the football field. She didn't disappoint him. Wearing boy's jeans and a plain robin's-egg-blue T-shirt, she looked ready for work. They were all business. No hugs, chit chat, or questions about the days of separation, but they did take time to hide their bikes behind some bushes behind the baseball dugout.

"I said she was nice, but all the lady ranger did was keep reminding us how she had sent several people to jail for 'digging pots.' Those were her words. Not stealing pots or selling pots or damaging pots, just 'digging pots.' She was so rude, and she kept staring me in the eyes when my mom wasn't watching. I know she recognized me from the time she caught us."

"I saw a pot while I was in Colorado. It was just like ours, only not quite as big. It was in an old antique store. The lady let me touch it and look at it up close. It had a few chips and somebody had tried to write their name in it with a knife or nail."

"Did she want to sell it?"

"Her husband traded it for a pickup truck. She said it was worth at least ten thousand dollars," Dalan said, waiting for her response, but she was too surprised to speak.

"Just think! If we could get just two of those pots out of the cave, clean them up and sell them, we could both be rich," said Marie.

They didn't notice the scorching heat as they walked and talked. When they arrived at the cave entrance, it was still covered with dried tumbleweeds just like they had left it. Carefully, they rolled away the biggest tumbleweeds. In their excitement and rush to get inside, they forgot to roll them back in front of the entrance. The cave seemed to have gotten smaller than before. For some strange reason they didn't have to sweep away cobwebs as they made their way through the cavern, but in their excitement they didn't notice. To the kids' relief, the pots were still in their original places, and were every bit as big and as beautiful as the two had remembered.

Dalan and Marie went straight to work. They placed two pink candles in little holes he made on the opposite ends of the pot shelf and lit them. The whole cave began to glow, giving off eerie shadows as the two moved around, filling the glass jars from the contents of the pots. They used spoons Dalan had borrowed from his mom's silverware drawer. The deeper they dug into the pots, the more bones, teeth, and tiny metal objects they discovered. He picked out one of the coin-sized objects and rubbed it against his jeans. A crust of soot and dirt fell away leaving a spot of shiny metal. He rolled it back and forth in his fingers inspecting it, but wasn't sure if it was a coin or some kind of ancient jewelry.

"Does it smell bad in here to you?" Marie asked.

"I can't tell. My nose is too stuffy. I think I'm getting a cold. Lots of people at the funeral were sick, leastwise they were blowing their noses a lot," he said.

They didn't hear the footsteps until the intruder bumped his head on an overhanging rock and murmured a cuss. Both of them froze with spoons in mid path. They looked at each other, then immediately reached and snuffed out the candle closest to them. Frozen in movement, they listened intently, trying to confirm having heard the sound. The footsteps had ceased and only the sound of their breathing was heard. Then they saw the darting flicker of a flashlight on the walls of the cave.

Unsure what to do, they acted in unison. Softly the spoons were slipped into pockets. Marie reached for his hand, squeezing his fingers so tight that they hurt. Slowly and carefully they inched deeper into the cavern, feeling for the walls in the blackness and trying to be silent.

They felt their way around the first curve, then froze again as a cough and then a sneeze echoed through the rocky cave.

"I told you you'd like it," they heard a male voice say.

"I have claustrophobia. It's way too dark in here for me." It was the voice of a young woman. "I'm not staying and don't ask me to ever come back."

"Come on, don't be such a chicken. It's just a cave. It's not like it's full of ghosts or something. At least give me a little kiss before we leave."

Ian? Dalan couldn't believe his ears. *Was it his brother and one of the girls he had seen at the grocery store? Could he have followed them here or learned about the cave from someone else?*

Marie was still squeezing his hand trying to reassure herself that they were safe. They heard a slapping sound, and then a moan, and then heard the girl yell something about leaving with or without the guy. Two minutes later the silence resumed.

They waited for what seemed like hours before Dalan turned on his flashlight. There was no sign that the intruders had come as far as the pottery room.

"What should we do?" she asked.

"Let's finish checking out the pots. If they come back, I'll sneak up on them and scream 'boo!'" he said.

Marie giggled.

They lit the candles, retrieved the spoons and went back to work sifting through the ash, getting more selective with what they put in the mason jars. When the lids were placed and the bottles packed in the backpacks, they took time to examine the pots again.

"I forgot to ask if you got the photos developed."

"The drugstore called and said the film was ruined. They gave me a new roll of film, but I forgot my camera. Sorry, Dalan."

He was touched by her sincerity. He reached over, giving her arm a pat.

"No problem. It's probably better not to have pictures around for someone to find. We have enough trouble now that somebody knows about the cave. I can't believe someone followed us. It kind of sounded like my brother Ian. If it's him, I may have to strangle him in his sleep."

This made Marie giggle even louder.

"Shhh! You'll wake up the monk," Dalan teased her.

"My grandmother told me not to say rude things about the dead," Marie mumbled.

"Sorry. Before we leave let's take a look at him; maybe there is something we missed. We didn't roll him over or check in the folds of his clothes."

"You go right ahead," she said. "I'll hold the flashlight."

Before they could get to the site where they had found the mummified monk at the far end of the cavern, an odor struck them both that brought nausea and fear at the same instant. Off in a side tunnel eight or ten yards deep, there was a buzzing sound.

"Shine the light over here," Dalan said.

"Oh my gosh!" she screamed, and then started to cry. "There's a body in there. Look at all the flies! It looks like blood everywhere."

Dalan stood beside her, too shocked and sickened to speak. Stretched out on the dirt floor of the cave was a body. A black plastic bag was pulled tight over the head and there was a massive wound in the person's chest. Lying on the ground beside the body was a pair of sunglasses. On his feet were black leather motorcycle boots with metal rings on the sides.

Not touching or disturbing anything nearby, the frightened youngsters fled from the side cave and hurried toward the exit.

"Stop, stop!" Dalan yelled at Marie. "We need to take all of our stuff out of here. We need to tell the police—but then they'll know that we were here and they will know about the pots. Someone else will get the pots."

They stood silent thinking then Marie said, "Think! We need to take the gold cross the monk was wearing too. Think! Think!" she said again in frustration.

"Get the glass jars and the backpack outside and wait for me. I'll go back and get the monk's gold cross and I'll dump that ash stuff out of two of the best-looking pots. That should make them light enough to carry. We'll hide the things somewhere nearby and then go tell our parents about the body."

Marie's lips were trembling when she looked at Dalan. His plan sounded logical. Quickly they gathered everything, choosing two pots from the end of the row, which seemed somewhat different than the others. Marie then moved toward the entrance of the cave to wait.

With his headlamp on bright, Dalan carefully walked back toward the deepest chamber where the monk's body had been. The first thing he noticed about the monk's body was that the ring was gone from the boney finger. Luckily, the old woolen robe had folded across the man's chest, covering the heavy gold chain and its bejeweled cross. With delicate motion, Dalan lifted the chain up and over the head of the corpse. He couldn't believe how heavy it was. Carefully, he walked back toward the main cavern. He couldn't help himself as he passed the side tunnel. He turned his head lamp toward the new body, casting the bright light on the scene. That's when he noticed the coat—the black leather coat.

CHAPTER 13

Harvey was ducking and dodging through the dry gully trying to keep out of sight. He no sooner had arrived at the desert arroyo than he heard the sound of a vehicle engine. A thin trail of dust followed a lime-green pickup heading toward him. He figured he was less than thirty minutes behind Dalan and the girl, but thus far hadn't caught a glimpse of them. Scrunched behind a blossoming ironwood bush he watched as the truck inched its way past. On the driver's door was emblazoned the large round seal of the National Park Service.

While he waited, a small swarm of honey bees had taken an interest in his aftershave scent and were circling close to his face, giving warning of a potential attack. He felt like he had at boot camp doing military war games of pursuit and evasion, thus requiring him being absolutely motionless to prevent being seen or stung. He waited until the sound of the truck's motor was gone then stood, moving slowly so as not to anger the pollen collectors.

A flash of black hair was the first sign that the kids were close to the cave. The girl was wearing a Los Angeles Dodgers cap with her hair in its usual ponytail. She poked her head out of a cave and started to move up the arroyo, hunched over by the weight of what appeared to be some kind of pack that bulged at its seams. Suddenly, the girl turned back into the cave.

Harvey was stuck. If he moved from behind the brush, she might see him, but the bees were getting angrier by the second. The renewed sound of the truck's engine was the next sign he was in trouble. Diving back deeper into the bushes he finally angered one of the bees enough that it stung him.

His right ear burned as he crushed the offending demon against his skull. "It's pretty dangerous to walk in these arroyos in the summertime. You really shouldn't be in there," a woman's husky voice said.

She was standing on the steep bank looking down at him, not twenty feet away. She was wearing a faded green shirt, with starched pleats that were being weighed down by the dark circles of moisture beneath her arms and pendulant breasts. Reflecting the sun, the silver badge on her left breast pocket removed any doubt she had the authority to speak up on the subject. Her hands were on her wide hips, making it obvious that she wasn't moving until he did.

Harvey cowered at first then stood, darting his eyes around to search for more attacking bees. He walked to the sandy open area in the middle of the arroyo and holding one hand on his painful ear, the other one up to shade the sun from his eyes, he glared back up at the woman.

"Is there some law against hiking around this part of the desert?" his tone was edging on belligerence.

"You are only fifty feet from National Park Service property. The land you are standing on actually belongs to the State of Arizona. They don't ban hikers, but there is enough vandalism over at the Indian Ruins that we keep an eye on whoever is around the perimeter. I need you to come up here and show me some identification."

Harvey could see that the woman was packing an extra thirty pounds, but not a gun. He thought about his navy record being scrutinized—and then he thought of the award he had won for the obstacle course at basic training. He pointed toward her north-facing truck and yelled, "What is that?" In the time the park ranger looked away and then back toward him he was sprinting southward at an Olympic-record pace. Before Alice Brown could get back into her truck and turn it around on the narrow dirt road, Harvey was out of sight.

❖ ❖ ❖

Marie was back in the darkened mouth of the cave when the ruckus between Harvey and Ranger Brown erupted. This was a busy place. When she first heard the voices she figured it was the unknown man and the girl who had been caught. Not until he walked into the middle of the wash did she see Dalan's friend, Harvey. By the time he took off running, Dalan was behind her, urging her to get moving.

"Hush," she said. "There are people out there. It's the park lady and your neighbor, Mr. Grimes. Wait. Oh my gosh! He just took off running away from her."

They both peeked around the mouth of the cave and watched the green pickup spinning its tires in the soft desert dirt as it made a tight turn and headed in the opposite direction, leaving a rooster tail of dust and flying gravel.

"Any sign of Ian and the girl, whoever she was?" Dalan asked.

"Ian? You still really think it was your brother in the cave?"

"I'm not sure," he said. "Even your voice sounds different echoing off of the wall of the cave."

"That is so weird because I could have sworn that the girl sounded like my sister, Kristen; did you get the cross and the pots?" she asked, and then looked back at him, answering her own question. He had a fat pot under each arm and had the cross stuffed in the front of his jeans just like the cowboys on TV stuffed six-guns in their belts.

"These things are heavy; can you take one?" he asked, then looking at the bulging backpack full of their tools and the mason jars, told her to forget it. "I can manage both of them."

❖ ❖ ❖

The new body inside the cave was now added to the rest of the young explorers' concerns, most immediate of which was finding a good hiding place for the pots. They would have to search out a good spot to hide the bulky vessels, and another one for the heavy gold necklace and cross. When they got the cross out in the sunlight they could clearly see the deeply embedded stones and appreciate their size and sparkle.

It took over an hour of biking back and forth and sneaking in and out before the two pot robbers had their loot securely hidden in gunny sacks behind some old lawn furniture in the Palermos' pool house. Hot, exhausted, and frightened, they sat with their feet in the refreshing water, drinking sodas and trying to decide what to do next. The options were limited and they didn't like any of them, but they had to do something. They knew that the hidden cave was no longer a secret. They hadn't even stopped to cover up the opening.

They considered and then agreed on telling their parents the entire story, but Marie had a swimming meet at the country club at five and by the time she got home it would be time for Dalan's family dinner. They figured that it would be eight o'clock before the families could get together. Dalan was seriously confused about whether or not to mention to Ian the possibility that he had heard his voice in the cavern. Ultimately he resolved to confront his brother when they were alone.

❖ ❖ ❖

The two sets of parents sat across the room appraising one another. At one end of the small room sat Marie, with Dalan on the other. Mrs. Dawson had changed from her house dress into a fashionable green and yellow frock and for once didn't wear one of her embroidered aprons. Gina Palermo, sitting at Marie's side, wore a sleek navy blue sleeveless dress with a hemline high enough for Dalan to see her whole knees. The dads had made small talk about some news out of Washington about nuclear testing in nearby Nevada. One could only guess what was really racing through the minds of the four adults ever since their fourteen-year-olds had called this urgent meeting.

Dalan felt his mother's discomfort hosting the well-heeled Palermos in her humble home. Sitting there, it was the first time Dalan had noticed that the carpet was threadbare in spots or that there was a rust-colored stain running down the far corner of the living room wall. Mrs. Dawson had offered coffee or ice tea or water to the group but no one was interested. "Get to the point," they had to be thinking.

The youngsters had vowed not to mention taking the pots or the cross unless forced into it. Marie started the meeting. She began with the story of chasing her Scotty dog down the weed-strewn arroyo and watching him turn into the cave.

They left out their first visit, the dead monk, and the Anasazi pots and kept the explanation simple.

"Marie was afraid to go into the cave by herself and asked me to come along. I had a good flashlight so I agreed," Dalan explained. "When we found the cave opening, there were lots of footprints outside so we guessed it was okay to go in. It was dark and there were lots of cobwebs and some old Indian stuff. We could smell something awful so we looked around some more. That's when we saw a dead person all covered with blood."

The tone Dalan used sounded like it was an everyday occurrence and that the punch line was yet to follow.

Franco immediately leaned forward, nearly breaking the legs on the chair. When he heard them creak, he carefully leaned back.

"What do you mean—a dead person?" Gina asked, giving a short gasp.

"There was a dead man—I mean that I think it was a man—lying on the ground covered with blood. There were lots of flies crawling on him," Marie said.

Dalan's father leaned forward almost as if he didn't hear the full story and was finally paying attention. "Are you sure it was a man and not some wild animal?" he asked, hoping that the kids had made a big mistake.

"I know he was wearing jeans and men's boots. I'm almost certain that it was a man," Dalan insisted. "It was definitely not some wild animal."

Mr. Dawson folded his arms across his chest and looked around the room realizing that he best shut up and listen.

Mrs. Dawson was looking pale. She blotted her forehead with a crocheted hanky and asked. "Dalan, dear, is there some reason that you didn't tell us about this when you first came home so we could call the police?"

"Well," Dalan said. "We didn't want them to arrest us and blame us for the murder."

That sobering thought brought a long silence over the room.

"Well, we certainly should tell them now," said Mr. Dawson in a take-charge tone of voice.

Gina, perhaps experienced in dealing with murders, volunteered and asked if she could use the hall telephone. Having received permission, she went into the hallway and then carried the long-corded telephone into the adjacent kitchen. She dialed a number then spoke in hushed tones, strangely hanging up once and then redialing. Again she spoke softly—everyone in the other room assumed—to the police. They waited less than ten minutes before they heard sirens and the neighborhood became a carnival of red, blue, and yellow flashing lights.

The two policemen were invited into the living room where they sat politely listening to the youths' story. Officer Roberts had to calm the elderly Chief of Police after the chief began to berate Dalan for not coming straight to the police with the report. Ten minutes later, the whole group made a parade out the door toward the cars. Ian, who had been in his bedroom—his ear plastered to the door during the entire meeting—came out and followed along.

Forensic teams were a luxury only to be found in the big cities that could afford them. Officer Roberts, two part-time deputies, and the chief were on their own to investigate the crime scene, and later, to help the coroner remove the body. Just like the flies had found the dead body, the news event-starved townsfolk were attracted to the desert crime scene. Word spread through the small community that something big was happening and they all wanted to see it firsthand.

❖ ❖ ❖

The rutted dirt road along the arroyo's bank jarred and jolted the occupants of the police car worse than Dalan could imagine. It had been hard spotting the opening to the cave in the dark, and from the perspective of the elevated road, even with the nifty hood-mounted spotlight. Everything at night looked so different. Once Marie confirmed Dalan's identification of the cave entrance, the police car was parked, and the engine and air-conditioning left running. Roberts rummaged around in the trunk before he found an extra flashlight for the chief.

Marie and Dalan were confined to the back seat of the police car while the investigation was proceeding. The four parents waited, as per police instructions, in Palermo's Fleetwood. People they had never seen before kept walking by the car and looking into the windows to identify who was inside. One man even had the nerve to try to open the Cadillac door, but Franco had it locked.

"My dad is probably driving your parents crazy with his stinky cigar," Marie said. "I wonder if my dad knows the dead man. He knows everybody."

"Do you think it's anybody we know?" Dalan asked her, knowing in his heart who they would find.

Marie shook her head and started to cry just a little. "Do you think we should have told the police about the pots and the gold cross?"

"What's done is done," he said. "No one will ever find them and if we just give them up, it might make us look like the murderers. We made a good plan. I think we should just stick to it."

Roberts came out to the Palermos' car, said something to the kids' parents, and walked over to the police car. He got in the driver's seat and using the radio, talked back and forth to the dispatch person in a garbled code neither of the kids could understand. However, the words "coroner," "blood," "murder," and "knife" were often repeated and clearly understood.

The chief of police surprised them when he opened the back door.

"Okay you two. Go back and get in the car with your parents. I will be by your house to talk to you tomorrow. Somehow, I think you haven't told us everything you know. You both better put on your thinking caps before I meet with you."

The ride back to the Dawson house was really weird. No one in the car said a word. It was the first time Dalan had ever been inside a Cadillac. It would have smelled good, with the new leather seats and plastic trim, but the residual smell of Franco's cigar smoke lingered. As they came around the corner the street was full of kids playing their game. Franco almost ran over the coffee can.

When the Dawsons got out of the car, the only words spoken were those of Gina Palermo.

"Marie obviously won't be playing the street game tonight," she said, looking straight at Dalan.

He stood by the side of the neatly-mown lawn and watched as the tail lights on the car's gigantic fins disappeared around the corner. For just a moment he wondered if he would ever see Marie again.

CHAPTER 14

Harvey sat on the porch watching the big black car pull into the Dawson's driveway. With his binoculars he didn't miss a single detail, especially of the sultry-looking Mrs. Palermo as she got out of the front passenger seat. Her dress was the latest fashion—on the short side of already short. When she walked toward the house her natural stride added a rhythmic sway to her hips, reminding Harvey of a Hawaiian hula dancer he had seen at a USO performance. The young daughter had what looked like wet hair, maybe just out of the shower or pool. The hubby in his tight slacks, black dress shirt, and white tie was the dead ringer for a bit player in a gangster movie. He even had a cigar stub stuffed in the corner of his mouth, which with apparent reluctance, he laid on the chrome fender of the caddy before he entered the Dawsons' house.

Harvey was exhausted and his swollen ear throbbed like a hammered thumb. With the Dawsons gone the neighborhood had been quiet. Someone had even moved the game down two houses after Mrs. Rawlings complained that her new plants were getting trampled. He was glad to see the neighborhood come back to life again.

Mrs. Dawson had left the lace curtains on her front window open, allowing Harvey a clear view of the meeting inside. There were a lot of hand motions and frowns, but only the saucy-looking Mrs. Palermo left her chair while everyone was in the house, disappearing for a few minutes. If only he could hear. Because of his encounter with that grouchy park ranger woman out at the arroyo, he hadn't seen the two kids until tonight. Now the six people were sitting quietly in the living room like they were at church or in court. He was standing up to get more ice for his throbbing ear when the sirens and light show started.

The town cops loved their lights and sirens. As if the house was on fire, the squad car and then the official chief's car approached way too fast and then skidded to a halt in front of the Dawsons'. Keeping a low profile behind the shrubs, he watched the cops rush into the Dawson house. Shortly thereafter, the parade of people headed for the cars and the departure, not toward downtown, but toward the high school—and he surmised—the arroyo. The older brother Ian was waved away by the dad and left standing on the side of the street.

A small group had gathered alongside the chief's car, some of them bombarding Ian with questions. Ten minutes later, Harvey melted right into the crowd. The conversations stopped as a fire truck and then an ambulance headed out past the school toward the desert. Rumors were rampant. Most thought that an escapee from the state prison over at Florence must have been captured. The previous presence of the Palermos' car, sitting in the middle of the official vehicles, started a rumor that there was a counterfeit money stash out in the desert. Only after the coroner's black windowless utility van rolled by on Main Street did a murder or suicide make the rumor rounds.

Harvey avoided talking to anyone. He was a good listener and by pulling his cap low on his ears, avoided any second looks by those who might have recognized him from the hamburger joint. By blending into the gathering, he gleaned lots of information, if not facts. It wasn't long before most of the adults on the street were headed toward the desert behind the Casa Grande Ruins. He followed along.

To say he was surprised when the word went through the growing crowd that there was a dead man in a hidden cave, would have been a mistake. What did surprise him was when three park service trucks showed up and began demanding that everyone leave the scene. It would have been easier to shoo turkey buzzards away from carrion. The townies were not standing on city or park service land, so they scattered just long enough for the rangers to move to the next cluster, then the crowd was right back together, trying to sift through enough rumors to solve the mystery.

Harvey thought it really weird that the two kids were stuck in the police car while the parents were in the Fleetwood. He was tempted to walk by and ask Dalan what was going on, just to pick his brain. He wanted all the information he could get, but then saw his buddy Officer Roberts and retreated back into the crowd.

Officer Roberts was the first one out of the cave, followed by the chief. They made a beeline to the squad car and after a short conversation, sent the two kids off to get in the Cadillac with their parents. Franco got out and apparently asked Officer Roberts if he could leave. Everyone watched as the limousine-sized car negotiated turning around on the narrow road and then disappeared into a cloud of dust and darkness.

A murmur went through the crowd as lights appeared at the cavern's mouth and the head of one of the deputies appeared, struggling with his end of a shiny black body bag. It was half-dragged, half-carried out into the open, then up the steep embankment to the coroner's van where it was laid on the ground while the attendant struggled to get a gurney out of the van. At last the limpid bag was lugged onto the gurney and loaded into the van.

Officer Roberts had a roll of yellow plastic tape that his deputies began stringing around and between the tumbleweeds at the entrance of the cave. One by one the officials re-entered and exited the cave. Finally, they got in their vehicles and pulled away, leaving a trail of dust hanging over the crowd. With only a few head lights illuminating the area, it was easy for Harvey to slip away. He would be back.

❖ ❖ ❖

The local weekly newspaper published an "Extra" addition, which disappeared from the counters of the cafés and drug stores like smoke in the wind. The front page showed a picture of the stooped-over officers dragging a black body bag out of an anonymous cave. Since the murder was so close to federal land, the newspaper claimed that the FBI would soon arrive in town to take over the investigation. The name of the victim wasn't released yet and the details of the story were still pure speculation. The only quote in the article was Franco Palermo warning that, "If anyone so much as speaks to my daughters or the Dawson boy, they'll have to answer to me."

Dalan slept in late. To his surprise, his mom had saved pancake batter for him—like it was his birthday. He read the newspaper article while he ate and started out the door to go see Boyd and, hopefully, Marie. He wanted to know who the dead man was and he had to talk to Marie. There would be a lot of questions to answer when everyone stopped feeling protective of them.

"Not so fast, Buster. Where do you think you're going?" Ian had him trapped between the bathroom door and the hall closet.

"Leave me alone," Dalan said, trying to push his way by.

"Not until you tell me everything about the cave and the dead guy and what you and your little girlfriend have been doing out there in the dark."

"How about you and your big girlfriend? What were you doing out there in the dark?" Dalan mimicked.

He ducked just in time to avoid the punch that hit the wall instead.

"You keep your mouth shut," Ian said, rubbing his knuckles. "I don't know what you even are talking about."

"Well, I don't know what you are talking about either," Dalan said, refusing to be bullied. He pushed his way by.

Factual news came to Dalan from an unlikely source. Fred Larsen, the old man from across the street, was walking up to the back door as Dalan opened it to leave.

"Hi, Mr. Larsen. My parents aren't home," he said, walking past the man on his way to the garage and his bike.

"Don't need to see your parents," Fred said. "Jest thought you might want to know that the dead man you found out in the desert cave was that bully kid that you hit with my fence post a couple weeks ago."

Dalan stopped dead in his tracks.

"You know who I mean?" Fred asked. "The kid that drives that hopped-up '32 Ford coupe? I heard his name is Real. Kinda Spanish sounding, don't you think? The guy at the Texaco said his first name is Billy," Fred added.

Dalan just stared at the old man, and then started to feel a bit dizzy. *Was it really Billy?* He staggered over to the rose bushes by the garage and started to vomit up his pancakes. Once he stopped retching, he could hear Ian talking to Fred, but Dalan didn't look up, he waited with both hands on his knees for the nausea to pass.

"Are you okay?" Fred asked, putting a hand on the boy's shoulder.

"He'll be all right," said Ian. "Did you know that it was my little brother here who found the dead guy's body?"

"You don't say?" mumbled Fred, paying no attention to Ian.

"Yeh, he's the town hero. They didn't put his name in the paper just in case the murderer wants to make sure there aren't any living witnesses."

"Well you better keep a close eye on him then," Fred said. "Oh, by the way Dalan, were you the one who told them about all those earthen pots or did you even know about them?"

"What are you talking about?" asked Ian.

"There's a whole team of archeologists coming into town today to study the cave where the boy's body was found. There was a collection of ancient Indian pots found in the cave. There also was the dried-up body of a priest or monk in there. The guy at the Texaco gas station says them pots are worth millions," Fred told the boys.

"Well, my brother didn't take them or else he would be riding around town on a new motor scooter instead of that bucket of rusted bolts. Right, Dalan?" Ian said, giving his little brother a solid punch in the arm.

Dalan went to the garden hose by the house and rinsed off his face, gargled and took a long drink of the warm rubber-tasting water. He thanked the old man for the information. Glaring at Ian, he grabbed his bicycle from the garage and rode down the driveway turning east toward Boyd's house. Less than fifty yards up the road, he took a right turn circling the block, and headed for Marie's.

❖ ❖ ❖

The two sat with their heads in their hands, feet in the warm swimming pool water. Marie had been looking out of the window when Dalan came around the corner. She ran out to meet him and taking his hand, dragged him toward the pool.

"What do you think?" Dalan asked after telling his version of old Fred's story.

She admitted that she now knew it was Billy's body in the cave, but she didn't have any idea who murdered him or how his body ended up there. She wasn't surprised that they had found the pots and the old person.

"I didn't know it was him until just a few minutes ago. How did you know?"

"We found out at midnight," she said. "Kristen came to the house, pounding on the door crying and screaming that her only true love was dead—although in reality she hated the guy. The only reason she was even seen with him was to make my daddy angry. Sometimes, he would pay her or promise her presents for not going out with Billy."

"Why did he care? She doesn't even live here anymore," Dalan said, kicking the water.

"Dad thinks Billy is a lowlife. He used to work for my dad when he was in high school. One time he even said that Billy was like the son he always wanted. Something bad happened last year. Dad sent Billy to spend the summer in New York with my uncles. Dad thought he needed to experience the sophistication of the big city. When Billy came back he was different. He even was mean to Harley. When he started dating Kristen, Mom said it was just to get back at my Dad. You saw how he treated her. Last Thanksgiving everyone was over for dinner, but Billy didn't show up on time. He had a place at the table with his name on it. My mom was real upset, and when he finally showed up while we were eating desert, he was dressed in jeans and a dirty tank top so Dad told him to leave or else. He's never been invited back to the house since then."

"What are we going to do with our two pots and the gold cross?" Dalan asked—he was losing interest in Billy Real's past domestic problems. "If there are archeologists here studying the cave, they will find out that some are missing. We'll be the first ones they suspect. We could go to jail for stealing them."

Marie merely shrugged her shoulders, apparently still pondering the loss of the one-time family friend. They sat by the pool for nearly an hour before they made a decision about their secret stash. The plan would be risky, but when they parted both kids were smiling.

❖ ❖ ❖

It was a long-distance toll charge to call all the way to Colorado. Dalan knew that he would be in trouble for calling from his house when his mom would eventually see the telephone bill. Marie's phone was an altogether different matter. She said her Dad used the phone for business and sometimes even called all the way to Sicily. For Franco, a phone call out of state wouldn't even be noticed. The next morning her parents left the house after breakfast and the housekeeper had the day off. Dalan came over as soon as he received the all-clear call.

He couldn't believe the inside of the Palermos' house. It was like some of the mansions he had seen on TV or in the movies. It had a carved marble fireplace and huge oil paintings with their own little lights shining on them. The wooden floors were glossy with wax and the kitchen was like a house out of the future with built-in ovens and refrigerators and even a food blender coming right up out of the counter top. When they went up the curving, wooden staircase to Marie's room to make the call, he was even more astonished. The carpet in her bedroom was so thick his feet sank deep into the fibers, making footprints with each step. It was an entirely new feeling to him.

"You have your very own telephone?" he asked, incredulous after spotting a tiny pink telephone on her bedside table.

"Here, I want you to do the talking; you already know the lady," she said handing him the phone.

He took the rumpled business card out of his hip pocket and dialed the operator. Moments later he was connected to the antique store in Colorado Springs and was speaking to the friendly old woman. She remembered his politeness and youthful smile and his curiosity about the ancient Indian pot. She listened carefully to his questions, then answered.

"Yes, there are places that buy old pots like that, but son, you need to know that it is against the law to sell those things. It's not illegal to buy them, just to sell them. If you really have found something special and want to be rewarded for finding it, the best thing to do is to call the Smithsonian Museum in Washington, D.C., and offer to let them have it, suggesting that they might pay you a reward. It's not exactly selling it and it's not exactly extortion. That's the way a lot of museums do business. If they're not interested, try the museum in Chicago."

The woman had the phone number for the Smithsonian and even had a name to ask for, but she wouldn't admit having ever done business with them before. When Dalan hung up the phone his enthusiasm was gone.

"What's the matter?" Marie asked

"This whole thing is too complicated. We need an adult to help us. Maybe your mom will help us. She is always so helpful," he said.

"We are desperate, but not my mom."

"What about Harvey? He is smart and if we cut him in on the money we're going to make he could be a big help," Dalan suggested.

"I don't trust him, but he's probably better than Mom. Besides, I know what my mom will do. She'll turn the problem over to Daddy and he will give us each twenty dollars and tell us to forget it."

In spite of Marie's distrust of Harvey, Dalan liked the idea of including him. He might just be the perfect partner. They were about to leave the bedroom when the front door opened and footsteps were heard on the stairs. Before they had a chance to think, someone was at the closed bedroom door.

"Marie? Are you in there?"Marie put her finger to her lips and pointed for Dalan to head to the walk-in closet. She closed the door part way behind him, leaving him surrounded by pink and blue dresses, stuffed animals, and rows of girl's slips and petticoats.

Peeking through the crack, he saw Marie's sister come into the room. The girls talked in muffled tones for a couple of minutes, and then Kristen left. Try as he might, he couldn't get the image of her at the pool barbeque out of his mind. It was hard for him to imagine that Marie might look just like that someday.

"You can come out," Marie said. "She came to borrow one of my mom's outfits—she has a date for lunch. She said that if I tell my mom she'll tell Dad she saw me smoking, which of course, is a big fat lie."

"Why is she being so mean to you?" he asked.

"Forget about her. She's way too complicated. When do you want to meet with Harvey?"

"Meet me tonight in front of my house. He's always out on the porch watching the street games with his binoculars."

CHAPTER 15

Harvey had started hating his job. Not only were the other employees and his boss grating on his nerves, but the repeat customers in this hick town were reinforcing the age old rule that *familiarity breeds contempt.*

It came to a head when a fat, blue-haired woman and her cadaveric husband came to the counter and announced that they would be sitting by the front window reading the newspaper—like they had done for weeks—and expected Harvey to arrive promptly to take their order. It wasn't the first time they had pulled this kind of stunt, but it was the first time he couldn't get one of the other workers to wait on the couple.

He stalled as long as he could, but the woman started to holler in a high-pitched voice, demanding Harvey's presence.

"What were you thinking, young man? We have been waiting to order for ages," the pathetic woman said as he approached the table.

"You need to place your orders at the cash register just like everybody else," he said in a monotone voice.

"My, but you are a rude one. Can't you see that we are handicapped? We even have a handicapped license plate," she said.

"What do you want?" was the most courtesy Harvey could muster.

"Well, you could at least ask nicely," the woman snorted.

Harvey glared at her, and then asked the man for their order. When he walked back to the register, he was already formulating his plan—good thing they didn't ask for hot coffee. He rang up the bill then went back to the table to get their money. The woman argued about the amount, but finally gave him a five-dollar bill for the four thirty-five she owed. When he returned with their food and two large cups of orange juice she demanded her change.

"It's right there in front of you," he said, nodding at the tray.

Sure enough, there on the orange plastic tray, hidden by the napkin were sixty-five grubby-looking pennies.

"You are an idiot!" She blurted out for everyone to hear. "I'm not touching those filthy coins. You go and get your manager."

"That's not necessary, madam. I'll just wash the coins off for you," he said.

Carefully he removed the lids of both cups, and stepping back so as not to splatter the juice on his white apron, lifted the orange juice cups three feet above the tray of pennies and poured all twenty-four ounces of the sticky juice downward, in a double stream. The juice went everywhere, filling the plastic tray of food and pennies and splattering on the table and customers. Pinned in by the window and the snug booth, the couple wiggled out of their places, drenched in the sticky liquid. The woman was howling like a wounded dog, much to the delight of Harvey. To his surprise, the scattering of other customers seemed to be as entertained by the event as were the girls behind the counter.

The couple left immediately, vowing never to return and telling everyone in the store that Harvey was lucky they were peace-loving people; otherwise they would have called the police and had him "thrown in jail." Bill, having heard the ruckus, grabbed Harvey by the sleeve and dragged him into the back office.

"How about explaining your actions out there, Grimes," his boss said.

"They insisted on their change in pennies and then spilled the damn juice. I'm lucky they didn't get it on me," Harvey lied.

"I don't believe a word you are saying. You are a troublemaker and a bad example to the other employees. Empty your locker and get out. I'll mail you your final check. And Grimes—don't you ever come back or you'll regret it," Bill threatened.

It was not even noon when he wadded up his apron and threw it in the trash. He snagged two double cheeseburgers from in front of one of the cashiers and headed for the back. There was nothing in his locker worth keeping so he walked straight out the door. His bicycle was leaning against the wall alongside the boss's station wagon. Against his better judgment he let the bike drag alongside the car as he drove it into the open, leaving a two-foot-long scratch in the Chevy's paint.

Without stopping to think, he hopped on his bike and headed in the opposite direction from his rented room. He stopped at a gas station and bought a Coke out of a machine and took a moment to sit in the shade and eat his stolen burgers. He needed a plan for his life. There was a bright spot on the horizon, but he wasn't sure how to magnify it.

Without pondering the consequences, he got back on his bike and rode up the highway northbound toward the Casa Grande Indian Ruins. There was a good reason that those two neighborhood kids had been out at that cave and there was a good reason that the three lime-green National Park Service trucks had shown up at the scene of that hot rod kid's murder. For the last two days a whole fleet of official-looking cars with official-looking people had been pouring into town. There had to be more to that cave's secrets than the local newspaper was printing. Puzzles were like a person's life. There were a finite number of pieces to each. How they were put together determined the ultimate outcome. Harvey had decided that he wanted a piece of this particular puzzle, whatever it might be.

❖ ❖ ❖

The sun's setting rays, mixed with a few tall thunderheads sitting on the far horizon, produced a spectacular late-evening display. Good sunsets were a way of life in the Arizona desert, but this particular one drew whole families out of their homes to stand in the wide streets of the little town and gaze at the last light of the day. Harvey had stopped in front of Fred's to take a look.

He had come home exhausted, wondering why everyone was standing out in the heat. He spent most of the afternoon learning everything the National Parks Ruins' exhibits had to teach. Looking through the plexiglass windows of the visitor center he could see a flurry of activity around the old Indian Ruins and in the open desert behind it. He read the printed explanations under the artifacts in the glass display cases and listened to the plump ranger woman who had been eager to help him learn all there was about the ancient dwellers of the area and their habits.

He had recognized her immediately, but guessed that when they had met that first time, the sun glaring in his eyes had hidden her appearance. He was wrong. Toward the end of the conversation, he asked her if the Indians had any caves around the area. Suddenly, like a switch had been turned off, she asked to be excused and went inside a heavy door marked private. She never came out.

By the time he rode his bicycle back to Fred's, he had a plan worked out in his mind. He knew he would need some serious help and now he had decided just who to ask.

He ate a supper of some fried Spam and eggs then sat down on Fred's couch to watch *Dragnet* when the telephone rang. It was on its third ring before he could get up to answer it. A woman's sultry voice made him stand up tall in spite of his fatigue.

"Have you seen the sunset?" she asked. "Are you going to be out in front for the kick-the-can game? Did you have a good day at work?"

Not only were the questions coming fast and personal but also the voice was unfamiliar. Maybe it was one of the little cute girls he had met at Bill's. Maybe it was one of the young married women who were always dragging their kids in to avoid their stuffy houses. Some of them tended to practice their flirting with any available male around.

"Are you sure you have the right person?" he asked.

"Isn't this Harvey, the hamburger man?" she asked.

"Yeh, who is this?" he asked again, curious yet slightly annoyed.

"You probably don't really know me. At least we haven't been introduced. I've seen you around town though. You always sit on the porch and watch the kids in the neighborhood, right? How do those binoculars work? I'll bet you can see right through the neighbor's windows," she said.

"What's your name?" Harvey demanded, frustrated and embarrassed.

"Just call me Miss Know It All, for now."

He almost hung up on the voice then couldn't help asking, "What is it you know and how did you get my phone number?"

"Getting Fred's number was easy. Everyone knows Fred. As for knowing it all, that's not that hard either. For example, I know that you got fired today and I know that you have been out to the Indian cave where they found Billy Real," she said.

"I have no idea what you are talking about," he said, once again on the verge of hanging up. "How could you possibly know anything about me?"

"I know all kinds of things about you, Harvey; such as knowing that you own a knife. You did hear that Billy was stabbed to death?"

"This conversation is stupid. You have ten seconds to tell me your name or I'm hanging up."

"Don't be in such a hurry. You might like what I'm willing to share with you," she said, the voice even more sultry.

Harvey's mind went blank trying to put together the faces and names of the girls and women he had met at work. Then the answer hit his brain like a sloppy, wet dish rag in the face.

"Sorry I was being impatient," he said. "Fred doesn't like me tying up the phone line. He's on a party line. Maybe it would be best to have this conversation in person."

"That would be great!" she said. "I always like to look into a guy's eyes when I talk to them."

"Tell me where and when you want to meet," he said.

"You may not know it, but there is more than one place in town to get a cheeseburger. Have you heard of Tag's? It's on the highway across the street from the Chevy dealer."

"I've seen it," he said.

"Meet me there at noon tomorrow, or have you already found another job?" This time her voice was on the sarcastic side of sultry.

"I'll be there," he said. "Maybe you better tell me what you look like. I wouldn't want to wander in and sit down next to the mayor's wife, now would I?"

"Maybe I am the mayor's wife," she said with a lusty laugh that was followed by the dial tone.

CHAPTER 16

Just like Dalan had predicted, Harvey was sitting out on the porch, rocking back and forth and watching the neighborhood's activity through his war surplus binoculars. When the two youngsters approached him, he acted as though he was expecting them.

"Well, how are the two town celebrities doing tonight?"

Marie and Dalan looked at each other like they didn't know what he meant.

"Don't you go being so humble now. The whole town knows that you are the ones who led the police to the body of that bully kid. By the way, did you hear that they found another body in the cave?"

The surprise on their faces was evident. They hadn't been privy to all the town gossip. Although they hadn't forgotten the mummified man for a minute, his being a topic of public knowledge seemed strange.

Dalan looked at Marie to lead the next part of the conversation.

"Mr. Grimes," she began.

"Hey, sweet thing. You can call me Harvey."

"Well, Harvey, we were wondering if you could help us with a little problem we have."

"Well, that's what friends are for. Right, Dalan? Just like when we needed to hide old Harley and that cute Scotty from that dead kid. What can I do for you?"

Dalan was distracted, watching two of the fifth-grade boys yelling and punching each other over who had kicked the can first. One of the moms came out of the shadows of the alleyway and grabbed one kid by the ear and marched him toward home. After the noise settled down the three turned to face one another again.

"Just tell me what it is that I can do for you two?" Harvey asked in a most pleasant tone.

Marie cleared her throat and was about ready to speak when he interrupted her. "Don't be shy, Marie. Tell me how I can help. Are you two in some kind of trouble?"

"We have certain items that we need some expert help with. We want to sell them," Marie finally got the words out.

Harvey's eyes got big and leaning forward in his rocker he asked, "Are you the ones who took the missing pot?"

The two looked at each other, then at Harvey. Either one of them, had they been on their own that day, probably would have denied the accusation, but caught together and having come to get Harvey's help, they nodded in unison.

"How did you find out that one of the pots is missing?" Marie asked.

"Oh, I have my sources. I spend a lot of time studying archeology and happened to be at the ruins today when some of the park service folks were talking about the cave and all that they found in it."

"Actually, we have two of the pots. The biggest and best two," Dalan said, feeling an enormous sense of relief at the confession. For just a second he felt a spark of pride.

"Dalan thinks that if we call one of the museums, we can sell them or return them for a reward," Marie said.

Both kids looked at Harvey expectantly. He casually put his hands behind his neck, locking his fingers, and then leaned back in his rocker, studying the faces of the two mastermind thieves. This was hardly the secret he had suspected they were hiding, but it certainly had potential.

As a noisy farm truck rattled by scattering the kids in the street, Dalan took the opportunity to turn away from Harvey and whisper in Marie's ear.

"Should we tell him about the gold cross and the bottles of bones?"

She shook her head and made a tiny frown.

Harvey, in the meantime, was doing his own mental questioning. *Just how much did these two little Sherlocks know about what really happened in the cave?* There were lots of questions the police would love to ask the two, he guessed.

"So what exactly are you proposing?" Harvey asked, leaning forward again.

Suddenly hesitant, Dalan looked at Marie who offered an affirmative nod.

"If you could help us sell the pots and a couple of other things we found, we could make you a partner in our plan. Mr. Larsen told us that those old pots could be worth millions of dollars. I don't know how much they are worth but I saw one in Colorado and the lady told me that her husband had refused to sell it for ten thousand dollars," Dalan said. "That lady told us it was against the law to sell ancient stuff, but recommended that we contact the Smithsonian Museum in Washington, D.C., and offer to donate them for a reward; that's what we could use some help with," he finished explaining, nearly out of breath.

"The problem is that we can't drive and we would like an adult to help us make a phone call to the Smithsonian Museum in Washington, D.C. Also, we need you to help us dispose of the pots, hopefully for a nice fat reward," Marie said.

The idea of ever having ten thousand dollars sent a wave of excitement through Harvey like the jolt of a cattle prod. He had never seen a thousand dollars at one time in his or anyone else's hands. Ten times that much was incomprehensible.

"Where else do you expect to sell the dirt pots? There's got to be better places to get that kind of money."

"Dalan told you that we shouldn't sell the pots. But I guess if the right opportunity came along and we were sure they were going to a good pers—"

"There is no way any museum is going to give you anything close to what they are worth," Harvey cut her off. "We need to find a buyer with a fat wallet. How about your dad?"

Marie immediately shook her head.

Dalan looked over his shoulder toward the inside of Fred's house and then scanned the street assuring him that there weren't any eavesdroppers.

"If you will help us either sell the pots—like to the lady in Colorado—or donate them to one of the museums with the agreement that we get a big reward, we will give you ten percent of whatever we get," he said.

Marie nodded in agreement.

Harvey considered himself a wise and street-savvy guy. He wasn't about to let two punk kids short change him on a business deal. He looked at them both, standing on the porch with their dusty shoes and Dalan with his threadbare shirt collar—stretched out and chewed on. If he could pull off a deal and these two naive kids got anything out of it, they would be lucky.

"Sure sounds like a fair deal to me," Harvey lied.

❖ ❖ ❖

The following morning was Harvey's busiest in months. He actually had to shower and shave, then get dressed in his best pair of jeans all before ten o'clock. He even borrowed Fred's iron to press the wrinkles out of his only button-up shirt. He had decided to meet the two little instigators at the post office where a row of phone booths lined the back wall. He had to be done by eleven thirty so he could make his date with the mystery woman at noon. He wanted to be outside observing her when she arrived. He had decided to walk to both places. Riding the junky bicycle didn't seem too sophisticated. He remembered the oppressive heat he would encounter, so he applied extra Right Guard and walked out the door.

"Don't you look nice," Marie said as Harvey approached.

Marie was dressed in light blue jeans and a bright pink, Minnie Mouse T-shirt. Dalan was wearing his usual cut-off

Levis and plain white shirt with a stretched-out neck. He was holding a small note pad. He had been busy finding the phone numbers of the Museum of Natural History in Chicago, and the Heard Museum in Phoenix, just in case the Smithsonian didn't pan out.

Harvey just nodded toward the two and kept walking toward the phone booths.

Dalan's pockets were sagging with the weight of ten dollars in quarters. He was nervous and suggested they start with the nearest museum in order to save money. Marie quickly changed his mind when she unfolded three ten-dollar bills from her front pocket and insisted on paying for the call. He told her he already had the quarters so she gave him a crisp new ten.

As the Chicago Natural History Museum's phone began to ring and the operator asked for more money to be deposited, Harvey cleared his throat.

"Yes, this is Mr. Harvey Grimes. I need to speak with the director of early American antiques. Yeh, antiquities is what I mean," he said, nervous about being corrected.

Dalan and Marie looked at each other, surprised that he suddenly sounded so sophisticated.

"Yes, I'll hold but I'm calling from Arizona so make it snappy, please," he said. Moments later he was speaking into the payphone mouthpiece.

At first he was smiling. The kids thought he was doing a wonderful job of explaining their situation and how they just happened to find the pots. Yes, the museum was interested in looking at the pots and yes they did purchase artifacts from time to time, he was told. Then they dropped the bomb.

"What do you mean October?" he yelled into the mouthpiece. "We can't sit around waiting for you to make a visit when it gets cooler here. Are you stupid?"

The loud dial tone on the phone receiver announced a sudden disconnection.

"You can't talk to people like that!" Marie whispered in an impatient tone. "Now they will never even take a call from you. Don't be so rude!" It had been all she could do not to call him "stupid," instead of "rude."

Harvey flattened the palm of his hand looking as though he might slap her, but Dalan stepped between the two, forcing a page of his notebook into Harvey's hand.

"Call this museum in Phoenix," Dalan said, trying to sound enthusiastic. "The park lady said they have a big collection of old Indian stuff. Maybe they'll be interested and they're real close by."

The next call was brief. The person on the other end of the line said that they were aware of the finding of several rare pots but since the pots were part of a murder investigation the museum wasn't interested for now and the caller should do his civic duty and call the police immediately. As Harvey reiterated the conversation to his young partners, Dalan dug into his pocket for another handful of quarters.

The third call was a charm. The Smithsonian operator switched them to the woman they were calling without question. The person on the other end of the line took the call like a hungry fish taking a worm. Not only was the museum interested, they were opening a brand new exhibit on Native American art and habitats. It just so happened that they had an archeologist who would be traveling by train from Los Angeles this very week. The person on the phone asked Harvey to wait, and moments later reported that the woman archeologist, a Miss Laura Linger, could be there in Coolidge the day after tomorrow. Since the train—the famous California Zephyr—would be passing right through town, it would be an easy stopover for the woman. More quarters were fed into the pay phone and more information was exchanged.

"What about a hotel for the woman for the night she's here?" Harvey asked, but Marie waved her hand in his face and mouthed that the woman could stay at her house. It would be a problem but she had confidence that she could make it work. There wasn't a decent hotel in town anyway.

When Harvey hung up the phone, the bottled-up excitement was boiling over in all three of them. Outside the post office Dalan and Marie had a million questions, almost none of which Harvey had answers for.

"No, they didn't mention anything about money. We'll just have to wait and see what the woman thinks," he said, trying to act like he was in full control.

"Thanks, Mr. Grimes," Marie said, giving his arm a squeeze. "You sounded just like a banker or the lawyer my dad pays lots of money to. Nobody could have done a better job."

Dalan couldn't believe the adoration she was expressing. The conversation didn't sound all that good to him, but he was still excited, so he smiled and thanked Harvey anyway.

"I've got to run and meet somebody," Harvey said. "Let's meet at the train station the day after tomorrow at two. That's just before the train makes its stop."

"Maybe we'll see you tonight," Marie said. "It's the end of the month when we have the championship game."

"What are you talking about? 'Championship game'?" Dalan asked.

"It just popped into my mind. We'll tell all the kids to be there. It will be a ball," she said, tugging on his arm in the direction of their bikes.

Dalan felt his pocket. It was significantly lighter to the tune of nearly nine dollars, until he remembered the crisp new ten-dollar bill.

❖ ❖ ❖

Tag's Café was a bright, airy diner that specialized in American breakfasts and Mexican food lunches. Just walking downwind of the place gave one the feeling that it was time to eat; the food smelled terrific. Depending on who was cooking that day, the food actually could taste great too. Not having a wife or girlfriend, Harvey had eaten lots of meals at Tag's. He entered the door, scanning the main room as he proceeded. There was no one in the place who could have been mistaken for the woman on the phone, so he took a booth near the far corner with a view of the entrance.

Twelve o'clock passed by. He was finishing his second Coke and was about ready to leave when he saw the car pull up to the front of the building, but it wasn't exactly her car. It was the '32 Ford hot rod—Billy's deuce coupe. When the door opened he saw the long tan legs first, and then the short skirt as she slid out of the narrow doorway. The long blond hair, not curly red hair, came next. He had guessed wrong.

Inside the door she smiled at the waitresses and waved to a man in the back, never glancing in Harvey's direction. Nonetheless she strolled straight toward his booth, never looking him in the eye. Sliding into the booth—her bare thigh making a strange flesh-on-plastic sound—she looked back at the waitress and mouthed, "Cherry Coke." Finally, she looked straight at Harvey.

"Sorry to keep you waiting," she said. "I had trouble getting my car to start. The man at the Texaco told me somebody might have loosened the battery cable. By the way, we've never officially been introduced. I'm Kristen."

Harvey looked at her freckled nose and cheeks, her dark blue eyes, and the glossy, light red lips; her words were exciting and he began to melt. It had been a very long time since he had sat across the table from anyone so attractive. He could smell her shampoo and a hint of perfume. Her nails were long and painted the same color as her lips. Even her in-person voice wasn't what he had expected.

"I'm Harvey," he said.

"Oh, I know," she said.

"So, why are you driving Billy's car?"

"It's my car now. Billy doesn't drive anymore," she said with a slight shrug.

"No kidding?" he replied, with equal amount of attitude. "How'd you end up with it?"

"Daddy loves me. By the way, why did you get fired from Bill's?"

"I resigned," he lied. "I'm ready to move on to a more intellectual line of work."

Her drink arrived and she waved off ordering anything else. When she offered to buy, Harvey ordered the enchilada lunch special and apple pie à la mode. The two just sat playing with their straws for a while until he finally asked why they were there.

"It's really simple. I know that you know stuff about the cave and about Billy getting killed. Since he was sort of my friend, I want to know too."

"I don't know crap!" he said, looking away from her.

"I just happen to know that you were stalking my sister and her little friend. You even had the nerve to come to Daddy's looking for them. Either you are really brave or really stupid."

"You are so full of you-know-what. I live across the street from the kid and we talk. I even kept your dad's dogs while they were gone to the beach. He and I are like this," he said, crossing his index and middle fingers. "But stalking? Where did you dream that one up? It seems that you have been stalking me."

Not denying his accusation, she reached across the table and touched his hand, which he nearly jerked back.

"I would think you would be flattered to have someone like me interested in you enough to even know that you were alive," she said, her voice slow and of an even tempo. There was no anger or malice, not even a tone of conceit; just a stating of what must have been to her a simple fact.

The steaming plate arrived and their drinks were refilled. He stirred his chopped salad into the enchilada sauce and cut off a bite of the enchilada, immediately burning his mouth.

Kristen giggled at his discomfort, then leaned in closer.

"There is some kind of a treasure missing from the cave," she said. "I heard the police talking to Daddy. They aren't sure whether it was the murderer who took it or if you and your teeny-bop friends stole them. Rumor has it that they are worth a lot of money. My guess is that you know all about it and are playing dumb. Maybe you murdered my poor Billy to get your hands on the riches."

Harvey was intrigued by the comments this strange, yet gorgeous girl was making, and was bewildered as to what the real facts were regarding the cave and Billy's death. Nonetheless, a shiver ran down his spine when she accused him of the murder.

"How is it that you 'know it all'? I believe those were your words," he said.

"I've lived here most of my life and know everybody in town. This is small town USA, Harvey, not the ghetto projects of Chicago or the Kentucky hill country or wherever you were hatched. If something out of the ordinary happens here, everybody knows it. They may not really give a darn, but at least they know."

Harvey might have gotten angry if he really had caught the insult she just had leveled at him, but his mouth and ears were temporarily in a state of chemical cremation from the green chilies in the enchiladas. Downing a whole glass of ice water he recovered enough to continue the inquiry.

"Now girl, you just told me you already know it all, and yet you invited me here to what, eat enchiladas and look at your legs? What could I possibly know that you don't?"

This time she didn't lean across the table but instead stood and moved to his side of the booth. Sliding sideways, her hips bumped him over a space. Hip to hip, shoulder to shoulder, she put her red lips against his left ear.

"I know that you helped Marie and her little boyfriend make some long-distance calls from the post office this morning. I have friends in high places, but not at the Smithsonian or the Heard museum, so knowing you made the calls didn't tell me what they were for. My guess is that my bratty little sister has something to sell and is willing to cut you in on the deal for your help. Am I getting close?" she said, pressing her body against his arm.

"I don't have a clue what you're talking about, but I like your form of interrogation," he said with an intentional, stupid grin.

"I'm starting to really like you, Harvey. We could make a dashing figure here in town, with Billy out of the picture and you unattached. You don't have a girlfriend do you? Maybe some chubby hometown girl back in Arkansas or wherever you came from."

Harvey's mind was racing a hundred miles an hour. How could he ever keep a secret from this woman? He knew he should get up and leave before he was in deep trouble, but physically he was trapped—short of shoving her onto the floor—and emotionally, he was beginning to take her bait.

"I'm not at liberty to discuss the phone calls right now," he added. "Besides this isn't a good place. And no, I don't have a girlfriend, but I'm accepting applications."

"Do you like to swim?" she asked.

"Sure. Who doesn't?"

"Tomorrow, my daddy is taking the little princess and the witch—I hear you have already met her—to the movies in Phoenix. Meet me at the pool just after sunset and I'll give you a swimming lesson you won't forget, and you can tell me the story of the phone calls."

She didn't wait for an answer but slid out of the booth, planted a ten-dollar bill under her Coke glass, and sauntered her way to the door. Harvey looked at the check and the bill, glanced at her driving away, and then took six rumpled ones and a quarter out of his pocket to cover the check, pocketing the ten. This dinky little town was starting to get real interesting.

CHAPTER 17

Of all the times for his parents to take a major interest in Dalan's life, the night after the museum phone calls wasn't a good one. Yet there they both were, beckoning him into the parlor after the tasty dinner of tuna and creamed peas on toast.

"Have a seat on the couch, Dalan," Mom said. "Dad and I have something to talk to you about." His first thought was a moment of panic, thinking she was going to announce that she was pregnant.

Never one to beat around the bush, his dad asked, "Son, do you know who killed the kid they found in the cave?"

There was dead silence in the room until Dalan actually shook his head to clear the thought that his parents might be thinking that he killed Billy.

"No," he said, staring at the linoleum floor.

"The policeman, Sergeant Roberts, thinks that there are some items missing from the cave and wants to know if you know anything about them."

A cramp squeezed his stomach as he first thought and then said the only thing he could possibly say under the circumstances. "I don't know anything," he lied.

"Well, your mother and I don't like you hanging around with that older fellow, the boarder across the street. I think the guy works at the hamburger stand? You need to find friends your own age. Someone like that older fellow will just get you in trouble," said Dalan's father.

"We haven't seen your friend Boyd around the house lately; you need to invite him over to play," Mom said.

Dalan hunkered down in the couch with his arms wrapped around his knees and stayed quiet. He had learned long ago that whenever he or Ian got in trouble, trying to defend themselves with logical explanations was a wasted effort. It was best to let the parents say their piece, give their sage advice, and feel they were in absolute control. Sooner or later they would forget the problem and get back to their ordinary lives.

"Son, you know you can talk to us if you ever need to." With that said, Dalan's mother bent down and gave him a peck on the cheek.

His dad stuck out his hand to shake, which required Dalan to stand up. That was the family rule—real men shake hands to seal an agreement, standing and looking one another in the eye.

Dalan knew that his parents loved him and he loved them as well, but there was no way in the world that they would ever understand the plan he, Marie, and now Harvey, had instigated. When all was said and done and he had thousands of dollars to show for it, they were going to be so proud of him. He gave them both his biggest smile and ducked out of the room to the phone in the hall, and promptly telephoned Boyd in a raised voice inviting him to come over for kick the can and a sleepover.

❖ ❖ ❖

It was another marvelous summer sunset in the desert with the western sky a flaming orange blending into pinks in the eastern mountains. There had been the tease of an evening thunderstorm, but the giant, white puffy clouds had stayed in the distant mountains to the east.

Harvey had watched the sun's spectacle from the ditch bank of a cotton field a quarter mile from the Palermos' house. He had a good view of their driveway. Just like promised, the black Fleetwood left the driveway a half hour earlier. Now where was Kristen?

The light was fading and he was getting tired of waiting for the young woman to show up. He pulled his rattletrap bike out of the weeds and started pedaling back towards Fred's when he heard the low rumble of the hot rod. He didn't want her to see the bike, but he was caught in the head lights anyway.

She drove past him without slowing down but did give him a wave to follow. She parked the car behind the pool house and was holding the gate open for him when he arrived. Harley charged across the yard threatening an attack, but instead gave them both a good sniffing and smeared slobber on Harvey's pants.

Kristen obviously knew her way around the pool house. She turned on an inside light but not the pool light. Carrying a couple of sodas she led the way to a glass-topped poolside table.

"I hope you have a swimsuit under those baggy jeans," she said.

"I hope you don't have one under that cover-up."

She laughed then laid down the drinks and two small towels. She removed the oversized, men's button-down shirt she was wearing, revealing a skimpy, yellow polka-dot bikini.

"Just like the song," he noted.

"Why not?" She said.

"Nothing itsy-bitsy about you," he said.

"Thanks a lot," she said with a bit of a huff in her voice.

He hadn't been swimming since he had left the navy. She kept her distance from him, which was fine. He thought her swimsuit looked silly, but then he hadn't ever paid attention to girls in swimsuits. Forgetting the suit, her total look was much more than he had ever hoped for.

The water felt great! They had a couple of races that she easily won. Out of breath, they both slipped out of the water and perched on the pool's edge. The meeting was called to order.

"So what is the deal with the cave?" she asked. "And don't give me any more of your evasive answers."

Her entire tone and persona had changed. She wasn't playing the sultry co-ed anymore, but instead that of a no-nonsense interrogator.

"I'm just being a good guy and trying to help your sister and Dalan stay out of trouble," he said, sliding back into the pool and treading water as he spoke.

"Why would they be in trouble? Did they see you hide Billy in the cave?"

"I don't know anything about what happened to your Billy and neither do they. They found some stuff in the cave long before they ever found the bodies. They just want to see that it goes to the right people."

"What bodies are you talking about? There was more than Billy?" Her surprise was sincere.

"There was an old, mummified priest or monk in one of the back branches of the cave. There were lots of cooking pots and some other stuff too I guess. The kids have a couple of the pots which they want to go to a museum, not just end up in some rich guy's trophy case."

"And what's in it for you?" she asked, not beating around any bushes.

"Absolutely nothing, other than the satisfaction of helping a couple of nice kids," he said.

"That's baloney and you know it. How stupid do you think I am?"

"Think whatever you like," he said. "The problem with you is that you've been hanging around with the town losers too long. Not every guy slaps girls and little kids around like your old boyfriend did. There are still a few of us who do good things just because it's the right thing to do."

She looked at him and shook her head in obvious disbelief. She dived back into the pool and swam a couple of laps before surfacing next to him. This time she put her hands on his shoulders and playfully tried to push him under. He didn't resist. As far as he was concerned, the interrogation was over.

Kick The Can

He swam to the shallow end, letting her follow, and then he turned on her, pinning her up against the side of the pool.

With both hands on her shoulders he put his face right in front of hers, and in a very cold tone told her to listen to his words.

"What I just told you about Dalan and your sister stays between just you and me. Do you understand?" His tone left no doubt that he was dead serious.

She glared at him and tried to move away, but couldn't.

"Do you understand what I said? Just between me and you."

"I can keep a secret," she said softly, turning her head and pushing him away.

❖ ❖ ❖

Dalan heard the hot rod prowling around the neighborhood. He and Boyd were lying on top of their sleeping bags in his backyard. The street games were long over and the ice cream floats his mom had made for the boys were long gone as well. At first the unmistakable sound of the hot rod sent a jolt of fear through him, until he remembered that Billy wasn't around to hurt him anymore.

"Hey, Boyd, who do you think killed Billy Real?" he asked out of the blue.

"Everybody knows who did it."

"What do you mean? I don't know and I'm the one who found him."

"Well you're new in town. Live here another year or two and you'll understand how things work around here."

"So who did it?"

"If I told you, you would tell your mom or your dad and then it would come back to me and the next thing you know some coyote would be chewing on my body," Boyd said.

"Come on, you're pulling my leg."

"Think what you like, but don't ever ask me to tell you again."

The air was calm and the town quiet. Boyd was soon breathing heavily and making little snorting sounds. Dalan lay still, looking up at the stars and wondering about this town and all the people he had met the last two months. He couldn't get to sleep. It seemed like hours had passed when he heard the hot rod again. This time he was sure that it stopped out in front of Fred's house. He heard the car door shut and then the throaty engines started up and drove away.

❖ ❖ ❖

The next morning he was surprised to see Harvey outside trimming the shrubs in front of Fred's. He sent Boyd off toward home then walked across the street.

"Why aren't you at work?" Dalan asked.

"Got fired. Thought I told you yesterday," Harvey said, keeping the clippers active.

"I'm sorry if you are," he said. "Are you still going to be here to help us talk to the lady from Washington? I checked the train schedule; it gets in at two this afternoon."

"I'll be there just like I promised. How are you going to get her to where you have the stuff hidden?"

"Marie and I are counting on you taking us. Do you think Fred would loan you his car?"

Harvey put down the clippers and wiping his brow, looked Dalan in the eyes and asked him, "Are you sure you don't want to tell your mom and dad? They seem like nice people. Maybe your dad could get off work and take you. Or maybe tell Mrs. Palermo?"

"My parents would be real mad, and Marie's dad would probably kill us."

"You know that they are going to find out anyway," Harvey said. "You don't really think that the lady from the museum is going to just peel off a bunch of thousand-dollar bills and hand them over—do you? She will have to take them to some place to have a lot of tests done. Then you'll have to sign a whole stack of papers giving them the ownership. Probably some lawyer will have to get involved and be paid. Don't you think that somewhere along the way those adults will want to talk to your parents?"

Dalan was studying the ground during the whole conversation. He looked up at Harvey with little tears in his eyes.

"That's why we invited you to be our partner. You are an adult and can sign papers and everything. Even if she doesn't give us money right away you can get a bank account and she can send the money there. Don't you see—we're counting on you to help us."

Harvey started to argue again but couldn't get over the innocent look on Dalan's face. Later, he would wonder if he hadn't just been duped by the world's youngest con man.

CHAPTER 18

Marie was wearing a fancy, light-green dress with a lace collar when she came to the door. Dalan was in his usual cut-off jeans and white T-shirt. He hadn't thought about wearing anything different. She hadn't shown up at the street games for two days, and he was worried that she was sick or had forgotten about the train arriving that afternoon.

"Are your parents here?" he asked, worried that they would ask questions about his visit.

"I told my mom that I was going to play at a friend's house and would be coming home late, so she went shopping in Tucson."

"What about your dad?"

"It's working out perfect," she said in an excited tone. "Daddy went to Los Angeles and won't be back until tomorrow. What time is Harvey coming to get the pots?"

"He still hadn't talked to Mr. Larsen when I saw him last night. I had to ask him two different times before he agreed to ask for the car. He'll probably show up, but if he doesn't get to borrow the car we might have to ride our bikes to the train station and then pay for a taxi to bring us here. I brought some money," Dalan said.

"Let's call him right now and find out," she said.

Fred's phone rang four times before he answered. He said that Harvey wasn't around, that he had left and wouldn't be back until dark. "That boy borrowed my Plymouth. I hope he knows how to drive better that he knows how to work," Fred said.

With the phone back on its cradle, Marie and Dalan danced around the phone table celebrating the good news. Not sure when their ride would show up, they went out to the pool house to check on the pots. Marie used an old pool towel to brush off the accumulated dust, and then they covered them again. Dalan wanted to wash them off with the hose but then thought better of it, worrying about washing off some of the writing or even making them fall apart.

They were still undecided about what to do with the gold cross. They had never mentioned it to the Smithsonian lady or to Harvey. They took it out of a back cupboard and Dalan polished it with the towel. They talked about it, but just couldn't decide what was best. Finally, they wrapped it in a towel and Marie put it in an old beach bag.

"We need to get it out of here before someone finds it. Can you take it back to the desert where we hid the glass jars?" she said.

"When should I do it? He asked.

"Yesterday," she said.

❖ ❖ ❖

Harvey was getting cold feet. When he walked out of the house with the keys he almost turned back. He drove to the gas station to top off the gas tank in Fred's car. While the attendant was washing the windows, three official-looking park service vehicles cruised by, followed by an unmarked black Ford sedan. Something very out of the ordinary was going on. He pulled onto the highway headed to meet the train, and was almost at the station when he remembered that he was supposed to pick up the kids, but he couldn't remember where. He headed back toward the neighborhood hoping they would be in front of Dalan's house, but it looked empty. Forcing his courage up a level he drove out to the Palermos'.

His action was rewarded when the young tomb robbers came running from the swimming pool toward the car. The glistening water of the pool reminded him of his swim last night. A new wave of apprehension added to the afternoon heat.

"We thought you had forgotten about us," Dalan said.
"Or maybe you chickened out," Marie added.
"What's to chicken out about? All I'm doing is playing taxi driver for two insane teenagers and some museum lady who is probably older than most of the things in her museum."

The kids laughed and snuggled into the narrow front seat. Everyone was quiet for a couple of blocks, lost in their own thoughts.

"How do you think we'll recognize her?" Dalan asked.

"We'll know," Marie answered, keeping her eyes on the road ahead.

❖ ❖ ❖

The train was thirty-five minutes late, but finally arrived with a loud screeching of brakes and a trailing cloud of dust. Only a few passengers got off at the little whistle stop, among them a stately but somewhat disheveled woman wearing a snug-fitting grey skirt, and a white ruffled blouse which needed the weight of an iron. Her large "Jackie"-style sunglasses deflected the late afternoon glare of the sun, hiding most of her upper face. A porter set her suitcase and travel bag on the siding and stepped back onto the train. She barely looked toward the waiting area when the train whistle blew and the giant steel horse was off again.

Marie was the first to take the initiative and move toward the woman.

"Excuse me ma'am, are you Miss Linger?"

"Why yes, I am, and you must be Marie. Am I right?" the woman said, smiling as she brushed her hair out of her eyes.

Marie blushed at the thought that the woman knew her name. Like the little lady she was, she made formal introductions to Harvey and Dalan.

"I would like all of you to call me Laura. Miss Linger sounds so formal for partners, doesn't it?"

Dalan glanced at Marie, wondering what he had missed in the phone conversations. She just shrugged. Harvey was standing a little gap-mouthed. Instead of the wrinkled old-maid he had expected, he was looking up and down at a one-time possible calendar girl. Her flaxen, shoulder-length hair glistened in the afternoon sun and the hour-glass figure was better than anything he had seen in town for months. She even made the sultry Kristen Palermo look bland, plus she was much more mature. He caught his reflection in the ticket office window and did a quick check of his hair. She was a good ten years older, but he once had read that older women often preferred younger husbands.

They carried Laura's bags to the car and the teens scrambled into the back seat. Harvey, showing his best manners, held the heavy door of the Plymouth for the woman, glancing at her knees as she slid into the rough wool car seat. He had a grin lingering on his face as he walked around the car to the driver's seat.

It took three tries to get the old Plymouth started, and even with the windows down everyone was briskly perspiring before the dry desert air flowed into the car.

Blotting her forehead with a hankie, Laura said, "Perhaps we should drop by the hotel to check in and leave my bags. I could use a little freshening up."

"Which hotel might you be speaking of?" Marie asked, wondering if she had used the correct English.

"Oh, goodness! I just supposed that you would make a reservation for me at one of the nicer local places; my next chance to catch the train is in twenty-four hours. I'm sorry; I guess I should have asked."

"Actually, there ain't any nicer places in town," Harvey said. "This town is a dump. When God was planting his garden and got to this county, he ran out of seeds."

This lame joke brought a little giggle to Laura's dry lips. Marie and Dalan were hunkered down in the back seat in panic mode, and couldn't understand why God was to blame for the smallness of Coolidge. They were more concerned with the immediate problem—where would the woman agree to spend the night?

"Well, maybe we should go and look at your pots," Laura said, trying to maintain her air of control.

"There is a bathroom at the place where the pots are hidden; you can freshen up there," Dalan spoke up, wishing he had said "located" instead of "hidden."

Miss Linger didn't answer, but turned toward the car window, taking in the dry grass in the yards and the dilapidated buildings of the downtown.

Dalan wondered if she was having second thoughts about getting off of the train. He had to come up with another idea for a place for her to stay, but was afraid to mention it.

"Have you ever been out West before, Miss Laura?" Harvey asked.

"Yes I have. But I seemed to have missed this place," she answered, still staring into the window.

"Well?" Harvey persisted.

"Well what?" she asked, turning to face him.

"Well, where have you been?"

"It's not important. We just need to get to the artifacts," she answered.

"I ain't trying to get personal," he said. "I was just making conversation. It's not like I'm asking you how old you are or how much you weigh."

Dalan thought the lady was going to slap Harvey. Her tone of voice was as cold as the air conditioning at his dad's office.

"San Francisco, older than you, and too much—since you had to know," she snapped back. The answers put a freeze on further conversation for a while.

It was quiet for several minutes, and then Marie spoke up. "The artifacts are in a room behind my house. That's my house right there at the end of the road."

The car pulled around to the side of the Palermos' house, next to the pool gate. Harley bounded across the yard, ready to attack until he saw Marie. Jumping up on the chain-link fence he gave a robust bark, which kept Miss Linger in the car. Dalan went in the yard and threw the dogs' play sock a couple of times to distract them while the others made it into the pool house.

"They're right in this closet," said Marie, opening the cupboard and removing the dirty towel.

"Why are they so dirty and old looking?" Harvey asked. "Those things look like junk to me."

"Oh, Mr. Grimes, you couldn't be more wrong," the woman said, going down on her knees to get a closer look. "What was in them, or were they empty?"

"All of them were filled with dirt that looked like it had dry chicken bones mixed in," Dalan said. It suddenly dawned on him that he hadn't even thought about the bottles of the dirt he and Marie had hidden.

"Where might the dirt be?" she asked, turning to Marie. A quick glance at Dalan confirmed that she hadn't given the dirt any further thought either.

"Who gives a rat's . . . a . . . tail about a buncha dirt? How much will you pay us for these two pots?" Harvey interrupted.

The woman's look cooled the hot stuffy room.

"In order to know the value of any archeological find, Mr. Grimes, it is necessary to build as much history and concomitant data as is possible. Only when I have examined everything associated with the find, will I be able to establish a provenance, and thus, the value," she said.

She spent the next ten minutes turning and twisting as she examined the pots, looking them over with a small magnifying glass that she removed from her travel bag. Finally, getting to her feet and brushing the dust off of her knees, she asked to use the bathroom. She took her time freshening up, causing the other three to have time to worry about her decisions.

The trio was waiting outside in the waning daylight, arguing about where Miss Linger was to spend the night, when she emerged from the pool house. Harvey was insisting that they ask Fred Hansen if she could use the empty third bedroom in his house. She would have to share the bathroom with Fred and Harvey, but that didn't appear to be a problem until it was offered and she flatly refused.

"What are you thinking?" she asked, and then came back with her own suggestion. "Marie dear, I'll bet you mother won't mind me spending the night here in your lovely home, now would she?"

"Ah... she doesn't exactly know anything about the pots. Neither does my dad. I didn't want to worry them."

"I surmised that the three of you were in on this on your own. Trust me; I can make up a very good story to satisfy your parents—a woman at the train station in distress. Don't you agree that it will work? Otherwise I'll have to call a taxi and the three of you can pay for my fare to Phoenix and we can forget about the pots and whatever other treasures you haven't told me about."

Dalan and Harvey looked expectantly at Marie as though their bright shining faces could convince her to indulge the woman. Marie ignored all three of them and whistled for Harley, who had lost interest in the humans. She petted her dogs, threw the Dane his chew toy a couple of times and then turned to Miss Linger.

"That was just horrible—and to think that some misinformed person told you this was the train stop for Phoenix. It was certainly fortunate that Dalan saw you dragging your suitcase down Main Street and thought to call me. We have lots of room for lost strangers at my house." With that she gave Laura a big grin.

"Atta girl," said Harvey, patting her on the back. "Now why don't you show me and the nice lady what else you found in that cave?"

CHAPTER 19

When Gina Palermo walked into her house, Miss Laura Linger, curator for the Smithsonian Institute in Washington, D.C., was sitting at the kitchen table making collect, long-distance calls and probably wondering what kind of a mother would leave a young teenage girl home alone, long after dark. It was just plain bad luck that Marie had picked this very moment to run upstairs to the bathroom.

"Excuse me, just who might you be?" Gina asked in a pleasant but commanding tone.

Laura looked up with a rather critical eye, just as Marie hollered from the stairway, "Mom, you're home. How was the meeting?"

"My meeting was fine—who is your guest?"

"My name is Laura Linger," she said, standing and extending her manicured hand. "I presume you are the mother of my little guardian angel."

Gina stepped to the table and introduced herself, giving Laura and Marie a look requiring an explanation. The fabricated story, many times revised, seemed to satisfy Gina, who put her arm around the girl, giving her a proud squeeze.

"Have you offered our guest something to eat?"

"Sure, Mom; we finished off the cannelloni and tossed salad. Miss Linger even liked the capers," Marie said with a smile.

"Did you show Miss Linger the guest room sweetheart?"

Truth was that Marie had shown her much more than that.

❖ ❖ ❖

She and Dalan still hadn't had a chance to decide whether to tell this likeable but somewhat aloof woman about the gold cross. Liking her was one thing. However, they still weren't convinced that they trusted her. Around seven o'clock Harvey looked at his Timex and about had a heart attack. He had promised to have Fred's car back in time for Fred to make it to Bingo. He blubbered an apology then left the Palermos' house in a trail of blue smoke and dust.

The teenagers' resolves were weakening as the sun settled on the horizon. They were standing on the front porch under the portico as he said good night. He got a nod of approval from Marie and said, "We really didn't tell Harvey about a certain thing. I mean he didn't find anything himself. He really wasn't a part of our partnership but kind of pushed his way into the situation."

"I can only imagine," Linger said. She had freshened up a bit and was almost feeling at home at the Palermos'.

"We should have told you about the murdered guy that we found out in the cave and about the old dried-up man in the robes."

Linger's eyes widened in eager expectation of what other wonders these kids had found. She had been on her feet for hours and her high heels were killing her.

"Why don't we sit down while you explain it to me?"

"Actually the other thing we found isn't right here," Dalan said. "We buried it with the other glass jars of dirt. It's out by the hidden cave," Marie lied.

"Well, what exactly is it?" Miss Linger said, showing a combination of fatigue and impatience.

"It's a fancy gold cross with some glass chunks buried in it. It was hanging around the neck of the mummy."

The museum curator gave a suppressed gasp, then once again collected her thoughts.

"Marie, could you draw me a picture of the cross?"

"I can do better than that. I got my film back from the drug store today; sorry Dalan—I forgot all about telling you. It turns out one of the pictures wasn't ruined and turned out really clear. It's up in my room."

Kick The Can

Dalan, already late for supper, excused himself and rode off on his bike, leaving the females to go into the house for the photo display.

His mother was furious with him. She had spent the late afternoon frying chicken and peeling potatoes for Ian's special birthday dinner. Luckily, the plates were still on the table and she hadn't lit the candles on the cake. Dalan was starved but couldn't concentrate, worrying about how they were going to get Miss Linger to see the cross tomorrow and how they were going to keep it a secret from Harvey.

The candles were lit and the traditional "Happy Birthday" song was sung, then Mom and Dad and Ian left Dalan with the dishes—his punishment for being late—and went off to see a new movie which his Mom said was for more mature audiences—there would be too much violence for a fourteen-year-old. Dalan guessed finding mummified priests and town hoodlums stabbed to death in caves wasn't enough to qualify him as being mature. He started to protest, but remembered he had plenty of unfinished business planned for the evening. Having his parents gone would make it easier. He finished off the dishes, ate an extra piece of cake, and found his dad's best flashlight.

He needed a good excuse for getting his clothes dusty and dirty so he joined in the kick-the-can game. Fifteen minutes into the thing he made a dash for the can and intentionally tackled an older, nerdy kid. They both went rolling in the dirt and the kid came up swinging and crying. It was enough for an alibi. Dalan let the kid hit him once in the shoulder then took off into the dark.

He had taken a gunny sack from his garage and had it wrapped around the bike's handlebar. Even though there was no moon, his eyes accommodated to the dark and he could see the road as he passed the high school football field. When he parked the bike and stopped to listen there was dead silence. A cricket or two restarted their love songs, and then a barn owl swooped by, whooshing the air with its wings. He turned on the flashlight and started moving away tumbleweeds with his feet. Reaching too close to the ground was inviting a scorpion sting.

There, under a thin layer of dirt were the two additional glass jars of bones, broken pottery, and who knows what. Beside them, wrapped in an oily rag, were the cross and its gold chain. Dalan had forgotten all about the heavy links of the gold chain which had held the cross around the neck of the mummified priest. Carefully, he placed the objects in the burlap bag and wrapped the end in a knot on the bike's handlebar. He was just passing the junior high when he heard a car's engine start.

Just like some indelible smells associated with events of one's past, sounds too can etch an inerasable groove in the brain. Dalan's brain screamed Billy and yet he knew Billy was dead. As the throbbing sound of the car's full race cam drew closer, Dalan pedaled faster. Although it made sense that the car was still in town, it still sent a chill through his sweaty body. Then he saw the lights. No matter how innocent of a story he might create, he didn't want to face whoever the car's driver was. But on the wide dirt road, it was too late to hide.

Blinded by the bright light filtering through the ambient dust, Dalan had no choice but to stop. Straddling the bike's post, it was hard to keep his balance. He turned his eyes away from the glare, hoping the car would pass by, but his hope would be in vain.

"Hey kid, where have you been and where are you going with that sack?" the female voice asked.

He was pretty sure the voice was Kristen's, but then who could tell with the noise of the un-muffled V-8 idling inches away, and the pounding of his heart drumming in his ears?

"You're a long way from home for this late at night," she said. "I'd offer you a lift but there's no room for the bike. Maybe I could take the gunny sack home for you. I know where you live."

He could see her now in the glow of the dash light. She wasn't alone, but the other person didn't speak.

"Thanks, but I've got it," he said subconsciously grasping the bag tighter.

"Well you be careful out here. There can be all sorts of dangers out here at night. The rattlesnakes do their feeding in the dark."

The tinted window went up and the car crunched its way down the gravel road. Its tail lights stayed in view for a long time. Dalan wasn't sure why Kristen had frightened him, but he couldn't make himself start peddling again until the car was completely gone. He had planned to take the gunny sack to Fred's garage, not trusting leaving anything around his place for nosey Ian to find.

It was another ten minutes of peddling to his neighborhood. As he rode around the corner, the kids were still in the street shouting and laughing. He stopped at the corner unsure where to turn. The bulky burlap bag would not go unnoticed. He made a quick U-turn and rode back a half-block, ditching the bike in a clump of pinion shrubs. He decided to sneak up the alley behind Fred's and hide the treasure in the garage.

In the months he had lived on the block, he felt he knew every bush and building in everyone's yard. He made it to Fred's clapboard garage and opened the side door. He still had his dad's small but powerful flashlight and put it to use finding an empty five-gallon paint bucket. He stuffed the burlap bag into the bottom and replaced it on the shelf. Retrieving it in order to show the contents to Miss Linger would be a problem to deal with tomorrow. Tonight, he was too exhausted to think any more about it.

With his bike back safely in his own garage he went into the house. Boyd yelled from the street for him to come join the game, but Dalan ignored him.

He showered, ate another piece of birthday cake, and crawled in bed. He didn't hear his family come home, but did awake to the sound of the hot rod speeding around the corner, tires squealing, exhausts roaring. He looked at the clock, surprised that it was a few minutes short of midnight, then he heard the car come around the corner again. This time it stopped right in front of Fred's. He lifted the shade to be sure that he wasn't mistaken.

Surprised and then overwhelmed with fear, he saw Harvey get out of Billy's hot rod and walk toward Fred's house. The car drove away and the neighborhood was again silent. Dalan tried to go back to sleep, but the haunting feeling that it was Harvey in the car out by the junior high wouldn't leave. *Did Harvey know that he and Marie were holding back on the secret? What would he do if he knew?* The image of Harvey sitting in the rocker on Fred's porch, sharpening the hunting knife, wouldn't leave his head; then the thought started going around and around in his mind that it was Harvey who had killed Billy Real. *But why?* Billy had threatened Dalan and Harvey had vowed to protect him. *But how did Billy or Harvey or Ian find the cave?* The whole affair was becoming too much for his young mind. When he finally crashed into a deep sleep, the paperboy had already thrown the morning newspaper onto the porch.

In the back of his head he heard a ringing, but all he wanted was for it to go away and let him keep his face buried in the soft pillow.

"Dalan, your little friend is on the telephone," his mom said, giving his shoulder a little shake. "I told her you were asleep but she says it's very important. She sure is a pretty little thing. Also, don't forget that today is lawn mowing day. Don't wait until it's too hot or you'll get a heat stroke."

❖ ❖ ❖

Miss Linger's brain was still on Eastern Standard Time. She had been up at the crack of dawn and had gone for a long walk up and down the farm roads and then into the closer neighborhoods. When Marie came downstairs there were coffee cups on the kitchen table and the paper was scattered. She could hear the TV blaring from the sun porch and Jack Lalanne, the new age fitness guru, telling Gina and a nationwide audience to stretch harder and breathe deeper. She filled a bowl with frosted flakes, poured in some milk and sat down at the table. The news headline on the paper's front page was staring her in the face.

Ancient Burial Pottery Found Among Old and New Human Remains
Additional Priceless Artifacts Missing—
Murder Weapon Found?

"Great," she mumbled under her breath. "Miss Linger probably has told Mom everything." But she was wrong.

When Miss Linger came downstairs from the guest room a few minutes later, she smiled at Marie and waved for her to leave her breakfast for a moment and follow her outside.

The sun already was heating up the desert town. Linger faced Marie, her arms crossed in front of her, eyes glaring, and sweat dripping from her brow.

"You didn't tell me that you were part of the focus of a murder investigation and that the items you want to sell to the museum were probably stolen," she said. "Is that the truth?"

The question was left hanging in the air as a car honked several times and approached the front of the house. The black Fleetwood pulled into the driveway and Franco Palermo got out of the car. With a smile and a wave he approached the ladies.

"Bon Giorno, my beautiful Marie," he said, sweeping his daughter into his muscular arms and giving her a 360-degree spin. He set her feet back on the ground and turned to Laura Linger. "And who do we have here?"

❖ ❖ ❖

Still rubbing his eyes, he put the phone to his ear and listened as Marie poured her state of panic out to him over the telephone line.

"We are going to go to jail!" she said, trying to hold back the tears. "Miss Linger says she wants nothing to do with the whole thing. My dad came home a few minutes ago and she has already asked him to take her to the train station this afternoon. The newspaper says that whoever stole the two missing items must have killed Billy. Oh Dalan, what are we going to do?"

His brain was still numb from the late night before but he could feel the adrenaline starting to surge. He stretched the phone cord over by his kitchen table and saw the same headlines Marie had just mentioned.

"Did you get the two jars and the cross?" she asked.

"Yes, but your sister saw me carrying them on the road. She was driving Billy's hot rod and someone else was with her in the car, but it was dark and I couldn't tell who it was. Maybe it was Harvey," he said. "I just don't know."

"Where did you hide the stuff?"

Dalan told her and then they agreed to meet Miss Linger in an hour. Marie said she would try again to get Miss Linger to agree to at least look at the cross. As he hung up the phone he looked at the newspaper again; the situation was looking pretty scary, but he made a silent resolve to push forward. It was too late to retreat.

He got dressed, ate a couple pieces of toast, and then told his mom he had to go for gas for the lawn mower. He got the gallon can out of the garage and hopped on his bike. He didn't like lying to his parents—even little white lies—but what else could he do? Fred's car was gone and the garage door was wide open. Dalan devised a quick plan. Should he get caught, he already had another lie in mind. He rode straight up the dirt driveway into the garage. Within seconds he had the gas can hanging from the handlebar in one hand and the gunny sack balanced in the other.

Where to meet Marie was a problem without many options. They were pretty much stuck again with the pool house. He took a roundabout way to her house, approaching the pool from a back farm road. He dropped his bike and the gasoline can in some weeds, then hoping not to be seen, went through the back gate and into the pool house. To his relief, Marie was waiting inside, but she wasn't alone. Standing toward the back wall with her arms folded across her chest was Miss Linger.

"Good morning," Dalan said, his eyes trying to adjust to the decreased light in the room—his eyes not quite able to meet hers. "I've got them," he said, nodding toward the gunny sack in his hand.

There was a silent moment then Marie gave a little stutter-sob. It was obvious that she had been crying, which instead of adding to any sense of shame or remorse, infuriated Dalan.

"What have you been doing to her?" he demanded of Miss Linger.

"The question is: What have you been doing to me? I can't believe that you two children talked me into involving myself and the world's most famous museum in this web of apparent criminal intrigue." She paused for a moment, as though trying to make a decision. "But since I'm here, I might as well look at what else you have. By the way, where is your friend, Mr. Grimes? He must be part of this crime ring, if I'm not mistaken."

Dalan ignored the question and carefully removed the two quart-size jars from the bag. Setting them on a small table he stepped back, allowing her access to the dirt-filled jars. Marie remained a few feet away in the corner, still sniffing and rubbing her eyes.

The expert took her time poking and prodding the contents then asked Dalan to find a piece of paper so that she could pour the jars' contents out. With this done she took a small magnifying glass out of her purse and studied the sample. Marie, now focused and curious as ever, stepped closer and looked over the woman's shoulder. She was unimpressed with anything she could see with naked eyes.

Linger folded the paper such that she was able to pour the powdery dirt back into the jar, then she stood up straight and turned toward the teens. She glanced at the gunny sack now lying on the floor and again at the two.

"I must give you credit for courage. This material is probably ashes of a cremated dignitary. There are specks of gold and silver and a few shards of bone, but not enough to add any historical value to the pots. Nobody wants to collect ashes of dead people, no matter how old they are. Now Dalan, show me what's left in your bag."

It was crunch time for the two teens. Thus far, the woman had made it a point to distance herself from the reported stolen pots. She paused to explain to them that the best thing Dalan and Marie could do was to call the National Park Service and return the pots with a return promise not to prosecute them. Then, at the end she gave herself an out. "Give me a chance to make a couple of phone calls, and maybe I can help you stay out of trouble with the law."

Again, she pointed at the gunny sack and said, "Dalan, show me what else you have."

He glanced at Marie for confirmation but received only a wide-eyed look. No nod or smile or even negative shake of the head. He was on his own with this decision. He looked at the folded burlap then bent down to pick it up. Inside he could feel the dense weight of the gold cross. He looked Linger in the eye and with a shrug and a smile told her, "That's all we've got."

Astonished at his answer she reached out to grab for the sack, but he was too quick for her and turned away enough to prevent her taking it. Then, to both females' surprise he bolted for the door. He didn't stop to look back nor did he heed Miss Linger's angry demands that he not leave. He lifted his bike out of the weeds, picked up the gas can, and holding the gunny sack in the other hand he pumped his legs as hard as he could. Off down the road he went.

This move on Dalan's part placed poor Marie in a very awkward situation.

"Where does he think he is going?" Linger demanded.

"He's a boy. How am I supposed to know?" Marie said, giving a shrug and turning toward her house.

"You can't just walk off. We need to resolve the situation about the pots—and what else is in the bag? Does he have the cross you showed me the picture of? Why all the mystery with that burlap bag?" Linger demanded.

Marie didn't know what to do. In a way she was proud of Dalan's decisive but rude action. At the same time she was mad at him and resented that he had left her to deal not just with Linger, but also with her parents. When she got to the pool gate she turned abruptly, causing Linger to nearly crash into her.

"Are you sure we should just give the pots back to the park service? Can't you find a way to at least get your museum to give us a reward for returning them?"

They stood in the now blazing sun facing each other like two gunfighters at high noon. Marie was in the half open gateway blocking the path.

Linger finally spoke. "Now that is an idea that could have some merit. First I need to know everything else you found. Why don't you just tell me?"

Again Marie turned away. There was no way she was going to tell anything more about the gold cross until she and Dalan agreed that it was the right thing to do. She had shown the woman the picture, but as it turned out, the flash bulb had made a glare that obscured most of the relic, and she hadn't even photographed the chain with its large, heavy, gold links.

Harley came to her rescue, bounding up behind Linger with a loud but friendly bark that nearly paralyzed her. Marie began laughing and finally Miss Linger did as well. The door to the house opened and Franco walked out onto the patio.

"It's way too hot to stand out there in that sun. It's kind of early, but you might think about going for a swim. I need to run into town but I'll be back to take you to the train station at four," he said to the woman. "Mrs. Franco has a board meeting at the country club. We could meet her there for a late lunch if you like."

Marie made a dash for the back porch. "Daddy," she said. "I need your help."

"What's the problem sweet pea?" he asked, putting his muscular arms around his baby daughter.

Marie hated the nickname but snuggled into him anyway. She went up on her tiptoes and whispered into his ear.

"Excuse us just a minute, Laura," he said, using her first name to diminish any sense of superiority she might mistakenly feel. "I think Gina has a fresh pitcher of ice tea on the table. Why don't you get in out of the sun? Your light skin is already looking pretty red."

He held the door open for the woman to enter. Then, with his arm around his daughter's shoulder, they strolled away from the house toward the shade of a large cottonwood tree.

"Daddy, you have always trusted me to make grown-up decisions—right?

"Absolutely, sweet pea. What can I do to help?"

"Will you promise me you won't get mad at me if I tell you something important?"

"What could a loving father say to a beautiful fourteen-year-old daughter but, 'yes'?" he thought. He had already screwed up his relationship with his only other child. He wasn't about to mess up this kid too.

Marie went into a moderately editorialized version of her and Dalan's adventures over the past few weeks, making it clear that Dalan was not the instigator of any of the events and that they were both the victims of a cascade of tragedies that led them to their present conundrum.

She mentioned Harvey only to the point of his being a taxi driver of sorts and trying to protect Dalan from the evil, but now very dead, Billy. She told how Miss Linger had promised to help the teens but was now mad at them, and was threatening them with exposure to the authorities.

"All we ever wanted was to return the pots for a reward, because Dalan really needs the money. He's hoping to use it to go to college. He wants to become a doctor and come back to Coolidge to help the poor people here," she said—the idea just then popping into her head. "As you saw, Daddy, Dalan's parents don't have much money."

Marie looked at the ground most of the conversation in a repentant stance with occasional glances at her father's dark-brown eyes, just to be sure he was following every word of her confession and plea for help.

"I'm sure that I can convince your museum friend to cooperate with whatever plan we decide on sweet pea," he said, giving her a reassuring squeeze.

"Daddy, there is just one more thing. Dalan and I have pondered what to do with the other thing we found in the cave. It was a long way from the pots and we don't think it has anything to do with the Indian stuff."

"You need to tell me everything," he said.

"Do you really have to go somewhere right now?"

"My time is your time," he said in a Sicilian dialect that she had heard before enough times to know the meaning.

"Would you consider driving me over to my friend Dalan's house and we can show you something very special that we found. But Daddy, I don't want Miss Linger to see it."

CHAPTER 20

Harvey was headed out the door with a bag of dirty laundry over his shoulder, on his way to the town's only Laundromat, when he saw the black Fleetwood Cadillac. He was surprised to see it ease to a stop in front of the Dawsons'. He saw Dalan look up from pushing the lawnmower and then bend over to press the kill switch. Suddenly the neighborhood became very quiet. Harvey ducked back behind an oleander bush to hide while he investigated. What the heck was happening?

He hadn't heard from anyone since he had left the kids and that snooty East-Coast woman at the Palermos' house the night before. He had planned to stop across the street to talk to Dalan on his way to wash his clothes—now this strange event. He watched as Marie, then her mother, then the big man, Franco Palermo himself, exited the car and walked toward the Dawsons' front door. Franco raised his hand to give a short wave, and then with his index finger, motioned for Dalan to follow. There was a short pause at the door until Mrs. Dawson opened it, wearing a simple blue house dress, standing in bare feet, and her hair in curlers; she stepped aside to allow them all to enter.

Harvey snuck back into Fred's house and emerged on the front porch taking up his usual place in the rocker with his binoculars in hand, but ducking down low to avoid being seen—it being daytime. Mrs. Dawson had opened the living room curtains letting daylight into the room, giving Harvey a clear view of the show about to begin inside. Unfortunately, there was no sound for him to hear. Just like the old silent movies.

It hadn't been ten minutes when a power and light company truck roared around the corner and pulled into the

Dawsons' driveway. Mr. Dawson jumped out of the truck and headed straight for the front door. Harvey could see all six of the people in the room. None were sitting. All were animated. Not being able to hear the conversations was almost too much to bear.

❖ ❖ ❖

Dalan was getting pretty good at predicting adult behavior, but never in a million years would he have predicted that Franco Palermo, supposed Mafia Don and gentleman farmer, would take time from his busy day of making millions to help Marie and Dalan out of their convoluted mess. Dalan's dad, with his engineer-minded, organizational manner insisted that everyone sit at the table. With pencil and paper in hand, he recorded the high points of "the story" part three—the gold cross. To Dalan and Marie's surprise, both sets of parents immediately dismissed any consideration of just turning the thing over to the authorities.

"Where is it?" Marie asked. "Is it over at Mr. Larsen's?"

"No, it's under my bed," he said, taking quick glances at the four adults to gauge their reactions. He also looked at Marie, wondering if she thought he was trying to hide it from her after taking it from the pool house and then telling her that it was in Fred's garage.

It was Gina who placed a gentle hand on his arm and with a smile asked, "Would it be all right with you if we have a look at it?"

Dalan went to his room feeling a mixed sense of relief and frustration. With his hands shaking, he lifted his mattress, brought out the twelve-by-eight-inch cross and unwrapped it from an old, tattered T-shirt. He laid it on the dining room table, where for the first time in hundreds of years, the sacred work of art was given a thorough inspection.

"Magnificent!"

"Incredible!"

"Look at all of the perfectly cut gemstones!"

"I've never seen anything like it!"

When the oohs and ahs died down, it was Dalan's dad who posed the ultimate question to the two teens. "What are you going to do with it?"

It was like a rite-of-passage for Dalan, and most likely for Marie as well. Rather than making demands or even suggestions, their parents were actually deferring this enormous decision to their children.

Marie had had time to get used to her parents knowing about the pots and cross, but for Dalan it was like waking up from a dreaded dream, only to find that most of it wasn't a dream.

He looked at Marie and then at the adults and said, "Marie and I need to talk it over. When we have decided, we'll let you know about the cross. I think both of us agree that we need to return the pots to the park service or maybe even the Heard Museum in Phoenix. I read that they have a real big collection of Indian stuff. Our friend Harvey is involved in the thing with the pots so we need to get his approval."

"What about the woman—Miss Linger?" Franco asked, looking at his daughter.

Gina raised her hand like a school girl in class. When everyone looked at her she said, "Why don't we simply go back to the house and invite Miss Linger to accompany us to the park service rangers at the Anasazi ruins. We can talk to the people there and if they think it's best, we can turn the pots and those bottles of dirt over to the rangers. That is, of course, if your friend, Mr. Grimes, agrees."

"I don't give a . . . I don't care if he agrees or not. We'll do what Marie and Dalan think is best," said Dalan's dad.

There were no immediate objections but Franco interjected, "I'm pretty good friends with Officer Roberts. I think we should invite him to the returning presentation of the pots. It might diffuse any type of criminal questions."

"I could give him a call right now," offered Mr. Dawson.
"I still think we should get Harvey to agree," Marie said.
None of the adults answered, but finally nodded in the affirmative.

❖ ❖ ❖

Harvey apparently had watched all that he needed to in order to figure out that there was something serious going on across the street. He had the creepy feeling that his name was part of the conversation. Fifteen minutes later, when Franco Palermo knocked on Fred's front door to insist that Harvey join the party across the street, Harvey was long gone.

Dalan's dad needed to attend a mandatory meeting at the power plant and begged off staying with the group. Mrs. Dawson joined the others in the Fleetwood, settling back into the plush seats and taking a deep breath of the new leather. They were heading back to the Palermos' to fetch the pots and, if she agreed to come along, to fetch Miss Linger as well. It was decided that if they couldn't find Harvey by making a pass or two along Main Street, that they would proceed without his permission. As far as Miss Linger was concerned, she could join them or not. In either case, Franco would drop her off at the train station in time to catch the four-fifteen to Phoenix and Los Angeles. She had become a non-entity as far as Franco was concerned.

The one strange thing, which Dalan noted as the Cadillac turned around, was that Fred's garage door was open and his car was gone. It was especially curious, in that Fred was standing on the front porch holding a pair of binoculars.

❖ ❖ ❖

The Plymouth crunched onto the driveway by the pool and the engine was shut off. The only sound was a ticking sound as the engine cooled. Harvey saw the monster dog, stretched out in a shallow dug-out hole under a grapefruit tree. The Dane lifted his head, opened one eye, and then went back to sleep. The Scotty was nowhere in sight. Harvey got out of the car, and moving as slowly and quietly as possible, went through the chain-link gate and into the pool house. The door was ajar and a light was on. Kneeling in the corner by the open cabinets was the woman.

"So the little snots double-crossed you too," Laura said.

"What are you talking about?" Harvey said, unable to not stare at the woman's dripping body in the tight-fitting, black, two-piece swimsuit.

"Your little friends have taken the pots and the jars of funeral ashes."

The last of the puzzle pieces fell into place. Maybe this woman wasn't just interested in returning pots or obtaining them for her employer.

"And why were you out here on the sly snooping around? The family isn't at home. I jest saw them in town. If they don't want you to have them then that's their business."

"Well if that's so, Mr. Honesty, what are you doing here, if not trying to steal the pots for yourself?"

The two had a short stare-down ending with Harvey looking her up and down again. "That swimsuit is a little small for you isn't it?" "Mind your own business and keep your eyes where they belong," she said, turning away from him—looking for a towel to cover up.

"Maybe your business is my business too," he said.

"What is that supposed to mean? Surely you aren't proposing some kind of partnership. I saw the little princess talking to the godfather this morning. I doubt that he will tolerate anyone sticking their noses into the family business."

"That kid, Dalan, has something he found in the cave that he hadn't shown to anyone except Marie," Harvey said. "Now both sets of parents know all about it, whatever it is. I tried to get a look at it but the best I could do was, to see how heavy the thing was hanging in a burlap bag. I heard it hit against his bike frame, too. It sounds like something metal and he his guarding it like it's the silver chalice."

"Maybe it is," she said with a smirk, thinking that Harvey wouldn't know the silver chalice from a box of Rice Krispies.

"Well, you and I were supposed to be a part of the deal with the pots and I'm not about to walk away from an opportunity to make a big score," he said.

Laura started laughing at the man standing in front of her. He was a loser if she had ever seen one: worn-out clothes, scuffed shoes, a two-day-old beard, and driving a borrowed clunker car. Now, he wanted to be in on an underhanded deal, which, if anything, would yield peanuts and could put them in jail. The whole affair here in Tumbleweed Town was a joke. She couldn't believe that she had let herself get talked into getting off the train in the first place. The only good thing was staying in this nice house and getting to swim in the pool. In her mind she had already dismissed the whole thing—except now she knew that the pots were missing.

"I'll tell you what, Harvey. While you are checking every inch of this pool house for anything else they might have hidden, I'll go get dressed and then we can go try to find them. My best guess is that they are headed to the police station to turn over the pots. I was shown a photograph of something last night and if they really have what was in that picture, it could be more valuable than any pot. If we get there in time, just maybe we can persuade them to wait until I can get a closer look."

❖ ❖ ❖

The black Cadillac cruised the mostly-empty streets of town with no success spotting Fred's Plymouth. When it headed back toward the Palermos' house, Dalan was getting very nervous. He was having second thoughts about them having shown the parents the cross and its heavy chain, but realized that Marie's parents hadn't given him an option. His dad had been surprisingly supportive and had wished them well. Now, his mother was staring out of the car window, seemingly lost in her own world.

As the car turned the corner approaching the Palermos' estate, Dalan spotted the Plymouth sitting beside the pool house, but remained quiet. He felt satisfaction for having transferred the pots into a cardboard box in which he carefully packed them with crumpled newspaper. There was no way anyone was going to find the pots, now safely hidden in the back of Harley's dog house, covered with an old rug. The cross however, Dalan had left hidden back in his room, under the mattress. Since Ian was already at work he had missed the entire drama at the house. Dalan thought the cross would be safe in its hiding place.

❖ ❖ ❖

"Isn't that the car we're looking for?" Gina asked the group, pointing at the old Plymouth with the oxidized green paint.

Franco reacted by swinging the Fleetwood's steering wheel to the right, away from the driveway and around to the side of the pool house. Momentum compressed the passengers to the left.

Harvey looked up from behind the steering wheel of the Plymouth and nearly had a stroke. The Cadillac was headed straight for him.

Laura saved the day for him when she stepped out of the house, fluffing her wet hair as she walked toward the cars, squinting in the bright sunlight. Franco slammed on the brakes, sliding to a halt just feet short of the Plymouth then jumped out. From the backseat Dalan and Marie could hear Franco yelling and swearing at Harvey. Franco was obviously a man who was used to getting his own way, on his own terms. He had wasted time looking for Harvey and was letting everyone know it. Finally, Franco lowered his voice, letting Harvey get in a few words. Laura had stayed clear of the ruckus, but then approached the car.

Without any real invitation, Laura crawled into the backseat of the Fleetwood forcing Dalan, Marie, and Mrs. Dawson to squeeze together. Gina scooted over to the middle of the front seat expecting Harvey to join them, but Franco got back into the car, put it in gear and drove away leaving Harvey behind in the dust.

"Daddy, why were you so mean to Mr. Grimes? He's been nice to us and helped us," said Marie, from her sandwiched position in the back seat.

"He's nothing but a lowlife drifter. You kids shouldn't be hanging around with his kind," Franco said.

"Actually, your daughter is right, Mr. Palermo. That young man has been very helpful," Laura said.

Driving twenty miles over the speed limit, Franco wasn't about to be told his business by a teenage girl or an arrogant out-of-towner. He headed the car out a graveled back road that met up with the highway, past the edge of town. Once on the highway he headed straight for the Anasazi ruins. At the speed he was driving it didn't take long.

The guard at the entrance gate waved him to a stop. He might have ignored the man were there not double six-inch steel gate arms stretching across the road. They were closed and padlocked.

"Sorry, sir. The ruins are closed today," said the guard.

Franco started to demand that he speak to the director, but the man cut him off.

"I'm just a rent-a-cop. All of the park service people are at an emergency meeting. There is no way to get inside this place today without a cutting torch to remove the lock."

Franco was struggling to control his frustration. He was used to resolving problems immediately, but today things didn't appear to be going his way. The tires chirped on the hot asphalt as he left the scene.

"Just take us all home, Franco," Gina said. "The kids have things to do, as I'm sure Mrs. Dawson does. Miss Linger can get packed and I can drive her to the train station at four o'clock."

"What did you tell Mr. Grimes?" Laura asked.

"Don't you worry about that dirtbag. I told him to get lost and not to bother the kids. He didn't find the pots and neither did you, Miss Linger, so it's none of your business any more. It's best that you get on your train and forget about this dot-on-the-map town. We'll take care of our own problems," Franco said.

When the car stopped in front of the Dawsons' and Mrs. Dawson opened the door to get out, Marie squeezed Dalan's hand and nodded toward a battered coffee can lying beside the road. He took the hint and squeezed back. He politely said goodbye to the Palermos and Miss Linger, then got out of the car.

CHAPTER 21

Dalan was mad at himself the whole rest of the day. He should have insisted that the box with the pots in it be left with him. Franco Palermo had telephoned shortly after they returned home and demanded that Dalan tell him where the pots were stashed. *Who did he think he was anyway?* He wasn't Dalan's dad or boss or capo, and yet Dalan told him where the pots were hidden.

He finished mowing the lawn then turned on the sprinkler. He was hot and angry but mostly frustrated. Avoiding having to talk to his mom, he put on his swimsuit and rode his bike to the city pool. There he went straight to the water, immersing himself in the cool wetness, trying to wash away the stress of the morning. There were a couple of his new friends there, including Boyd, but to Dalan they seemed so young and immature right now. Trying to have an educated conversation with them would be useless.

He thought about riding his bike over to Marie's, but gave up that idea when he remembered Franco's scary voice, screaming at Harvey. That tone of voice had really scared Dalan. Once out of the pool, dried nearly instantly by the sun and low humidity, he headed to the grocery store to say "hi" to Ian—he was that desperate for someone to talk to. They shared a blue Popsicle on Ian's break and Dalan got up the courage to ask a question.

"Can I ask you something without you getting mad?"

Ian looked at him like he was crazy, but then said, "Sure, little brother."

"Remember the day that I found the dead guy, Billy Real, in the cave?"

"Sure, who could forget it in this boring town? What about it?"

"Something really weird happened that day. Marie Palermo and I were in the cave looking at the pots and the old dried up dead guy when we heard voices."

"I've told you a hundred times, there's no such thing as ghosts."

"It wasn't a ghost we heard. We both thought that we heard a girl's voice and there was somebody with her. We both could have sworn that it was your voice."

Ian took the news calmly. He didn't jump and start hitting his little brother or anything like Dalan had presupposed he might. Instead he put his hand on Dalan's shoulder and looked him coldly in the eyes.

"I'm going to tell you something that you must swear never to tell a soul."

Dalan nodded his head in solemn agreement, feeling a sudden closeness to his big brother that warmed his heart.

"I'm the head of the Sicilian Gambino crime family. I had Billy rubbed out cause he was trying to take over my heroin business." Ian burst into laughter and slugged Dalan in the shoulder. He kept laughing and laughing. "You better watch out little brother, or I'll have some of my boys come around and flatten your bike tires too." Again he burst into raucous laughter.

Dalan just stared at him and then got up and left the store, rubbing his shoulder as he walked out. Ian was a jerk and he sure could hit hard.

He rode around town until about four, then parked his bike by the post office and walked to the train station and found a shady place to sit where he could see the parking lot and the tracks. His shoulder still hurt from where Ian had slugged him. Maybe it was more than a joker punch. Maybe Ian felt left out.

He hadn't waited but ten minutes when he saw the Fleetwood round the corner and come to a stop. He couldn't tell who was driving, Franco or Gina. If it was Gina, he was considering going up to talk to Miss Linger. The car stopped for less than a minute. The trunk opened automatically and Miss Linger emerged from the back door and retrieved her suitcase. No one got out to help her with her bag or to say goodbye. There were no waves or audible farewells. The second the trunk closed the car was gone.

Linger walked toward the train station platform and stood waiting in the shade, blotting her forehead with a hanky. Dalan figured the train was soon to arrive, but instead of the sound of the train whistle he heard the throbbing of a full race cam and the barely muffled V-8 of Billy Real's hot rod.

The awesome-looking, '32 Ford pulled into a parking place and both doors opened. Kristen got out from the passenger side and to Dalan's surprise, Harvey, wearing big sunglasses and a baseball cap, opened the driver's door. He watched from his shadowed position as Miss Linger turned toward the two new arrivals and waved. They met without handshakes or embraces. Kristen stayed a couple of steps back while Linger gave an animated plea to Harvey who nodded in agreement and accepted a small envelope from the museum curator. Two minutes later, the hot rod was roaring off to the west and the train was screeching to a momentary halt. The woman stepped up into the Pullman car's doorway then paused, looking back in Dalan's direction. He wasn't sure, but for a moment he thought he saw her smile and give him a little wave. As the train pulled away, he hoped he would never see her again.

❖ ❖ ❖

There is something about the sound of children's voices at play that is both reassuring and irritating. They never speak in normal tones, but communicate in raised voices, demanding this or that with the authority of adults. When the neighborhood kids gathered that night to play kick the can, they were in great form, and having been cooped up during the heat of the day added to their energy levels. No closed window or humming air conditioning motors could mask the sounds.

Dalan listened and watched from his living room window, hoping for a glimpse of Marie. Ian had ignored him completely at dinner and his parents hadn't mentioned the morning's meeting with the Palermos. It was as if ten hours of his life hadn't happened. He had considered calling her, but the thought of what he would say if Franco answered was too much of a deterrent. As for Harvey, he hadn't seen him since the train station.

Marie finally made an appearance under the streetlight, looking wonderful. She was wearing a frilly white blouse, green pedal pushers, and a new pair of Keds. She stopped under the light to talk to a few of the other kids, but kept looking around, apparently searching for Dalan, then she stared straight at his house.

He came out the kitchen door, but instead of walking toward her, caught her eye and nodded toward one of his favorite hiding bushes next door. She stepped away from the circle of girls and was soon sitting immediately next to him.

"What happened after you dropped me off?" he whispered.

"You go first. Where is the cross?" she asked.

"It's safe. It's still under my mattress. Where are the pots?"

"I guess they are still in the trunk of Daddy's car. When we got home there was another distraction. Somebody had left the gate open and Harley was missing. Mom went completely whacko and wouldn't let anyone do anything until we found him. Even Miss Linger was forced into walking up and down the streets calling for the dog. I finally had to go in the house to—you know—and there he was, locked in the powder room, sound asleep. Somebody had taken him in the house while we were gone."

"Who would do that?"

"It wasn't somebody familiar with our house, because it would have been a lot easier to put him in the utility room where he wouldn't have barked. I'm thinking it was Kristen's friend, Candy Real. I thought I could smell her perfume," she said.

"But why would she do that?"

"I have no idea unless she was snooping around trying to find something."

Dalan took hold of her arm, pulling her closer to him. She was startled at first but then saw why. Harvey was standing in the driveway next door less than thirty feet away. He was with two women. It was dark where they stood, but as a car drove by the reflection from its head lights left no mistaking Kristen and Candy, each hanging on one of Harvey's arms.

The trio was standing in the shadows, watching the street game, which was getting more vigorous. The Bailey twins were back from vacation and standing a head taller than most of the kids, trying to dominate the game. A shouting match started, giving audio cover for Dalan to pull Marie out of the bushes opposite Harvey and run into the backyard of the next house. They dodged through to the next street, and then kept walking.

"I just can't believe that our partner, Harvey, is hanging around with my sister and her trashy friend. He's way too old and they are way too mean," Marie said.

"It's not the first time," Dalan said, telling her about the incident at the train station. "So where are our pots now?" he asked nervously.

"Like I said, the last thing I saw was Daddy carrying the box from Harley's dog house to the trunk of Mom's black car. Then he left in his truck and Mom took Miss Linger to lunch at the country club. When they got back Daddy was waiting for them and they took her to the train station. They said they were going to Tucson from there. I think they forgot all about the pots being in the car trunk," she said.

"No way!" he said. "Your dad was too upset with everybody this morning to forget about them. And I watched Miss Linger get her suitcase out of the car at the train station—the trunk of the car."

"Why were you at the train station anyway?" she asked.

"I had to be sure that she was gone," he said. "When are they going to get home?"

"It will be late. My regular babysitter is "on call" for me—meaning that if I need anything I'm to call her. Otherwise I'm on my own. I let her know that I was going to play kick the can and then be home. She won't even check on me."

"What should we do? I don't want Harvey to see us."

"Look where we are. We're only a quarter of a mile from my house. I'm hot and these bushes are making me itch. Let's go swimming."

Dalan was all for the surprising idea. He couldn't remember ever going swimming at night. Then he remembered he didn't have a swimsuit and said he guessed he better just go on home.

"You have underwear on don't you? That's all you need," she said, and she was right—at least for the time being.

They went in the gate and threw Harley a ball to distract him and then went into the pool area. The yard was dark being so far away from the downtown city lights. Marie slipped off her blouse and pedal pushers, tossing them on a lounge chair. He was used to seeing his mom in a bra, but still this seemed different. He tried not to look at her until she was in the water and without a word she dove into the pool. Dalan pulled off his T-shirt and threw it on a chair and followed her lead. The water felt awesome.

They splashed around at opposite ends of the pool for a minute, then she disappeared. At first he thought she must have gotten out; it was too dark to see, but then he felt his ankles being jerked out from under him. He barely caught a breath before she had his head under the water. He was amazed at how strong she was for a girl, but then realized he had no reference. He'd never wrestled with a girl before, especially under water. They both came up coughing and laughing. They swam to the shallow end of the pool and sat on the steps catching their breath.

Marie slipped her left arm around his back and laid her head on his shoulder. He froze in place at first but then reached his right arm up over her head and pulled her in closer to him. They sat still like that for several minutes. Dalan was sure he could feel her heart beating, or maybe it was his own.

"Do you wish I had never taken you to see the cave and the pots?" she asked.

The water was still and the air silent. Only an occasional sound of a distant truck could be heard from town.

"If you never took me to the cave, we probably never would have been best friends," he said.

"A lot of good being best friends will do us if we both get arrested and thrown in jail," she murmured.

They heard the phone ring inside the house, interrupting their thoughts and future conversation. She got out of the water, and in the dark pool house found them a towel to share. When they were as dry as they were going to get, they pulled on their clothes. She was hanging the towel up to dry when they saw the car lights. Ducking behind the patio furniture they waited for it to pass but it didn't. Instead it stopped at the far side of the darkened house. Although Marie had left on a light in the entryway, from the pool the house looked black.

"Whose car is that?" Dalan asked.

"I have no idea," she said. "I've never seen it before."

Then they saw the woman and the man sneaking around the back of the house. That's when chaos broke loose. The automatic security light on the back porch came on. Harley and the Scotty heard and saw the two intruders and went rogue, charging toward the strangers and growling at first, and then barking so loud that the woman began to scream. It was a voice familiar to both of the wet kids.

CHAPTER 22

Harvey was exhausted. He had experienced a very unusual day. It started off bland enough—not having to get up for work was a real luxury, but feeling the thinning of his wallet was making him nervous. Twenty-four hours ago he had dreamed of relative riches when he drove the teens to the train station to meet the woman. He, in his imagination, had envisioned her taking one look at the pots and then handing out thick stacks of hundred-dollar bills for each of the three conspirators in exchange for the ancient pots—the pots that he had yet to see.

But, today the woman was scheduled to leave and by the conversations he had heard thus far she wouldn't be leaving behind any king's ransom. Then the Fleetwood had arrived for the second time. When he saw that the woman wasn't with the Palermos, his thoughts started to blossom. Twenty minutes later he was at the Palermos' pool house trying to negotiate with the stuffy museum lady.

Their verbal altercation, followed by her running off to get dressed, had been another roller-coaster ride, especially when Franco Palermo drove up and started screaming at Harvey. There were a couple of moments when he was certain Franco would pull out a gun and put a bullet in his face.

He had gotten back in the car and waited until Linger came out of the house and got in the car and then followed the Cadillac, keeping his distance. When the car turned toward the ancient Anasazi ruins he figured the whole escapade was over. He turned the Plymouth toward home.

Fred had been mad at him for not asking to borrow the car, and later when he finally made it to the Laundromat his clothes wouldn't all fit in one washer. He didn't have enough change for two. He ended up snatching a quarter from a woman who had her money laid out in a neat row waiting for the dryer while she ran after one of her kids. Taking the money gave him a twinge of guilt but what else could he do? Then his luck changed.

On the way back to the house Kristen and Candy rumbled by in the hot rod—he could never quite figure out why Kristen had the car instead of Billy's sister Candy. When they asked him to hop in, the afternoon suddenly became much more interesting.

It was his idea to go by the train station and witness Miss Linger's departure. He guessed that would be the last he would ever see of her. The dream of all that money was replaced by his thoughts regarding the young women sitting next to him. They spent the rest of the daylight hours driving around, drinking Cokes and hanging out at a desert park. "Another lost opportunity," he thought when they dropped him back at Fred's with the excuse that she and Candy had plans.

He was sulking, sitting on the porch watching the kids' street games when the phone rang, and to his big surprise, he heard the voice of Laura Linger.

"Meet me in ten minutes at that greasy spoon on the corner by the Ford dealer. Bring a flashlight and don't say a word to anyone. I think I have a plan," she said, hanging up the phone before he could get in a word.

❖ ❖ ❖

Linger was driving a grey rental sedan with California license plates. She was dressed in a tight-fitting black shirt and black pants, looking like one of the evil women in a Flash Gordon movie. She was even wearing a black baseball cap.

The car lights flashed to get his attention, but he had already noticed her sitting in front of the café.

"Get in," she ordered.

"My, but aren't you the bossy one?" he said. "And look at that cat burglar outfit. Are we robbing a bank?"

"No, idiot, we are going to get the pots and whatever else the little snots stole from the cave."

"You need to know that I've fallen in love with you too," he said. "But, your terms of endearment aren't necessary. By the way, if you are going to burglarize the Palermos' house, I hope you have something more than your forked tongue to cut through the security doors."

"How about a key?" she said, "Gina forgot to ask for it back when she dropped me off at the train station."

"So where are the pots?"

"They were in the Cadillac's trunk, but when I left the house and I put my suitcase in, they weren't there. They've got to be somewhere in the house."

"And the mystery metal object I saw in the gunny sack—what do you suppose it is and where is it?"

"If they were trying to keep it a secret from me they weren't very careful. The kid showed me a poor quality snapshot and Dalan's mother asked me if an ancient gold cross was worth anything."

"You must be kidding—a solid gold cross?"

"Why do you think I went to the trouble to rent a car and drive the fifty miles back to this armpit town? If the cross is as old as the Indian pots it could be worth hundreds of thousands of dollars. These hillbillies haven't a clue what they have and what it's worth."

"I'll bet that the godfather has it wrapped up right next to his machine gun," Harvey said.

"I don't care if it's under his pillow next to his teddy bear. I plan on taking it back to Washington with me. If you help me and don't do anything stupid, I'll give you twenty percent of whatever I can sell it for."

Harvey couldn't believe his ears. Greed immediately kicked in and he told her in a timid voice that he didn't like the terms, but she ignored him. Then, reason set in. He was quick enough at math to figure that twenty percent of hundreds of thousands of dollars was a lot more than he had in his wallet at the moment. It was more than he had ever imagined in his wildest dreams and all he had to do was take a gold cross from a kid at best, or steal it from the house of a dangerous and probably mobster-connected bully at worst.

"Just tell me what you want me to do, boss," he said with a smirk.

Their first stop would be a couple houses away from Fred's. The street games were winding down—the younger kids already headed for bed. Linger insisted Harvey go in and exchange his white T-shirt for something black or close to it. When he returned to the car she started the engine but didn't move the car.

"I've been thinking. Why not try the easiest thing first?" she said.

"And what would that be, boss?" he said.

"Go knock on the Dawsons' door and ask Dalan where the pots and the cross are hidden. Make him think that you are there to help him sell them just like before. Tell him you have a buyer who will pay cash for everything he has but it has to be tonight. You know that I can't do it. If he sees me he'll wonder what is going on—why I'm back in town—and he won't cooperate."

"He probably doesn't even have them," Harvey protested, starting to have second thoughts about his new partnership.

"It's worth a try. After all, he is just a little kid. He's still afraid of the dark, let alone the police. If he does have them we're out of here in ten minutes. If he doesn't have them, he'll know where they are. Maybe he can help us get them from the godfather's house. If he refuses to help, tell him you are going to go to the police and tell them he has the stolen stuff."

"Are you going to pay him for them—if he has them, that is?"

"What do you think? You think I'd just steal them from the poor little kid and his rich girlfriend? I won't cheat any of you. I have a big roll of cash in my purse," she said. "But don't start daydreaming yet. And don't get any ideas about robbing me."

"So," thought Harvey, "at least she's not going to just steal them and she agrees that Franco Palermo could be dangerous." He could feel his pulse increase yet another ten beats per minute.

He walked across the street as instructed, and knocked on the Dawsons' door. He was expecting Dalan to be home. Mr. Dawson answered with a frown on his face and the news that Dalan hadn't come in yet from playing. Harvey didn't have a follow up question so began to turn away from the door.

"Was there a message I could give him?" Mr. Dawson asked.

"No sir. I just wanted to ask him a question," Harvey said.

"Perhaps you could ask me?" Dawson said, curious what this man wanted from his fourteen-year-old son. He didn't like or trust the man and certainly didn't want his son to have any association with him. There were too many strange events in town lately. Dalan's connection to some of them was getting downright frightening.

At a loss for words, Harvey started walking away from the door. This angered Mr. Dawson.

"Mr. Grimes, isn't it?" Dawson said. "My wife and I would appreciate it if you would leave Dalan alone. He is a young child. He has friends his own age and should be playing with them and not hanging around with someone your age. I'm not saying this as an idle warning. I expect you to heed it strictly."

Harvey looked up at the older man, noting the serious look on his face. For the first time he also noticed Mr. Dawson's thick forearms and wide shoulders. He had thought that Franco Palermo was scary, but now realized that Dalan's dad might be an even worse adversary.

It took Harvey a minute or two—he was already nearly to Linger's car—when he realized that Mr. Dawson might think that he was some sort of pervert.

"He's not there; let's get out of here before Mr. Dawson calls the cops," Harvey said in answer to Linger's questioning look. "My guess is that he is with Marie, probably at her house."

"What did you say to him to bring on a threat of calling the police?"

"Just forget it and drive," Harvey insisted.

Linger started the car and away they went. The streets were dark and abandoned. As they approached Palermos', the house was dark except for a front porch light.

"Perfect," she said. "I'll park on the far side of the house and we can go around to the back."

They should have known better, but in the excitement of the moment they forgot all about Harley. They were soon reminded of why he was sometimes referred to as a guard dog.

❖ ❖ ❖

"Marie, look! It's Harvey and Miss Linger! What's she doing back here? I saw her get on the train this afternoon," Dalan said, motioning for Marie to follow him into the pool house. But it was too late to hide when the yard lights lit up the area like a baseball park.

Harley was running in circles, jumping and barking, not biting—yet.

"Hey, what are you guys doing here?" shouted Marie, running across the yard with Dalan at his side. "Get down, Harley!"

Some twenty feet separated the two adults and the two kids as they stood in the bright light of the yard facing each other, the adults dressed in their black cat burglar outfits and the kids innocent and frightened, with their wet underwear soaking through their clothes.

"I said what are you doing here?" Marie asked again, looking at the flashlight in Harvey's hand and the house key on her mom's heart-shaped key ring dangling from Miss Linger's finger.

Harvey stammered and started to make some excuse when Linger cut him off. "And just what are you two doing—skinny dipping while your parents are away? Thank goodness we got here before you took off the rest of your clothes—or are you just getting dressed?"

Dalan looked at Marie with her wet panties and bra clearly outlined beneath her shirt and shorts. He didn't have to look to know that his Levi cut-offs were wet and dripping water down his legs. He felt like turning to run away but Marie grabbed his arm and again asserted her property rights, demanding to know why Linger was back in town and with Harvey.

"Why are you sneaking around my yard?" Marie demanded.

"Actually, I have come with some good news for the two of you," Miss Linger said.

"What could be good about you trying to break into my house?" Marie said in a tone of voice none of them ever had heard her use.

In the meantime Harvey had taken a step or two back from Linger and was trying to get Dalan's attention. This didn't go unnoticed.

Dalan interrupted the argument. "I'll be right back," he said and walked toward the pool to retrieve his shoes. Harvey followed close behind.

"Hey, Dalan, wait a minute," Harvey begged. "Don't get mad. I went by your house for you and your Dad said you weren't home yet so we came here. Listen to our plan. It will be worth a lot of money to you."

Dalan pulled on his Keds. He picked up Marie's flip-flops but didn't answer Harvey.

Suddenly, the timer on the motion detector lights went off, leaving the yard in the dark. All four of them stopped talking or moving as if the darkness was a new intruder.

"Can we sit by the pool for a minute and let me explain what I have in mind?" Linger said to Marie, trying to take control of the situation. No one answered, but slowly moved, Marie taking the lead and turning toward the reflection of the pool.

"So when I got on the train I started having second thoughts," Linger began. "I think I can get one of my friends in Los Angeles to buy the pots. There is no reason that the local museum needs all of them. Whatever my friend is willing to pay, I will take a small commission and the three of you can divide the rest, however you had agreed before I ever came here. In the meantime I will give you three hundred dollars cash as a deposit."

She waited for a response, but only Harvey had one, and his was more of a sigh of relief than an answer.

Linger then went on. "The other thing we need to discuss is the other object you found. Marie, your mother said that you found a gold cross on the old mummified monk?"

Dalan looked at Marie, surprised. "What if we did find something else? It's ours," Dalan said, his tone more belligerent than defensive. "Who else did she tell?" he said, looking accusingly at Marie.

"You don't need to get mad, kid," Harvey spouted. "These ladies here are just trying to help you get rich."

"Sneaking into the house dressed like burglars? I think you were both trying to rob the pots and cross from us," Dalan said. "And probably anything else of value you could find in their house. I hope you know that when Marie's dad gets home and sees that car parked on that side of the house he won't bother calling the police. He'll make both of you just disappear." Linger looked surprised at Dalan's implied threat.

Turning toward her, Harvey said, "He's probably right. You better move the car, Laura."

She huffed and stood up from the patio table. "Don't anybody go anywhere, unless you want to go get the pots and the gold cross so we can get on our way."

"Harvey, you stay right here. Dalan, come help me," Marie said, now walking toward the house.

Moments later the yard lights and then the house lights went on. By the time Laura had moved the car to the pool house gate and rejoined Harvey, Dalan and Marie were walking out of the house with a large cardboard box. Harvey nearly applauded when he saw that the kids were complying with Linger's request. Dalan walked straight to the back of the rental car and asked Linger to open the trunk. When she did he set the box down and started to shut the trunk.

"I'd like to look at the pots one more time," she said.

He closed the trunk anyway.

"What about the cross?" Linger asked, turning toward Marie for an answer.

"I think if," Marie began, "and I mean if, we had some kind of gold cross, it would be best for Dalan to hang onto it until we see if your friend wants to buy the pots."

"Might I just look at it before I leave town?" Linger asked, suddenly all polite and cheerful.

"Yeh, we need to see it," Harvey agreed.

Marie looked at Dalan, giving him the decision and silently communicating her feelings.

"I'm not positive what you are talking about, but I know for sure that if I'm not home in ten minutes I'll be grounded for the rest of the summer. Also, I know that if Marie were to tell her parents about what you are doing here, both of you might not like price you'll pay," he said.

"You little smart ass," Linger said, "I came all the way here to help you and now you are trying to threaten me."

"It's not a threat," Harvey said, coming to Dalan's defense. "Her sister says that their dad is not just a rich cotton farmer. He's a Mafia Don. I told you that before we came here. Just give us the three hundred dollars and let's get out of here. You can call me when you talk to your friend in California. I'll take the bus over and get the rest of the money if I need to. Just leave before her dad gets home and there is real trouble."

To everyone's surprise, that's what Linger did. She reached into the car and opened her purse. She counted out fifteen twenty-dollar bills and handed them to Marie. She then got in the car and drove away, leaving the three of them standing in the darkened gravel driveway.

"Go home, Harvey," Marie said, handing him five of the bills. Then she waited while he walked away in the direction of the lights of town. When he was several hundred yards down the road, she turned to Dalan giving him the rest of the money. He could hear her begin to sob.

"What's wrong? You need to keep your share," he said, holding half of the bills out to her.

She refused to take the money. "Why did you both say all those horrible things about Daddy? He's never hurt anybody."

"I had to say something to make her leave. I didn't mean it," he lied, putting his hand on her shoulder. When she looked at him he could see the tears on her cheeks. He wanted to hold her close and maybe even kiss her, but he was afraid.

"What if she looks in the box before she gets to California and comes back here to get us?" she said, pulling away from him and slipping on her flip-flops.

"Then we better hope that the things Harvey and I said about your dad are true."

CHAPTER 23

It had been nearly two weeks after the finding of Billy Real's body when Officer Roberts received the fingerprint report from the FBI headquarters. There were many different fingerprints found in the cave, yet there were no matches to anyone in the FBI's national registry. One set, however, matched the fingerprints found on a blood-covered butcher knife, which a worker at the cotton gin had discovered in a cotton trailer a couple of days after the murder. The cotton co-op's gin property and trailers sat vacant and empty all summer, waiting for the fall picking of the town's major income product.

Officer Roberts was one of the rare rural policemen to keep up on all the latest forensic technology. When the FBI fingerprint report arrived, he finally felt that he had a clue to the murder. He had asked a state police lab specialist to travel from Phoenix and take castings of the tire tracks around the cotton trailer. Also, he had the local hardware store take a look at the knife and make him a list of places one could buy the Henckels knife that was manufactured in Solingen, Germany. The list was very short. No local stores carried the brand, and there were only two stores in Phoenix and one in Tucson that sold Henckels knives. It only took him two phone calls to find the knife's owner, and only one phone call to get a court order to fingerprint everyone on his suspect list.

When he showed up on Fred Larsen's doorstep with one of his junior officers holding the fingerprint kit, Fred started to laugh. "The last time I saw one of them fingerprint things was on that TV show *Dragnet*."

When Roberts asked if Harvey Grimes was at home, Fred stopped laughing.

"Not only isn't he here," said Fred, "but he didn't come home last night."

"He's a young, single guy isn't he? Maybe he spent the night with some friends," the officer suggested.

"I haven't ever heard him mention any friends, male or female, and he for sure hasn't ever brought one home. Why do you want his prints anyway?"

"Police business, Fred. You ought to keep my visit just between the two of us for now."

❖ ❖ ❖

Harvey hadn't come home because he was lying in the bar pit alongside a farm road two miles from town. When he slowly became aware of his surroundings, the sun was blazing and a few ant scouts were checking out the dried blood on his face and sending "Food available!" alerts back to the queen. He tried to move but the pain in his knees was so intense that he turned to the side and wretched. He needed to get out of the sun and he needed a doctor.

It took all the courage and strength he could muster to pull himself up onto the side of the gravel road. When he pushed himself into a sitting position his hands were scratched and full of bullhead thorns. He needed help and prayed that he could just stop the first car to come by.

He tried to remember how he had ended up in the ditch, but he was missing pieces of the mental puzzle. He remembered walking away from the Palermos' house after that Linger witch drove off. Someone had stopped to offer him a ride—maybe it was Kristen—yeh, it was Kristen in the hot rod—or maybe it wasn't. He just was not sure. The thinking was making his headache worse—if that was possible.

He heard an approaching car—maybe a pickup—but couldn't identify it in the glare of the sun. As it drew closer he waved his arms frantically and the old white pickup truck came to a stop. He heard a man and a woman mumble something in Spanish. He had learned a few words at Bill's Burgers and was able to mumble, "a casa por favor," and his street name. They helped him into the bed of the pickup where he was content to lie back down, taking the pressure off of his knees.

A police car was sitting out in front of Fred's when the little white pickup turned onto Pinkley Street. Harvey banged his fist on the side of the truck bed and pointed then waved for the woman to stop the truck. The next few minutes was a jumble of pain and questions as Fred and that uniformed policeman that Harvey kept seeing around helped him into Fred's house. He tried to use his legs to walk but his knees hurt too much. Then he passed out again.

❖ ❖ ❖

"What happened to you?" Dalan asked for the third or fourth time.

Harvey was lying on a couch in Fred's parlor. Someone was sponging his forehead with a cool towel. He blinked his eyes and started to sit up.

"Not so fast," an unfamiliar voice said.

"Maybe he needs to sit up and drink some water," a girl's voice said.

Harvey opened his eyes and looked around the room. Fred, Dalan, Marie, and the policeman, Roberts, and another cop he had seen around town were all inspecting him from a distance. He felt a cool moist glass pressed against his lips and Marie's voice encouraging him to take a few sips. The water felt wonderful on his lips and cooled the burning in the back of his throat. He drank until the glass was empty, and then laid his head down again.

"If you'd like, we can take you to the hospital," the policeman offered.

Harvey shook his head indicating no.

"He ain't got insurance. He can barely pay the rent," Fred offered. "Harvey, this here officer came by to take your fingerprints. I reckon he can do it now that you are awake."

The assistant didn't wait for permission but opened his kit and proceeded to wash the stickers and dirt off of Harley's hands, then apply ink to his finger tips and press them one at a time against a thick divided pad.

The young policeman spoke up: "While these two are here," he said, indicating Marie and Dalan, "we could print them as well."

"We need their parents' permission. I already told you that," Roberts said.

"Our fingerprints?" Dalan and Marie said in unison.

❖ ❖ ❖

Mrs. Dawson was home when the doorbell rang. She took an extra breath when she saw the police uniform, instantly thinking the worst. Straightening the front of her smock, and then taking another, deeper breath to compose herself, she prepared mentally for his greeting. "This is probably just another aggravation on the long list of strange events which had occurred since the family moved to town," she thought—and here everyone had told her what a boring place it was.

"May I help you?" she said.

"Mrs. Dawson?"

"Yes. Is something wrong?"

"Not really. As you know, your son, Dalan, was involved in the situation at the cave where the body of Billy Real was found."

She nodded in agreement, her clammy hands folded over her chest.

"Well ma'am, we now have some fingerprints from the crime scene and need to get comparison prints from everyone who was in the cave. We need your permission to fingerprint your son."

"Are you implying that Dalan is a suspect in the murder?" she said in a cold voice—arms more firmly crossed, in a subconscious defensive stance.

"No, no, not at all, ma'am. It's just that since he was in the cave, his fingerprints are probably in the cave. We need to rule out some of the many prints belonging to innocent people like your son, and the Palermo girl, and even some of the first policemen who were at the scene."

Mrs. Dawson hadn't budged from the door frame. She looked the officer up and down and then looked across the street towards Fred's house and the two patrol cars sitting in front.

"So did Mr. Palermo give you permission to fingerprint his daughter?"

"Well ma'am, we haven't had a chance to talk to him yet. Dalan and Marie are across the street at Mr. Larsen's house. We thought that since we were close by we would get the prints from everyone possible."

"You're Officer Roberts, right?"

"That's right, ma'am."

"If you had a son who was barely fourteen and happened to walk by the bank during a robbery, would you let him be fingerprinted and interrogated and treated like a felon?"

Officer Roberts couldn't believe his ears, and even worse, he couldn't believe the cold stare and the body language this otherwise benign-appearing woman was exhibiting.

"What I would do isn't the point, Mrs. Dawson. I don't have any sons. What we need to do is just a formality. It doesn't put him at any risk or danger and only helps us identify the extra prints of who might be the murderer," he said, becoming frustrated.

"My son has civil rights. That's why you didn't just fingerprint him without asking parental permission. He also has the right not to have his fingerprints in some kind of Big Brother government file. As his mother and guardian I'm exercising his right to privacy. You are not to fingerprint him.

If you have already done so you are to show me the prints and destroy them in front of my eyes. Do you understand, Officer Roberts?"

"Hold on a minute . . ."

"I'll hold on all right. I'll hold on to the Constitution and I'll bet Mr. and Mrs. Palermo will do the same."

She looked across the street to see Marie and Dalan crossing the street toward her. When they came up onto the porch she stepped forward taking first Dalan's hands and then Marie's, inspecting their fingertips. All twenty were significantly darkened by black ink.

"Dalan, did the officer ask your permission to take your fingerprints?"

"That other policeman made us stick our fingers in some ink and then pressed our fingers against a paper. It hurt my fingers," Marie said.

"Well children, say hello to the man who just paid for your college education," she said, walking into the hallway and picking up the phone.

"Just a cotton picking minute, ma'am," Roberts said, but was too late to address anything but a closing front door. It took a while before he could get his assistant out from Fred's house. By then his car radio was barking orders for him to immediately call in to the station.

"Judge Hardy, the justice of the peace just called. He received a phone call from an irate woman. He has requested an emergency meeting with the chief of police, the city attorney, and the Dawson and Palermo families," the dispatcher said in a garbled radio transmission. "And you, Officer Roberts, are apparently the guest of honor."

❖ ❖ ❖

Judge Hardy was a salty old fellow who had been passed over for every good judgeship in the county and state. In spite of his personal setbacks, he was a man of integrity and ruled his courtroom with an iron hand. He didn't like it when the police started interpreting the laws, and he liked it even less when children's rights were in question. The single phone call from Mrs. Dawson to the town mayor's office had toppled a number of dominos. When she followed it up with a call to Gina Palermo, whole buildings were in danger of toppling.

When the dust finally settled, Officer Roberts was exonerated from the fray because he had left Fred's house before his assistant got heavy-handed with the kids. The other poor guy was lucky to come away with his head still attached. The chief of police took the brunt of the blame, and was given orders by Judge Hardy to set things right and to do it in a hurry.

By the time the entire hubbub over the fingerprints quieted down, the Palermos and Dawsons had been assured that a mistake had been made. The papers with the children's fingerprints were destroyed in their presence. The Palermos' New York attorney had strongly advised that both families forget about the whole thing.

"This is the kind of thing the small town newspapers love to write up and send into the Associated Press and UPI. Remember nobody here really wants your picture in the papers, Franco, especially you," he said.

"Just put the cop's screw up in your favor bank," Franco passed along to the Dawsons. "Who knows when you might be driving a bit fast in a school zone or lose count of the number of beers you have at the Christmas party and get pulled over. The way I see it, both our accounts at the court house are pretty full right now."

As far as Marie and Dalan were concerned, the whole fingerprint thing was a waste of time and hadn't solved any of their own problems. They still had two ancient pots and a bejeweled gold cross to worry about. They knew Miss Linger would have seen the old bricks by now—the ones Dalan had put in the cardboard box—and would be pretty mad.

"That's her problem," Dalan told Marie, though in fact

he felt a little bit guilty about the hundred dollars he had accepted and tucked under his bed next to the cross, but he couldn't very well just give it back.

Back at Fred's where both families stopped by to check on Harvey, the consensus was that he had been hit by a drunk driver—a very coincidental accident. So far, he couldn't remember much of anything from the night before, including being at the Palermos' pool house accompanied by Miss Linger. Dalan tried to jar his memory, but Harvey was either playing stupid or really did have amnesia. Fred had finally shooed them out, telling them that Harvey needed sleep. With a few whispers and nods, Dalan and Marie agreed to meet that evening at the kick the can game. They desperately needed a new plan. And they needed it soon.

CHAPTER 24

A late afternoon thunderstorm—preceded by near-zero visibility with dust and blowing tumbleweeds—delayed the start of the game. The kids were all huddled on the Dawson's front porch as the last of the storm cells passed with their spectacular lightning show. Dalan's dad had once warned the boys about the desert's lightning, emphasizing the fact that Kitt Peak National Observatory, less than one hundred miles from Coolidge, had recorded the most lightning strikes ever in a single day, on the entire planet. He also reminded them that more people are struck by lightning than are bitten by rattlesnakes.

Ian left work early because the power was out all over town. The store manager sent everyone home but the checkout lady, who was calculating sales on an old hand-powered adding machine. The family ate peanut butter and banana sandwiches for supper. Dalan was sent to take a bath in the dark bathroom, but couldn't find the shampoo, so he settled for a bird bath. Dad was at work trying to get the county's electricity back up and working, but had called on his two-way radio to report that the outage was widespread—several transformers had been struck by lightning.

When Dalan looked out the front window he was surprised to see Ian standing on the porch organizing the start of the street game. He was more surprised to see Candy Real literally hanging on his brother's shirt sleeve, as though she was afraid of the surrounding gaggle of little kids, the approaching darkness, or both. Dalan was less than five feet from her through the glass, but apparently she couldn't see into the darkened house from the twilit porch.

He had never seen her close up like this—certainly nothing like he had observed of Kristen. Candy was beautiful. Her long red hair was pulled into a thick, glossy ponytail and her ears had little, sparkly diamonds in each lobe. Her eyes were large and curious, never stopping their search of her surroundings. She wore a tight-knit shirt and short shorts with a wide white belt. Her sandals looked like old tire treads turned upside down held on by leather thongs. Dalan didn't take his eyes off of her until something alarming happened. Candy yanked on Ian's arm to get his attention. When he looked at her—somewhat annoyed—she snarled at him in a most vicious way.

Dalan felt anxious for his brother, who was a couple inches shorter and skinnier than the beautiful, muscular girl. He pulled on his T-shirt, buttoned the fly of his jeans and opened the door to step out on the porch.

"Ian?" he said. "Mom needs to talk to you."

Candy turned to face Dalan. She wasn't smiling. He could see tiny beads of sweat on her forehead and could smell what must have been the fragrance of her shampoo or perfume. The scent was enticing. Although he felt a sense of distrust for her, she was like a magnet. He wanted to stand closer to her, even touch her smooth tan skin or stroke her red hair. He didn't know what had come over him.

"Get the game started," Ian commanded his little brother, and then went inside on the contrived errand, the screen door slamming behind him.

"Candy? I'm Dalan, Ian's brother. How long have you lived here in town?" Dalan asked in an attempt to get the girl talking. He needed to hear her voice.

She gave him a sideways glance of dismissal but answered him anyway.

"We moved here two years ago," she said.

"Is the school pretty good?"

"No school is good," she said in a tone which surprised him. Her attitude matched the looks she had given his brother. "The best day of my life will be next May when I will be done with school forever."

    Dalan took another closer look—and sniff—of the angry beauty, then called the kids into the street to start the game. The streets were dark and the potholes were full of muddy water. It would be a wild night. Marie showed up as if on cue, "It" was chosen, and the backwards counting started.

    "Twenty, nineteen, eighteen," "It" shouted.

    The covey of kids scattered around corners and into bushes. Dalan and Marie headed for their favorite spot. As he ran, he looked over his shoulder at the redhead standing on his front porch again, grasping Ian's sleeve and visibly arguing with him. He felt a pang of jealousy and a chill of fear at the same time. He had heard that voice once before.

❖ ❖ ❖

Harvey sat on the rocking chair holding an ice pack to his forehead. He had slept away most of the day and awoke to a fearsome hunger and a throbbing headache. Fred had scrambled him a mess of eggs, and sliced him some fresh local cantaloupe. Three aspirin and the food had helped the pain in his head, but it hadn't entirely cleared his thinking process.

    As he tried to recall the events of the previous evening he just didn't remember how he got out into the desert. One minute he had been with the Linger woman and the kids. The next thing he knew, he was waking up with the blazing sun on his face and a huge red ant crawling in his nostril. Somewhere mixed in the jumble of his brain's memory bank was the sound of a big truck engine—or was it the sound of Billy Real's hot rod? He shook his head in a vain attempt to make some sense of the thing. So far it just wasn't working.

    When the rain let up, he was sitting on the porch watching the little kids all standing shoulder to shoulder under the cover of the neighbor's porch. He had been surprised to see

Candy, the tall redhead beauty, walk up the street holding hands with Ian Dawson. They were a very unlikely pair. He wondered if they would be together if the girl's brother were still alive. Harvey felt a little pang of jealousy and then his thoughts turned to Kristen Palermo, wondering where his relationship with her was headed. He liked her saucy attitude and her looks were first class, but deep inside he knew she was just using him. Maybe that door could swing both ways.

"Harvey," came a soft voice from the bushes.

"Who's there?" he asked, slightly startled.

"It's Marie, but don't look down here. How is your head?"

"It's not good. Every time I try to move it, my ears ring and I feel like I need to puke."

"My mom says that you had a concussion. You need to try to remember who hurt you. Was it Miss Linger?"

Before he could tell her he didn't remember, she was off running toward the middle of the street screaming that she was home free, then the can went sailing onto the grass and the little boy who was "It" started crying. What seemed like just moments later Harvey looked down into the bushes and Dalan was looking up at him asking the same questions.

"How's your head, Harvey? What happened to you?"

"Don't you kids get it? I can't remember anything! Stop asking me the same useless questions over and over," he said. Then he stood up, wobbling a bit, and went inside the house.

Without any warning, it started to blow and thunder again, followed by the rain coming down by the bucketful. Dalan ran up on the porch and waved for Marie to join him. The other children scattered to their separate houses.

"Did you see her hands?" Marie whispered, sitting close to Dalan, hips and shoulders touching.

"Whose hands?"

"Candy's. Your brother's new girlfriend," she said. "Her fingertips are covered with that black ink. Fingerprint ink."

Dalan didn't answer but stared into the dark, trying to let his brain process the myriad of facts and innuendos. Before, he had two big problems, the pots and the cross. Now the worry was added that his brother might be a part of the murder—or worse still, he might be the murderer. He knew that he had heard a voice like Ian's in the cave that night and now he was sure that the other voice was Candy's. It hadn't been ten minutes after Dalan heard both of the voices that he found Candy's brother with stab wounds all over his body. He didn't know about Candy, but was his brother a murderer? It was too much to think about.

Although Marie was becoming his confidant and functioned quite well as an alter-brain, he was afraid to share with her the conclusion he was now making. Then he shook his head to clear his thoughts. Better to focus on the antiquities.

"I think she did it," Marie said, interrupting the silence.

"Who did what?" he asked.

"Miss Linger, I think she hurt Harvey. Maybe she ran him down with her rental car, or hit him over the head with one of the bricks you put in the box."

"I don't buy her running him down. He would have other injuries. Maybe a broken leg, or arm, or his insides smushed. He looked fine when he left your house for home last night," said Dalan. "If she did hurt him it had to be with one of the bricks."

"Where do you think she is now?" Marie looked at him and went on, not giving him a chance to answer. "My dad says that the police are looking for her. He says that we better hope they don't find her. If they do, she will probably blame everything on us. We could be arrested for stealing the pots and the gold cross. Daddy first said that we should go to the museum and give everything back. Then later he said we should try to get a reward for finding the things. Have your parents said what they want you to do?"

"You have got to understand my parents. Dad works all day long and Mom takes care of my sick grandmother at her house. When Mom is home, she cooks and cleans house and also sews clothes for other people. That's why she lets me and Ian pretty much do what we want; she is so busy trying to earn money that she doesn't have the time or energy to worry about every minute of our day. She trusts us to be on our own. Dad didn't say anything about the pots, but Mom said she thinks it would be nice for us to get something for our efforts. Some extra money—just like you told your parents—could make the difference of whether I get to go to college or not."

Marie lowered her head and her voice even though the rain was noisy enough to cover their conversation. "Daddy said something to me just before I left the house tonight. He had this idea—if you agree—that he would send the pots and the cross to my uncle in New York who could donate them to a charity and take a thing called a tax deduction or sell them to one of the museums there. Either way, we would get paid something for them and wouldn't have to worry anymore."

Dalan didn't answer right away. The offer sounded too good to be true. He had to ask himself why her dad and uncle would be willing to step in and help. In spite of what he wanted to believe, he was pretty sure that Franco Palermo was part of the Mafia, just like the guys in the movies and on TV. Why he lived in Arizona instead of New York or Chicago or Sicily was anyone's guess. Maybe it was to hide from someone.

"How much do you guess we would get paid for them?"

"A lot less than they are worth," she said, "but a lot more than we have right now. You can have my share too," she said, putting her hand on top of his.

Her touch felt like a soft, warm kitten on the back of his hand. His instinct was to move his hand, but something stopped him. Slowly he turned his hand over and let her fingers slide between his. He didn't look at her or answer, but just sat there feeling something inside like he had never felt before. Her head settled against his shoulder and he inhaled the fragrance of her hair. It smelled way better than Candy Real's.

❖ ❖ ❖

Dalan could hear the phone ringing and ringing. He had gone to bed much later than normal and was in the midst of a dream when the telephone woke him the next morning. No one else was home. When he got into the hall to answer the phone, it had stopped ringing. On the kitchen table was a note from his mom saying that she would be home by noon. He supposed Ian had gone to work, and by the looks of the crumpled overalls lying on the washing machine, his dad had come home late and was now gone again.

He wandered through the house noticing how everything was straight and clean and even in Ian's room the bed was made. The room his mom used for her sewing was orderly, with a row of new dresses she had been working on. It was a nice place to live, but since they had moved here everyone was too busy to be a family. He thought about how more money could help everyone. Mom and Ian could quit work and Dad could refuse the overtime hours. But, when he splashed cool water in his face to wash away the sleep his mind was wiped clean of the unrealistic daydreams.

Then, the phone rang again. This time he answered it before the second ring.

"Is this Dalan?" Miss Linger asked in a polite voice.

"Yes," he said, instantly recognizing her voice and feeling like something was crawling around in his stomach.

"You have something that belongs to me, you little cheat," her tone was now angry and threatening. "Now, you listen very carefully. I paid you hard-earned money and you cheated me. Now, I want my pots and I want the gold cross."

Dalan started to press the hang-up button.

"Don't you dare hang up on me you little creep!" she yelled at him, as though she was actually watching him, not just talking. "I don't have the pots," he said, which was true.

They were at the Palermos' but he didn't know where Marie had hidden them. Maybe she had turned them over to Franco by now.

"I'm coming back to your decrepit little town this afternoon. I want to meet you in your driveway at three o'clock and I expect you to have the pots and the cross there waiting for me. If the cross is what I think it is, I will give you one thousand dollars for it and will forget about the bricks you put in the box. Do you understand?"

Dalan hesitated, wildly assimilating the information and thinking of a plan. "Do you understand?" she asked again.

"You can't come to my house," he said. "Harvey will see you and he'll want part of the money for the cross. He didn't have anything to do with it, so he doesn't deserve any of the money."

"Well, why don't you suggest a place to meet," she said in a sarcastic tone.

"I'll talk to Marie and you call me back in ten minutes. Give me a phone number." He wrote down the Phoenix area number and promptly hung up the phone before she said another word.

He seldom called Marie's for fear Franco would answer, but this time he didn't hesitate. Mrs. Palermo answered "hello" in a sweet voice and immediately recognized Dalan as the caller. She said that Marie was at piano lessons and wouldn't be home until after one.

"By the way, Dalan, Marie talked to her father last night. He is gone to the store for some special packing in order to send your Indian pots to New York. She asked me to tell you that she would stop by on the way home from piano to get the other thing—the gold cross. I think it is so nice of you to donate them to the museum in New York City," Gina said.

Dalan hung up the phone and sat down on the hall floor. He had less than an hour to decide who he wanted to fight with—Miss Laura Linger or Franco Palermo.

CHAPTER 25

Dalan had just finished a bowl of Sugar Pops when he glanced out of the window and saw Marie riding her bike toward his house. He put the bowl in the sink and ran out to meet her in front by the mailbox. She stood astride her bike smiling at him as they greeted—little beads of sweat glistened on her tan forehead—her piano books in the bike's basket. He had no idea how to tell her the latest bad news, so he just blurted it out.

"Miss Linger is going to be here in town in two hours and wants the pots and the gold cross. She doesn't want her money back. She says that if we don't give her the things she is going to go to the police and tell them we stole the pots and the cross from the cave and insist that we are arrested and put in jail."

Marie looked at him with a frown. "That won't be easy," she said.

Before she could explain, he heard the phone ringing in the house. "That's Miss Linger calling back. What should I tell her?" he asked as he ran toward the door.

"Why don't you tell her to meet us at the pool house? I'll tell Daddy that she is coming and he can chase her away," Marie said, catching the last of the conversation.

"She says she won't come to your house. She wants to meet us at the high school football field at eight o'clock."

"Tell her that is too late; our parents won't let us just wander around town after dark," whispered Marie.

He repeated the statement into the phone then held the phone away from his ear as Linger screamed. When she finally settled down she agreed to be there before dark. Dalan neither agreed nor refused. He simply hung up the phone.

Kick The Can

❖ ❖ ❖

Harvey observed the short interchange from the comfort of Fred's rocking chair. Something obviously was happening again, and even with his throbbing headache, he still needed to be a part of it. A fraction of his memory from the attack had returned. Laura Linger hadn't run him down with her rental car.

Hearing the phone ring and watching Dalan dash into the house to answer it jarred his brain. He knew that Linger had left him at the Palermos' that night because when he asked for a ride in her car he had faced a string of profanities followed by her driving off into the night. He had been alone on the farm road walking back into town when he heard a vehicle's motor. That's when the curtain of memory fell. The last thing he remembered was the sound of the vehicle; not the rental car, maybe not even the hot rod, but definitely a big horsepower V-8.

He could figure only one option if he wanted to remain a part of the kids' ongoing plan. He had to follow them everywhere they went until they retrieved the pots and the gold cross from their hiding places. Thank goodness whoever hit him didn't take the hundred dollars Linger had given him. It was safely tucked away in the coin pocket of his jeans.

He watched as the girl came out of Dalan's and picked up her bike. He was distracted by a fire truck on Main Street for a couple of seconds and when he looked back, Dalan was standing at the driveway watching her as she bounced down the gravel road, kicking up a little trail of dust as she rode away. Harvey sat abruptly upright in his chair when he thought he saw something new in the basket. He wasn't sure but it looked like a brown grocery sack. He had noticed the music books when she arrived but was almost certain that there was something new in the basket.

He rubbed his eyes and massaged his temples. He needed more aspirin and maybe something strong to drink. Then he needed to be ready to follow Dalan.

❖ ❖ ❖

Marie couldn't believe how easily Dalan had given up the cross. He still had it wrapped in an old T-shirt. He stuck it in a grocery bag and then handed it over to her to give to her dad. As she rode down the street toward home she worried that someone would stop her, wanting to visit. How would she explain the heavy bag?

It was when a green National Park Service truck started to follow her that she really became anxious. It was a long way from the ruins and the museum. It didn't speed up to pass her like the last two cars had done. For sure it had plenty of room to pass. She was practically riding on the adjacent lawns.

Instead of going straight toward home, she took a turn down one of the alleyways, which would bring her around to the farm road that led to the back side of her house. She held her breath, waiting to see if the green truck would follow. For a second it was out of sight as it passed the alley. Then with a roar of the engine, it sped back and turned down the narrow alley toward her. She pedaled as hard as her legs would go, although she knew that her legs were no competition for the truck's motor.

Toward the end of the alley with the roof of her house visible in the distance, luck came her way in the form of a tin garbage can, which was close to the edge of the alley. As she rode by, she stuck out her foot and caught the top of the can, knocking it off balance and tipping it over. As it fell, it rolled into the middle of the alleyway, leaving the truck with only two choices: either it had to stop, or it had to crash into the heavy can, crushing it under the truck.

Marie pedaled even faster, turning her head for the sound of the crashing can. To her relief, the rumble of the truck's motor died away as she approached the back fence of her home. She was startled by the sudden gruff bark as Harley charged across the acre of lawn, intent on attacking the bike rider. Once he recognized her, he gave several welcome barks and intentionally crashed up against the chain link, making a huge racket.

She looked back to see if the truck was coming, but the trees and a long row of oleander shrubs blocked her view. She rode the bike around to the side of the yard and set it up against the fence. Her plan was to use the hiding place in the pool house, but the green truck made her think again. She grabbed her piano books and the grocery bag and ran toward the house. Luckily, the back door was unlocked.

She could hear her mom upstairs exercising on their treadmill, loudly singing along to the music of Bill Haley and The Comets as she worked on her trim figure. Marie ran through the house to look out the front window. The green truck was nowhere in sight.

"Darn," she thought, squinting to see into the open barn. Her dad's truck wasn't there either.

As she started up the stairs toward her room she looked out the front windows again, this time seeing the green truck sitting up the road facing the house. She froze on the stairs, staring out of the octagon-shaped stairwell window and into the windshield of the truck. She wasn't positive, but she thought that the driver looked a lot like that woman, Alice Brown, who had spent so much time with her at the Casa Grande Ruins Museum. She also wasn't sure, but it looked like there was another person in the truck—another woman. The green truck didn't move; it just sat there baking in the hot sun, giving off shimmering heat waves.

She tried to make herself busy in her room, but knew that until her dad came back home, she and her mother were vulnerable. She let ten agonizing minutes pass then looked out the window again. The truck was gone.

❖ ❖ ❖

With the cross gone from his house, it seemed at first that a huge burden had been lifted from his shoulders. On the other hand he was bored, with nothing to do but wait for the sun to cross the sky. It didn't take long before he realized that he missed the stress of keeping the ancient artifacts hidden. He couldn't imagine a life with only mowing lawns and kick the can to think about.

Marie had promised that she would call the second she had any news about her dad. Relying on the secretive Franco Palermo for news could be like watching stalactites grow. He gave it an hour—straightening his room and sorting his clothes—then put on a clean new shirt Mom had set aside for the start of school and pedaled off toward Marie's.

It was one of the hottest days of the summer, and by the time he leaned his bike up against a huge Grecian pillar in front of the Palermos' house, he was soaked to the bone with sweat. He noticed that he also was beginning to smell a bit rank and wished he had borrowed a dash of his dad's Old Spice. "Maybe I'm just nervous," he thought as he rang the doorbell, silently praying that Franco wouldn't answer the door.

"Why, hello, Dalan," Mrs. Palermo said. She was wearing a purple, skin-tight, stretchy outfit and had her hair pulled back in a ponytail. Her usual make-up was missing and she was soaked with as much sweat as he was. She led him into the air-conditioned family room and offered him a drink of water.

"Marie and her dad have gone to run an errand. She mentioned that you might come by and asked that you wait for her. She said that she would have some good news for you when she gets back," said Mrs. Palermo.

Dalan watched her move around the kitchen as he inhaled the water and languished in the cool jet of air coming from the air conditioning vent. She was a very pretty lady and had a very nice figure. The thought occurred to him that maybe Marie would grow up to look just like her mom.

His daydreaming was interrupted by the sound of a horn honking out in front of the house. Gina smiled at Dalan and nodded toward the front door. Dalan thanked her for the drink and went out to investigate. Marie was getting out of the oversize pickup and hollering for him to come. She must have seen his bike, he supposed.

"Come get in," she said. "Dad is going to take us to meet a friend of his who wants to buy the pots and cross."

Dalan loved the look of the shiny new pickup, with its double head lights and its own spotlight mounted near the driver's door, just like a police car. He hesitated one minute to take a close look at the truck and listen to its powerful engine, idling like a purring lion, and then he crawled up into the front seat beside Marie. The truck was brand new and smelled really good.

"How ya doing, kid?" Franco asked, reaching across and patting his knee.

"I'm fine, sir," Dalan said in his most mannered tone. Try as he may, he couldn't force himself to make eye contact with the alleged son of a mobster.

"You okay with us selling your pots and that gold thing?" Franco asked.

"Yes sir," Dalan said.

"Well, we need to drive to Tucson. I want you and Marie to come along to agree to the deal. We better go by your house and ask if it's all right with your parents. Don't ya think?"

"My parents are gone for the morning, sir. Maybe I could just leave a note to tell them that I am with you and Marie. I'm sure my mom won't mind," he said.

As they drove toward his house he looked around the truck and saw a wooden crate on the back. It was padded with a heavy blanket and tied in place so it wouldn't bounce out.

Folded alongside the box was the grocery bag, now empty, which he had given to Marie a couple of hours before.

While Franco and Marie waited, Dalan ran into his house through the back door. To his surprise the door was open and the key was still in the lock.

"Mom, are you home?" he yelled, but got no response. He went into his room to get a sheet of paper and was shocked to see his room. The place he had just straightened up was a mess. All of the drawers were open and his clothes were thrown everywhere. Even his mattress was lying on its side on the floor. The throw rugs were pulled up and his shelf with his little league trophy and scout awards had been raked clean. Everything was on the floor. Worst of all, his hundred dollars was missing.

He felt a shiver of fear, but then remembered that the little town's best protector was outside waiting for him in the truck. He wanted to straighten his room before his mom got home, but knew he didn't have time. He wrote a quick note on the back of an old spelling test and laid it on the kitchen table.

> Gone with Mr. Palermo to Tucson
> will be back late.
> Dalan

He quickly used the bathroom and started outside when the man's voice stopped him.

"Where do you think you are going?"

Startled, he turned to look down the dark hallway. Harvey was leaning against the wall, smoking a cigarette, and looking unbelievably creepy with his swollen face and intrusive stance.

"Mom doesn't allow smoking in here!" were the first words that came to Dalan's tongue.

"I don't give a darn what your homely mother allows. I want that gold cross and them pots. You two little brats are trying to cheat me outta my share. Now, I found my own buyer, and you two are outta luck, so hand them over," Harvey said.

Dalan had an open run at the door and took advantage of it. Just like he had seen in a movie once, he grabbed a pot off of the kitchen stove and threw it at Harvey, then dashed out the door.

The big black pickup was idling at the end of the driveway. Running toward it, Dalan looked over his shoulder to see Harvey emerge from the kitchen door, and then stop abruptly. Neither Marie nor Franco noticed him. Dalan jumped into the truck and announced that he was good to go. His heart was pounding so hard that he could barely breathe. To his relief, Harvey didn't approach the truck but stayed back in the doorway until Franco put the truck in gear and they headed up the street toward Main.

"Is everything okay?" asked Marie, noticing his red face and rapid breathing.

He just leaned his head back against the seat of the truck and closed his eyes. He was leaving his previous friend—now his enemy—angry and alone in his house. His room was a disaster and he thought the teapot he threw at Harvey had hit the glass frame of his Mom's favorite family portrait. *What would she think and what would Harvey do next—kill his brother when he came home or worse, kill his mom?* He was about to ask Mr. Palermo to turn around and take him back home when he heard the siren.

❖ ❖ ❖

They were traveling down the highway just leaving the outskirts of town when the sheriff's car, an Arizona Highway Patrol car, and Officer Roberts in his black-and-white police car passed them heading south. The sirens had sent another chill up Dalan's spine. About two miles south of town, on a curving stretch of the highway, they came upon the police vehicles with their rotating lights, all parked at odd angles.

"Looks like somebody's been in a wreck," Franco said, slowing the truck.

The southbound lane of the highway was blocked and one officer was trying to direct the light traffic around the scene. In spite of his efforts, every car slowed to a crawl and some were parking to get out and examine the scene.

A cloud of dust still hung in the air above the cluster of cars, making visibility difficult, but finally they could see the problem. Four black tires were pointing toward the heavens, like the feet of a dead Louisiana armadillo. One of the tires was still slowly turning—refusing to concede to death.

Franco suddenly jerked the wheel to the right, wedging his truck between two of the official vehicles, and in spite of the frantic waving of the traffic director, came to a complete stop.

"Stay in the car!" he commanded, as he jumped out and ran to the scene.

Only then did Dalan see what Franco must have seen moments before. The crushed cab of the upside down car was tiny, and the shiny, candy apple red paint on the crumpled door announced its content. It was Billy Real's hot rod.

The lawmen and the gathering crowd didn't wait for a tow truck or the paramedics to roll the car upright. Dalan and Marie, free spirits as ever, didn't stay in the truck as ordered, but edged their way to the front of the crowd to watch as six or eight of the men from the crowd grasped one side of the car and in unison, heaved the car up on its side, holding it in place for the police to remove the driver. Dalan immediately knew what they were doing, and then saw the bodies.

"Pull her out!" shouted one of the men, straining to hold the demolished car upright before it toppled over again.

Franco and Officer Roberts rushed to the cab and manually twisted the door off of the coupe. Gently they eased a female body out from behind the crushed steering wheel and gently carried her to a blanket someone had stretched out on the desert ground.

"We've got the other one over in the ditch," someone else yelled. "He must have been ejected from the car when it flipped. Grab his legs and let's get him in the shade."

Dalan heard the car's groan and crunch as it was allowed to fall back in its place, once more resting upside down. He pushed forward between the legs of the adults and finally was able to clearly see the bloodied bodies.

Whether he or Marie screamed out first no one noticed. All eyes were on the two older teens, now lying side by side in the bright sunshine.

Ian Dawson and Candy Real were both unconscious and bleeding from their noses and ears, but both appeared to be breathing. Tiny shards of glass and clumps of dirt were ground into every visible skin surface. Candy's long, glistening red hair was tangled and her long tan legs were lying at an odd angle.

Unable to move, Dalan's knees gave out and he sat down hard in the gravel and weeds. He didn't hear the additional sirens or the shouts of orders from the lawmen. When an ambulance parted the crowd, and the ambulance drivers rushed forward, Dalan was astonished to see them take out equipment and start working on both unconscious victims. After a brief check and consultation with a tall highway patrol officer, the paramedics turned away from Candy, concentrating their efforts solely on Ian.

Within minutes they had intravenous lines in both of Ian's arms and an oxygen mask on his face. They brought a stretcher, and with a foam collar around his neck, carefully moved him onto the stretcher and into the ambulance. The last glimpse Dalan had of his brother that day was Ian's hand dangling off the side of the stretcher—clenching and unclenching his fist. When he turned back toward Candy's lifeless body, someone had respectfully placed a blanket over the girl's beautiful face.

"Are you sure there were only two people in the car?" Franco was grilling a County Deputy Sheriff.

"I'm positive," the man said. "They ran a stop sign and were nearly hit by a semi, so I started following them. They weren't speeding until I turned on my lights. I was nearly alongside of the car when she saw me and took off. I could see the boy trying to get her to stop but she just kept going faster. When they hit the curve of the road she started to spin, then she overcorrected and the car flipped."

Franco gave a big sigh then directed the two youngsters back into his truck. They sat waiting in the hot cab for what seemed like hours before he got in the truck and turned it around, heading back into town.

No one spoke for several minutes, then, Franco broke the silence. "The hospital radioed to say that your brother is awake and talking to the doctors. Your parents are headed to the hospital."

Marie finally started to come out of her shock and started to cry—quietly at first and then with big heaving sobs. Franco put his muscular arm around her, pulling her close to him. She still wouldn't let go of Dalan's hand.

Gina Palermo was standing in front of the house, waiting for them, when the truck pulled up. She was trying to give reassuring smiles but it wasn't working. She bent down and took both kids into her arms. Marie started another round of sobs, trying to tell her mom that Kristen wasn't in the car and that it was Dalan's brother and Candy, but that was unnecessary—the small town gossip web had already informed her of the details of the tragic accident. She ushered the kids into the house, giving a nod to her husband, who headed back to the truck to get the wooden box.

"I called your mother, Dalan. She was on her way out the door to the hospital. She was going to meet your father there. I told her that I would look after you until she gets back. Maybe, if everything is going well for Ian—that's his name right? Well, if he is stable, we can all go to the hospital and visit him later tonight. In the meantime why don't you two go in the game room and find a game to play or a show to watch on TV," she concluded.

"What about our trip to Tucson, Daddy?" Marie asked as he came back into the room.

Franco looked at his daughter and then at Dalan, then turned to Gina. "Why don't you make the kids and me some sandwiches and put some sodas in that little cooler while I wash up. None of us can do anything here right now anyway; we might as well finish up this clay pot business for the kids."

Gina started to protest, but recognized his statement not just as an order or suggestion but a wise decision. She turned and went to the kitchen as requested.

Dalan's mind was drawing a blank except that he couldn't stop thinking about his trashed bedroom and Harvey standing in the doorway, smoking a cigarette. What would Franco think of that, if he were told?

CHAPTER 26

They passed the residual of the wreckage on their way back out of town. The car was still upside down and there were several official cars still parked at odd angles. A wrecker truck with a rotating orange light was parked nearby awaiting its turn. Franco slowed his truck but didn't stop.

"What a waste of a nice custom paint job," he muttered to himself, surprising Dalan.

"Daddy, why was Candy driving the car instead of Kristen?" Marie asked.

It was the question Dalan had been dying to ask but didn't dare. Of course, he also had been wondering why Kristen had been driving Billy's hot rod, ever since the day he was stabbed to death.

"I called Kristen while you were getting washed up," Franco said. "She said that Candy borrowed it early this morning to go to the grocery store and didn't ever come back. I guess that's where she picked up your brother," Franco said Dalan.

Dalan had to swallow hard to clear his throat before he could get out the next question. "Did the car belong to Kristen?" he said, wondering why he asked.

Franco and Marie both looked at him as if he were retarded.

"Didn't you know that the hot rod was Daddy's?" Marie asked, and then went on to explain. "It's been my Daddy's hot rod ever since he was a kid back in New York. It used to be in our garage with a cover over it, but it didn't run. When Billy started working for Daddy he got interested in it and offered to fix it up if he could drive it sometimes. It was never Billy's car. He only drove it when Kristen was with him, but when he died, Kristen asked if she could use it for a few weeks until her eighteenth birthday. Then she was going to get a new car to take to college."

During Marie's explanation, Franco kept glancing over at Dalan and nodding his head in agreement. Dalan couldn't believe that he was being treated like an adult by the normally intimidating Franco. The discussion ended with a long silence.

"I'm starved," said Franco, after several miles travel on the arrow straight road.

Marie handed out the sandwiches and sodas. Dalan ate his food and stared out the window seeing the desert of Southern Arizona for the first time. The trees and cacti were different than around Coolidge and to the north. The truck sat up high so the view of the desert and mountains was good, and the air conditioning made it feel like springtime. Marie had become drowsy and had eventually fallen asleep, leaning her head on his shoulder. He wondered if Mr. Palermo minded, but nothing was said. Once he even thought he saw Franco smile after glancing at the teens.

As they arrived at the outskirts of Tucson, Franco broke the silence, talking softly, and just to Dalan. "How much do you think those pots and that gold cross are worth?"

He thought for a minute then said, "I saw a pot, just like the two we have. It was in a store in Colorado. The lady who owned it told me they wouldn't sell theirs for less than ten thousand dollars."

"That's what Marie already told me. What about the gold cross?" Franco asked.

"I don't know, sir," he said. "It has some diamonds and rubies and blue stones on it. My mom said that the stones—if they are real—are worth a lot more than the pots or the gold cross by itself."

"Well, just between you and me, and I do mean that, the guy I'm taking you to see is a pretty famous art dealer. He will know the value of the stuff or at least who to contact to find out. The truth is, he's famous but not necessarily in a good way, or for his knowledge of art. His name is Mr. Licavoli. When we leave there I want you to forget that I ever told you his name or anything about him, but you should write it down on a scrap of paper and put it away someplace safe when you get home. Someday, you can look up his name in the history books and tell your grandkids that you met him."

"Licavoli?" Dalan repeated. "How is he famous?"

"Back before the big war, he and his buddies took care of things in Chicago, and then later in Detroit, and sometimes in New York City. You ever hear of the Saint Valentine's Day massacre?"

"No, sir," Dalan answered.

"He was there in Chicago. He was the boss of some very bad people in Detroit too."

"They used to kill people who didn't want to do business their way," Marie added in a sleepy voice, still resting her head on Dalan's shoulder.

"Marie, you shouldn't say things like that. Anyways, he's retired now. If he likes the pots and the cross, he'll give you two the best price of anyone in the country. If that works we can go home tonight and the whole thing will be settled," Franco said.

"What about Miss Linger?" Marie asked. "I think I saw her this morning with that park service lady that works at the Casa Grande museum. You know, the lady who drives one of those green trucks?"

"If you ain't got the pots no more, what's she gunna do?" Franco said, reverting to his Bronx street language.

Silence filled the cab until the truck pulled down a little paved lane past a gate with a sign announcing *Grace Ranch*, and then below it a weathered sign that said *Catalina Arts and Imports*. At the end of the drive was an enormous, single-story territorial house constructed of stucco and round timbers. It had a flat roof and a wide porch surrounding the terra-cotta-colored building. There were thick steel bars on the windows and mature bougainvillea vines with their crimson flowers covering some of the walls. Oleanders and wild roses twisted and turned their way up, around, and through cracks and crevices of the old building. Unnoticed by the visitors were strips of silver tape around the edges of the window glass, all attached to a central security monitor.

An old stooped man hobbled out onto the porch as the truck approached. He waved for them to park by the front door and to come up to the house. Introductions were made to the wrinkled man, who Franco called Pete. He wore a shiny brown suit with double buttons and brown Sunday shoes with pointed toes, almost like cowboy boots.

Dalan didn't think the man looked all that scary, until Pete bent down and squeezed Marie's cheek saying, "so your old man says you to want to join the family crime business." He then laughed in what was more of a cackle. This produced a hacking cough.

When the chit chat ended and the "subjects" were mentioned, Franco suggested the kids wait in the truck. He walked them out, then reached into the back to retrieve the large box containing the pots and the cross and gold chain.

It seemed like hours sitting in the truck with the motor and air conditioning running before Franco returned and waved Marie and Dalan into the old house. It was dark and cool inside with real stone floors and the musty smell of leather, tobacco, and old wood smoke. Dalan was surprised that they could even see their way down the dark hallway, which led into a spacious parlor where a massive fireplace stood black and empty. They took seats around a heavy wooden table on carved wood chairs while drinks were brought out by an elderly woman.

When Dalan reached for the frosty glass of 7-Up placed in front of him, the old man put his yellowed fingers on Dalan's hand, stopping the action.

"In my old country," Pete said, in a raspy deep voice, "we drink a toast when a deal is made, not before. Let me explain what I have found."

He had the full attention of all three of the guests.

"The two pots you have brought are magnificent and very old, but also are very hot. There are lots of people looking for those particular pots right now. My suggestion is that you return the pots to the park service museum near your home. I've been there. It's a nice place. I'll have friends tell them you're coming. I'm sure they'll offer you a handsome reward. I can make a few calls and make that happen. Would you agree to that?" he said, looking directly at Dalan who nodded, and then at Marie who just stared but gave no indication of consent.

"What if they won't give us a reward?" she asked.

"Trust me, child. They will make you an offer that you will find very acceptable." The old man then went on talking about how the youngsters might otherwise get caught and even be sent to jail. "Jail is not a good place, believe me."

Dalan was already hurting from sitting on the rock-hard wooden chair and he was so thirsty. *Why couldn't this man get to the point?*

"The cross on the other hand is different, quite different," Licavoli said in a voice that was so soft Dalan had to lean forward to hear. "I have called around and it seems that no one knows anything about your cross. I have examined the stones, which appear to be real and very old—the cuts are primitive. I took the liberty of speaking to a friend of mine in Mexico City. He thinks the cross might be ancient Incan. Even before the Spaniards came to the new world they worshiped a white god and used the cross as one of the symbols of his power."

"So will he buy the thing?" Franco asked.

"Si, he is willing to pay you ten thousand dollars for the cross."

"For that price, I might as well buy it from the kids myself and hang it on my wall at home," Franco said.

The old man gave him a cold stare and then looked at Marie and Dalan. He arose from his chair and went to an old roll top desk in the corner, making a clatter as the top rolled up. He brought a leather case to the table and laid it in front of Marie. He nodded for her to open it. She struggled with the stiff buckle and strap, then with Dalan's assistance pulled out a stack of crisp hundred-dollar bills.

"Would you be so kind as to count them, dear? All of them," he said.

It took several minutes before she finished. Dalan's eyes got bigger with each pile of ten. "There are five hundred of them," Marie said, looking up at him.

"That's fifty thousand dollars where I went to school," he chuckled at his own joke then went on. "I will give you the fifty thousand for the cross. My Mexican friend is a cheapskate. That will pay for a good education—maybe Harvard or Duke, young man, and will buy this pretty little lady a rich, handsome husband someday."

Marie reached under the table and took Dalan's hand. Their eyes met and held the gaze as they pondered the offer. The ticking of a pewter clock on the fireplace mantle became the only sound in the room. Silently an apparently unanimous decision was reached.

"We are going to hold onto it for now," Dalan said in a soft but firm voice.

In spite of the previous warning, he couldn't sit still any longer and his throat was powder dry. He stood and reached for the bottle of 7-Up and took a long pull.

Marie also stood as the two adults, astounded at the decision, pushed their chairs away from the table. Dalan went to the fireplace hearth and looked into the box. Both pots were there and carefully padded. He turned toward Mr. Licavoli and offered his hand.

"Thank you for your valuable time, sir. Could I please have the cross back?"

Franco started to say something but Marie slipped her arm through Dalan's and watched as the moment played out. Licavoli paused then took Dalan's hand, shaking it firmly. He went back to the desk and brought the cross—still wrapped in the old T-shirt—to Dalan who unwrapped it and laid it on the table.

"It is too beautiful to be hidden in someone's private collection," he said. "It needs to be studied and then put in a glass case for everyone to enjoy." He then wrapped it up and laid it on top of the pots. He lifted the box, then turned toward the door. Without another word, he walked away from the table, the stacked fifty thousand dollars, and the astonished Mafia legend.

The drive back home was uneventful. To both kids' surprise, Franco voiced no criticism of their decision, but visited quietly with the two, making complimentary statements about their motives and decision. Marie had taken Dalan's hand as soon as they were seated in the truck and hadn't let go. Their problems were far from over, but their resolve was firm.

CHAPTER 27

It was ten days before Ian was released from the hospital. No mention was ever made to the Dawsons' about a hospital bill. The funeral for Candy was held in Clovis, New Mexico. The Palermos' left town for the funeral and didn't return for almost a week. No one had heard a word from Miss Linger or the park rangers. Dalan was back to mowing the neighbor's lawns for two dollars a week, thinking every minute of every day as he pushed the lawn mower—eating the Bermuda grass dust—that he could have been the richest teenager in the county.

He and Boyd had been to the city pool a few times, where everyone was talking about how great it would be when school started. They all had a boring summer. Dalan however, was dreading the thought of school.

Marie had come by a few times in the evening to play the street games, but something in their relationship appeared to have changed. They didn't run off to their secret place to hide anymore. That would have been fine with Dalan, but now she went a different direction to hide, and didn't ever stay for more than a few kicks of the can.

A late evening thunderstorm interrupted the game the night after Ian came home. Marie ran to Dalan's porch to stay dry and then remained after the cloudburst to talk.

"How is Ian doing?" she asked.

"He's okay. He says his legs and head still hurt all the time. He is real grouchy and wants me to wait on him like the nurses in the hospital did."

"Has he said anything to you about the accident—you know—how it happened?"

"He won't talk about it to anybody. Mom told me that the police came to the hospital the day after the accident and he wouldn't even talk to them."

"I wonder if he would talk to me?" she said.

"He is right inside the door. You could at least say hello."

"Before I go in, we need to decide about the stuff. Ever since we went to Tucson it's been sitting in my room. My parents act like they are afraid to talk about it and you haven't returned my calls."

"I didn't know that you even called," he said.

"I talked to your dad twice," she said.

"My mom and dad are so freaked out about Ian and the accident. Now, the policeman says he now isn't positive who was driving the hot rod. There is a chance it might have been Ian, mom said. So my parents are afraid that we are going to get sued, or that Ian will be arrested and blamed for Candy dying. Nothing around our house has been normal."

"What did you tell them about the trip to Tucson?"

"I didn't tell them anything. Things were so crazy that day that I don't even think they knew I was gone. Maybe we were wrong when we turned down all that money. I must have been crazy," he said.

"You weren't crazy, and besides, we decided together. Now we can decide together what to do. But we need to talk it over. Why don't you come over swimming tomorrow and bring Boyd? My cousin is coming to visit and he can keep her company while we talk about it. I'm going to make a list of the options. Why don't you do the same thing?" she said. "Mr. Licavoli called my dad the day we got back from the funeral and said his offer is still good. So that's one option."

"Do you still want to see Ian?" he asked.

She nodded, so he opened the door and let her inside.

Kick The Can

❖ ❖ ❖

From across the street, the old navy binoculars were in use, trained on the two lovebirds. Harvey was wishing he could read lips because he knew that they had to be telling important secrets. It had been a difficult ten days for Harvey, too. First of all, Fred had threatened to kick him out of the rented front room if he didn't get a job and pay his rent. Next, there was the funeral, and both before and after, Kristen had started coming by for Harvey to be her crying shoulder and spiritual advisor. She called Fred's phone at odd hours and insisted on meeting him to talk, but that was all she ever wanted to do. Then there were the serious threats. The long-distance calls from that witch, Laura Linger, were coming at all hours of the day and night. Poor Fred was about to stop the phone service.

Linger was back at work in Washington, D.C., but hadn't forgotten about the double-cross in the desert and the thousands of dollars she had missed out on—"been cheated out of," by her words. She was insistent that Harvey be her eyes and ears and find out what had become of the ancient treasure—or else. She implied that a friend of hers in the FBI could find a crime to fit Harvey's actions, or lack thereof.

He had taken a job—mostly to get away from the phone—at the Ford dealership. They had him washing cars and trucks, moving them around the lot, blowing up balloons and sweeping the floors in the shop and showroom. The pay was worse than at the hamburger joint, but they promised him a commission if he brought in some of his friends and they bought a car—fat chance that would ever happen. He had mentioned it to Fred who got a big laugh out of the idea of buying a new car when the only one he ever owned had one hundred and eighty thousand miles on it and was paid for.

Harvey became real curious about the whole treasure thing. So much so that he had gone back to the cave. He had trouble finding it at first, but finally found a piece of yellow crime scene tape someone had left behind, tangled in a tumbleweed. He found the cave completely empty except for a thousand footprints and the wrapper from a piece of Beemans chewing gum in a little side room near the front of the cave. He could see where the old monk had been found, but not the scene of Billy's murder. Dalan had told him about the various rooms in the cave and the earthen shelf that had held the clay pots. The shelf was undisturbed, but the pots were obviously long gone. After returning home late that night, Harvey had experienced nightmares for the first time since boot camp.

The night of the rainstorm he watched Dalan and the girl talking on the Dawsons' porch and then saw the girl go into the house by herself. "How strange was that?" He thought. The boy rejoined the rest of his little friends kicking the can up and down the street, but the girl didn't come out. He waited and watched until his eyes hurt. Harvey had come to hate watching the game. It was a stupid game. They played and played but they didn't ever keep score, thus no one ever really won.

Sitting there in the dark, he decided that he couldn't postpone learning the fate of the pots any longer. Miss Linger was scheduled to call the next day and would be expecting some progress. He changed into his black T-shirt and went out through the back door. As he left, Fred looked up from the TV, but only grunted something about leftover tuna casserole.

Marie came out of the Dawsons' house through the kitchen door and walked toward her house at the far end of the darkened town. By then, Harvey was standing in the shadows, watching her from the side street. He kept his distance from the girl, planning a surprise meeting a block or two away. He was sure he could threaten her into telling him what had happened to the pots. He knew that the stubborn Dalan would never give up the information he needed to satisfy Linger.

"Hi, Marie," he said from the dark, watching her jump at the sound of his voice. That was a good thing. It would weaken her resolve.

"Mr. Grimes! What are you doing here?" she said.

"How many times have I told you to call me Harvey? I'm just out for a little fresh air," he lied. "How did kick the can go? Did you win?"

"No, I let Jaden, that nine-year-old girl, win. Did you know that she is a national chess champion?" Marie said as she kept walking.

"Slow down for a minute. I need to talk to you. I swear, those short legs of yours can move three times as fast as mine. Tell me something," he said, trying to keep up with her. "What ever happened to those Indian pots?"

When she didn't answer he ran for a few paces to get ahead of her, then turned and stood, feet wide apart, blocking her way.

"I need to get home, Mr. Grimes. Please move out of my way," she said, beginning to divert around him.

"Just tell me about them pots, and then you can run on to your fancy house and your fancy room with its little dolls and bunny rabbits."

"How did you know I have rabbits? Have you been in my room?" she said in an accusatory tone.

"I just wanna know about them pots. That lady you stole the money from wants them back. She says that they are hers and that she paid for them fair and square."

Marie started to walk away faster, frantically looking around for someone to help her.

Harvey had lost his patience. He started swearing and screaming at her, using words she had only heard in a few bad movies or when her daddy's business partners closed the door to his study. It frightened her and she started to run into the field to get away from him, but he cut her off again, screaming, just like Billy used to do.

She looked up and saw what was about to happen before Harvey felt it. Out of the pitch-black night came the flying object, smashing into Harvey's back. It knocked him to the ground where he hit his head, and for the second time in as many weeks Harvey lost consciousness and his short-term memory.

No words were exchanged, but as the squeaking of the bicycle chain filled the night air she hollered after it. "Ian told me that Billy was dead when he got there."

The bicycle stopped for a moment and then continued moving away from her in the dark. There was moaning coming from Harvey, so she did the only thing she could think to do. She ran the rest of the way home.

"Daddy," she shouted as she burst through the door. "There's a drunk guy about two hundred yards away lying at the side of the road on the way to town."

"I'll take care of it," Franco said, getting up quickly from his recliner. "I've told you a dozen times that you shouldn't be out on the street late at night. Now you head off to bed and I'll take care of the man."

He picked up the phone, mumbled something to someone, then turned the sound on the TV back to normal.

❖ ❖ ❖

"Harvey's been in another accident," Fred said to Dalan. "He asked me to call you and ask you if you could come by and talk to him. I'm going to the post office. The front door is open."Dalan hung up and looked out of the window, wishing he had ignored the ringing telephone. He finished up the dishes and then took his time making his bed. Finally, he got up the courage to confront Harvey and walked across the street.

Harvey said he felt like he had been hit by a truck—a big truck. He remembered the flashing lights of the police car waking him up but no matter how hard he tried, he couldn't remember how he fell down in the road, or how he had even ended up there. Of course the police thought he was drunk, but the test they gave him and the blood drawn at the hospital proved them wrong. When the doctors discharged him, just after midnight, he had considered calling Fred for a ride home, but lucked out when the evening nurse who had cleaned up his cuts and scratches offered him a ride. Fred was still awake when he got home and told Harvey that the police had been by and searched his room for drugs and booze.

"They even had a search warrant, just like on TV," Fred told Harvey. "The policeman said that they didn't find anything but your knife. They took it but left a receipt. They said you could come down to the police station in a couple of days and pick it up. What's gotten into you young man? I told you when I rented you the room that I didn't want any funny stuff going on; now I feel like I'm living in the middle of a mystery movie."

Harvey was too shaky to talk about it, so he just apologized for the trouble he had caused and went into his room.

When he woke up in the morning, every inch of his body hurt—especially his back and the back of his legs. When he took his shower, there were marks on his legs that looked like small tire tracks—bicycle tire tracks. Nothing made sense. The last thing he remembered from the evening before was putting some floor wax on the showroom floor at the Ford dealership.

Dalan had avoided Harvey ever since Candy's wreck, but even more so since Harvey had stolen the hundred dollars and called Dalan's mom a bad name. But, he knew that a failure to appear would not go over well. Even his parents would expect him to pay his respects to Harvey. He finished drying his hands and headed across the street. Who knew what was going to be said, but he might as well get it over with regardless.

"What happened to you, Mr. Grimes?" Dalan asked. From the half-smile on Harvey's face, Dalan wasn't a hundred percent sure that he had been recognized the night before.

"I tripped on a tree stump and hit my head," said Harvey, slowly shaking his head from side to side, like he was embarrassed. "And what's with this Mr. Grimes stuff anyways?" He was sitting in Fred's recliner holding an ice pack to the back of his head.

"Sorry. How'd you get all those scrapes on your face?"

"There must have been branches on the tree," Harvey muttered.

"Fred said that you needed to see me."

"Yeh. You and Marie have been making yourselves pretty scarce lately. I need your help. That Linger witch keeps phoning me and wanting to know what happened to the Indian pots. She won't quit calling. She says that she is going to tell the police that we stole them from her if she doesn't get them back."

Dalan pondered the situation, then found a chewed-on pencil and a scrap of paper on Fred's table and wrote out his parent's phone number. "Have her call me the next time she phones," he said. "Maybe I can get her to leave us alone."

CHAPTER 28

The phone call came early the next morning. It was Mrs. Dawson who took the call. At the woman's insistence, she shook Dalan's shoulder until he was fully awake. "Son, sorry to wake you, but you have a long-distance phone call."

He bolted upright and rubbed his eyes, staggering to the hall phone. The voice sounded distant, and trying to wake up and listen at the same time, Dalan was having trouble hearing. He didn't get all of her words but got the gist of the conversation and the identity of the caller—Miss Linger. There was no hint of candor or politeness. She wanted her Anasazi pots and she wanted them right now.

Dalan played dumb for a couple of minutes, until finally a light went on in his head as a plan took life in his mind.

"I don't have them," he said, there being an element of truth in the statement.

"Well, I don't really care where you and your little friend have them hidden. I'm giving you one week to get them safely crated and shipped off to me. The train trip will take three days. That's ten days. If they are not here in Washington, D.C., I'm calling the police and have you and your parents arrested. The girl too!" Linger said.

Dalan was barely listening, staring out of the window across the street at Harvey sitting on the porch staring back. He must have received an early call too.

"What if my friend Harvey brings them to you? You'll need to pay for his ticket, but then they would for sure be safe. It would be harder for someone to steal them or to break them than if they are just shipped," he said.

There was a long pause. For a moment he thought they had been cut off. More likely, she was surprised that Harvey was still around—or even alive.

"What's to guarantee that he won't steal them from both of us?" she asked.

"Our families just want to be rid of them. School starts in a couple of weeks and we won't have time to worry about them. Harvey will take care of them. Mr. Palermo can give him his travel instructions. Could you give me your address and the address of the place where you work? Also, give me your phone number. I'll talk to Harvey and then we'll call you back."

To his surprise she gave him the information he asked for, repeating the numbers slowly as he wrote them on his mom's note pad.

"I'm not changing the time frame," she threatened. "You had better not double cross me again," she said. "I want my pots, not a pile of bricks, and I want that gold cross."

"What are you talking about, lady? We never mentioned anything about a gold cross," Dalan said in an innocent voice.

"You know good and well what I'm talking about, you little liar. Harvey told me that he heard all—" The phone started giving off static which was timed perfectly for Dalan. "I can't hear you—the connection is breaking up. If you can hear me, I'll go see Harvey right now," he said.

Dalan hung up the phone and turned to his parents who were in the hallway behind him listening. They were both standing with their arms folded, watching their son communicate long-distance with an adult, thinking how their little boy was all grown up. They patiently waited to find out what the heck was going on. He looked up at them with a smile and said, "Dad, Mom . . . Marie and I need your help."

After a twenty-minute discussion the three of them embraced; Marie was called, and a meeting time was set for that evening. In the meantime, Dalan needed to once again visit the recovering neighbor across the street.

❖ ❖ ❖

"Harvey, how come you're sitting out here in the middle of the day? I heard you had a job selling cars," Dalan asked.

"I told you I got hurt. I still don't feel any better. When I look at you I see two of you."

Dalan didn't comment, but took a seat on the floor of the porch and looked out toward the street. He was a little afraid of making too much eye contact while he pitched his plan.

"I need to ask you to do something for me and Marie," Dalan said.

"I ain't borrowing Fred's car again and I ain't tending them dogs."

"It's not about the car or the dogs. It's something lots more important," Dalan said.

"I'm listening, but I got a real bad headache so make it fast."

"You know that lady, Miss Linger, called me? Well, she wants those pots really bad. Mr. Palermo tried to help us sell them to a friend of his in Tucson but it didn't work out. I was hoping to get a good price and we were going to give you your third just like we always said." He turned his head to note Harvey's reaction.

At the mention of Franco Palermo, Harvey sat up a little straighter in his chair. "Who'd you try to sell them to anyway?" he said, changing the subject.

"All that's not important," Dalan said, looking Harvey in the eyes. "What is important is that we get those pots returned safely to Miss Linger so they can be put in the museum, and before she tells the police, and we all get arrested."

"So get to the point," Harvey said, frowning and rubbing the ice pack on his forehead.

"We each had a hundred dollars that Miss Linger gave us, right? At least I had a hundred dollars until it disappeared. Something you know about, right? Well, Marie and I would like to give you more money so that you can take the train to Washington, D.C., and deliver the pots to her. We think it is safer than trying to mail them."

"Me! Take the train all the way there and back? You've got to be joking," Harvey said in a disgusted voice.

"Marie can't do it and I can't do it. The ticket costs about sixty dollars and my mom can fix you a basket of food for the trip. Mr. Palermo said that he will make it right with your boss so you'll still have a job when you get back," Dalan persisted.

The discussion went on for several minutes until every pro and con had been tossed about. Finally, very reluctantly, Harvey said he would consider it but wouldn't promise to make the trip. He wouldn't admit that he had Dalan's money either. He did agree to think about it and to let Dalan know that night.

Later in the day, Harvey received a phone call from the Ford dealership's general manager telling him that he was sorry that Harvey had been injured in the accident. The man on the phone said that they wouldn't be needing Harvey anymore. They would mail him his paycheck. During the conversation, Harvey could hear a voice in the background, which sounded a lot like Franco Palermo's.

Ten minutes later there was a knock on Fred's door. Harvey answered and was shocked to see Marie and her mother. Mrs. Palermo was in a yellow tennis outfit with a scooping neckline that made it difficult for Harvey to keep his eyes where they belonged, and his mind on the conversation. Marie handed him an envelope and a train ticket. He opened the envelope and found it full of twenty dollar bills and a ticket for a one-way trip to Baltimore.

"My daddy said he would have Miss Linger meet you in Baltimore. She will pick up the pots there. Daddy says he has a friend in New Jersey who needs a good worker to help manage his restaurant, and you should see him about going to work there," Marie said.

"Mr. Palermo will be by at eight tomorrow morning to pick you up," Gina said, making it clear that there wouldn't be any backing out of the deal. "He will have the pots all wrapped up nice and tight. You might want to take most of your things with you. Should you decide to stay and work for our friend, we can send the rest to you if necessary."

"But I like it here," Harvey said.

"The job pays three times what you can earn here," Gina said with a smile which masked a tone of dead seriousness. "You should take the deal, Mr. Grimes. Mr. Palermo thinks you might have worn out your welcome here in Coolidge."

He started to say something, but the mother and daughter already had turned away. As they walked toward the shiny black Fleetwood, Harvey realized that his headache was gone, replaced by a profound abdominal cramping sensation.

"Who was that?" Fred asked.

"That was my connection," said Harvey, realizing that his life was about to change forever.

CHAPTER 29

To his surprise, Dalan's parents never once complained about the high telephone bill that he incurred over the next few days. Before they had left Tucson and Mr. Licavoli's place, the old mobster had given Dalan a copy of a magazine called the Smithsonian, which the old man said might be of help. In it were lots of articles and also lots of names of important people.

Dalan and Marie worked from the Dawson kitchen table writing notes and making numerous calls to the information operator, and then phone calls to speak to the people they thought would solve their problems once and for all. The next step took lots of courage.

They carefully wrapped the gold cross and packaged it into a shoe box. This they taped up and carried together to the post office, which at that point in time they trusted more than most anyone they knew. When the clerk asked if they wanted insurance on the package, Marie said yes.

"How much do you want to insure it for?" the clerk asked.

"What is the highest amount possible?" she asked.

And so the ancient Anasazi cross, taken from the neck of a dead holy man, wrapped in a ragged T-shirt, dumped in a burlap bag, and finally wrapped in cotton batting inside a stiff cardboard box, was finally sent off to what it's discoverers hoped would be a place of honor. It would be a long wait for Marie and Dalan to know if it had reached its promised destination.

❖ ❖ ❖

The following morning, Harvey Grimes, carrying a wooden crate with a hemp rope handle, a rucksack full of his clothes,

Kick The Can

and his ear full of warnings, boarded the Union Pacific's California Zephyr, heading east. Franco Palermo waited patiently at the railing until the train was out of sight before he got back in his truck.

It has often been said that important events, whether good or bad, happen in clusters of threes. And so it was, that late afternoon of the departure of Harvey Grimes, Officer Roberts came across something fascinating. He was just pulling his cruiser out of Tag's Café after a satisfying lunch of chicken enchiladas and a chocolate shake, when a green parks service pickup raced by. Curious, he smoked the tires to get up to speed, and had almost caught up with the speeding truck when the driver saw him in her rearview mirror and accelerated even faster.

Roberts turned on his flashing lights and siren, causing the rest of the traffic in Coolidge to scatter. Nevertheless, the pickup continued speeding, heading northwest toward the open road. Roberts picked up his radio mike and called in to the station dispatcher explaining that he was in pursuit of a green National Park Service pickup and could use a back-up from the state highway patrol.

Once out of the city limits, the traffic thinned and he pushed the Ford's big V-8 in an attempt to catch up to the truck. It didn't take long. However, every time he tried to pull alongside, the truck's driver would swerve wildly into his lane. The fenders of the two cars scraped and the bumpers almost hooked one another.

This is insane! Roberts backed off a couple hundred yards, but continued to follow the government vehicle. At this distance and speed he had time to glance at his speedometer. It was still over eighty-five miles per hour.

His radio squawked. "The highway patrol has two cars ahead of you on Highway 89 and is setting up a road block as we speak," the female dispatcher explained over the two-way radio.

Relieved that he wasn't going to kill himself and the person ahead in a hot pursuit accident, he slowed to seventy. That's when he saw the cloud of dust. He could barely see the green truck as it skidded sideways, then started tumbling. When it finally came to a stop, it was upside down and over two hundred feet from the pavement. The driver's door was pinned against the side of a giant saguaro cactus; one front tire was still spinning.

Getting out of the cruiser, Roberts could hear sirens coming from both directions, but no amount of assistance would prove to be of any use. Hanging upside down, suspended by her seatbelt, Alice Brown took her agonal breath.

Scattered among the debris in the pickup, Roberts would eventually find some very curious clues, not the least of which included a handwritten note signed by a Laura Linger, offering Brown half of any proceeds from the sale of ancient Indian artifacts. Very suspicious was a small empty cardboard box that looked like it had once contained a bloodied knife—the label on the box said Henckels. Most interesting of all, buried deep behind the contents in the glove box, was a tattered leather wallet. It was empty except for a faded social security card. The name on the card had been rubbed off, but the number was quite clear. Once back at the station, Officer Roberts phoned in the number to the Phoenix Social Security office and after a typical run-around, was told the name of the Social Security number's owner: William Ruiz Real.

Three thousand miles away, just like clockwork, a passenger train pulled into Baltimore's central station. It was a muggy afternoon as Harvey Grimes stepped down onto the platform carrying a wooden crate by its makeshift twine handle and his battered duffel bag. He had a two-day stubble and persistent nausea from the motion of the train. He searched the crowd for any sign of Laura Linger, but didn't have to wait long for his ride. He saw the two men before they saw him.

"Grimes," said a burley-looking man half a foot shorter and fifty muscular pounds heavier than Harvey.

"Who wants to know," he retorted—a verbal challenge he had learned in the navy.

"Listen, wise guy, I'm Marco. Mr. Palermo sent me and my gorilla friend here to pick you up," he said, nodding to a similarly built but much younger man. "We needs to take you for a ride. Don't bother talking to Antonio unless you speak Siciliano."

A black Lincoln was waiting in front of the station. Harvey was sweating, and at the same time had chills thinking about what could possibly happen next. When they got out of the car half an hour later, the unmistakable profile of the Washington Monument was on his right and the nation's Capitol building was on his left.

A security guard took Harvey's name, checked his clipboard then escorted him and Marco into a brick building's conference room where they were told to wait. Soon three middle-aged men and an older woman, all dressed in business attire, entered the room. Introductions were brief, with Harvey not remembering any of their names. While one of the men opened the crate, Harvey's pulse pounded in his ears and finger tips. Harvey could hear mumbles and whispered comments from the foursome; then at last the woman spoke up.

"These are fabulous examples of the pre-Anasazi era," she said.

The others nodded their heads, as though that was all that needed to be explained to the delivery boy. They then left the room, instructing the men to wait. Fifteen minutes later, even Marco was getting frustrated. He started to leave when a door opened and the older woman entered. She handed Harvey a business-size envelope and thanked him for coming.

Two minutes later, the men were back on the street where Marco was trying to wave for his driver. Only then did Harvey actually see the sign directing pedestrians to the Smithsonian Museum of Natural History.

"Where we going from here?" Harvey asked Marco.

"Where I'm going ain't none a you's business," Marco said, not even making eye contact as he reached into his breast pocket and withdrew a thin white envelope which he handed to Harvey.

As the black Lincoln drove away, Harvey hefted his duffel bag on his shoulder and looked for a bench in the shade. He was dripping sweat when he finally sat down next to a pale old woman wearing a bonnet covered with silk flowers. He turned to the white envelope first. Inside was a letter which he spread out on his lap to read.

> Harvey. Now that you have done a good thing for my kids, I'm going to forget the threats to my kid and the window-peeking at my wife and your other stupid acts. But don't think for a minute that I'm not keeping a close eye on you. Do not travel west of the Mississippi or I'll start remembering stuff. Below is a phone number of a guy in Brooklyn. Give him a call and he'll put you to work. 555-3579. Don't call me.
> Franco P.

Harvey's hands were shaking as he folded the letter and turned his attention to the manila envelope.

"Is everything okay, young man?" the elderly woman asked.

"I'm fine," he said turning toward her as though he hadn't even noticed her before. Then he opened the larger envelope.

Inside was a brief note thanking him for transporting the pots and a typed check bearing his name for the amount of two thousand dollars. The letterhead on the check said simply "The Smithsonian." No mention was made of the woman, Miss Linger, who had caused so many problems for him. He took a deep breath, put the envelopes in his duffel and stood.

"Could I bother you to ask which way to Union Station?" Harvey asked the woman.

"Walk straight up to the last street in front of the Capitol building, then turn left, Mr. Grimes. By the way, Laura said to tell you that she will be in touch."

CHAPTER 30

The next two weeks dragged by for Dalan. The Palermos had gone to Northern Arizona's White Mountains to escape the heat. They hadn't asked him to tend Harley or the Scotty this time, which kind of hurt his feelings. He guessed that Mr. Palermo was mad at him for getting Marie involved with the whole thing; Indian pots and murders and all.

He and Boyd had gone swimming a few times at the city pool. Marie had told him he could swim at her house, but he didn't feel comfortable going there and didn't want to know who was tending the dogs. He still had lawns to mow and injured Ian still called him every ten minutes to bring him stuff, or to run to the Tasty Freeze for him.

On the last Friday morning before school was to begin, while Dalan was throwing an old white tennis ball against the garage door, the mailman came by in his funny little Jeep with its steering wheel on the wrong side and honked the horn. He waved at Dalan and then motioned for him to come to the Jeep. He was holding a little yellow card.

"This is for a special delivery package. You have to go to the post office to pick it up," the mailman said.

Dalan sat in the shade on the porch to read the card and was surprised that it was addressed to both him and Marie. He wasn't sure what to do now. Should he wait for her to come home or go get it and investigate it? The weekend was coming and then they would have school. He showed it to his mom, who offered to drive him to the post office later when his dad got home from work. He guessed that she was as curious as he.

The postmaster woman was just getting ready to pull down the glass window when Dalan and his mom walked in. "Sorry," she said, "we're closed until Monday."

She continued pulling the obscure glass closed, and then paused, having seen the disappointed look on Dalan's face, and the yellow card he held out.

"Hold on just a minute," she said, from behind the frosted window. She opened the side door. "I suppose you came for this. It's all the way from Washington, D.C.," she said, holding out a large manila envelope. "I'll take that yellow card and you'll have to sign for the envelope."

Back in the car his mom didn't say anything as he sat staring at the thick envelope on his lap. He started to look at the sealed flap as though ready to open it, when he mentioned that Marie's name was also on the envelope.

"What if it had come addressed to her and you were out of town?" his mom asked.

"I guess she would wait until I got back," he said.

He left it on the dining room china cupboard, in plain sight, warning Ian to keep his hands off. Then he rode his bike to her house and left a note on the front door.

Marie telephoned late Saturday afternoon to tell him that she was home.

"My mom and daddy would like to have you and your parents come to our house after dinner, and we can open the envelope together. They think they should be there when it's opened," she said.

He couldn't disagree, but still, it was another agonizing three hours to wait.

❖ ❖ ❖

Gina Palermo looked fresh and cheerful as she opened the door, inviting the Dawsons into her luxurious home. Franco was in his den smoking a cigar, but left it behind when he joined the group. They sat around the dining room table as Dalan presented the envelope to Marie and insisted she do the honors. Gina got a letter opener for her and she proceeded.

Inside were two separate letters. Each letter had two separate checks attached. The first was regarding the pots. It thanked them for delivering the pots in such good condition. The checks were made out to Marie Palermo and to Dalan Dawson, each for two thousand dollars.

"Just like we thought," Marie said to the Dawsons and Dalan.

"Daddy said that Harvey got his share also."

The second letter was lengthy. Marie read it out loud to the group.

Dear Marie Palermo and Dalan Dawson:
The Board of Directors of the Smithsonian would like to thank you for finding and returning one of the finest fifteenth century Christian artifacts ever found in the Western Hemisphere. The cross with its precious stones is believed to have been a gift from the Queen of Spain to one of the early explorers. Since its value can't be calculated in dollars, we wish to reward the two of you with your name on the plaque that describes the cross when it resides in a new exhibit. It will be the focal piece. In addition, we would like to invite you and your parents, at our expense, to attend the opening of the exhibit in October. At that time, we will present each of you with the Smithsonian Merit Scholarship, which will pay for all expenses for four years at the university of your choice.
Congratulations,
The Smithsonian

The six people sat in silence for a few minutes, perhaps trying to calculate what the reward meant, whether in dollars or in experience or in the long view of all of their lives. For the Palermos the prestige might have outweighed the monetary value, whereas for the Dawsons and Dalan it opened a floodgate to an entirely new world of opportunity.

"Can we leave now?" Dalan asked his parents, not wanting to sound rude, but feeling unable to sit any longer. "I mean me and Marie?"

Gina looked across the table with a smile and nodded her consent to Mrs. Dawson, who in turn got the nod from Mr. Dawson. Franco shrugged his shoulders.

❖ ❖ ❖

Outside the house, the two young teenagers walked toward the swimming pool, with Harley and the Scotty tagging along behind. The night air was hot but dry and the moon was just clearing the horizon.

Marie kicked off her sandals and sat down on the pool's edge, dangling her feet in the lukewarm water. Dalan paced back and forth for a minute, burning off the adrenalin, then finally joined her. She reached for his hand, grasping it with both of hers, then leaned her head on his shoulder.

"Dalan," she said, "I was just wondering . . ."

"What, Marie?"

"If maybe next Saturday, you would go with me and Harley, to see if we can find another cave?"

The End

About The Author

After thirty years of medical practice—delivering over seven thousand babies—and raising five children with his wife, Paula, Doctor Dahl now splits his time between their homes in the Arizona desert and the mountain peaks of Utah.

Their most recent travels took them to central Europe, where for over a year they managed the medical care of the Latter-day Saints missionaries and researched the health care systems in such fascinating countries as Poland, Romania, Moldova, and Serbia. These European adventures added to Dr. Dahl's experiences of living on the tiny islands of the Pacific, his Viet Nam experience on a navy hospital ship, and time spent in a struggling Liberian hospital.

His previous fascination with ranching, flying, scuba diving, sailing, and serving his country as a Major in the U.S. Army all add credence and a realistic twist to his stories.

The best days of his life are those spent with his wife and family, especially with their children and grandchildren. With his fifth novel penned, and another taking shape, he and Paula will stay put in the U.S.A. for a while to watch the grandkids grow.

Order Kick the Can
for your friends!

Or other books written by
Steven I. Dahl, M.D.

Please visit: www.PublishAtSweetDreams.com
and click on the book title to order online.

Available at:
Amazon
Barnes & Noble
Sweet Dreams Publishing of MA
and other online bookstores

Visit us at: www.PublishAtSweetDreams.com
Contact us at: info@PublishAtSweetDreams.com

CPSIA information can be obtained at www.ICGtesting.com
Printed in the USA
BVOW011055170212

283170BV00001B/3/P